I Am in Urgent Need of Advice

# I Am in Urgent Need of Advice

by Josephine Lawrence

HARCOURT, BRACE & WORLD, INC.
NEW YORK

*I Am in Urgent Need of Advice*

The Carpenters, a city family, rely on astrology, marriage counselors and syndicated columns to solve their trivial calamities.

## Chapter 1

"If we lived in a house," Amanda said, "everything would be simple. Parents could stay upstairs, out of sight."

Pearl sighed. The Carpenter family would be nervous wrecks before Amanda finished planning her fourteenth birthday party. This latest idea—that a two-story house offered advantages for entertaining lacking in an apartment—was a sample of Amanda's thinking.

"Your father isn't going to move out of this nice, comfortable place just so you can give a party." Pearl reached for the tongs as a split muffin popped up in the toaster. "Why don't they just go out?" she suggested.

Amanda glared at her, but the effect was spoiled because she was trying to butter the muffin at the same time. Amanda's after-school snacks, unless she had first stopped at one of the fountains near Miss Mary's, were carefully assembled and Pearl never hurried her.

She spread the buttered muffin thickly with raspberry jam and fished two sweet pickles from the glass jar on the breakfast table. A bottle of root beer and a slice of layer cake—"your grandma sent it up," Pearl said—completed the repast.

"Parents are supposed to put in an appearance," Amanda said, leaning back against the settle seat with the air of one at ease for the first time in a busy day.

She and Pearl had no difficulty in following each other's mental processes. Their best time for the exchange of confidences was in the afternoons, either before Pearl started preparations for dinner or, with the actual cooking under way, when she waited for six o'clock and the word that she might begin to serve.

*1*

Pearl had worked in other women's kitchens for nearly twenty-five years, ten of which had been spent with the Carpenters. Her two marriages had afforded her only brief intervals in a home of her own, but the divorces had not killed her faith in romance. She was a short, stout woman with a round face, round, pale-blue eyes, and a nose that managed to look round, too. No one considered her a good cook, but as Elaine Carpenter said to her husband, she was at least reliable. To Amanda this was also Pearl's most endearing quality; except for Wednesday, her day off, she was always on hand.

"How do you mean, put in an appearance?" Pearl demanded. She glanced at the wall clock above her ironing board and decided she could do the table mats.

Having finished the raspberry-covered muffin, Amanda ate a pickle without shuddering. Parents were not supposed to "go off" when their children entertained, she said, although that didn't mean they should hang around and spy upon the guests.

"Mirabelle Marilyn Meeks says they should be around when the kids come, then go upstairs, if there is any upstairs. Or stay in another room. With the door shut, I guess. It's all right to come in once, maybe, to pass potato chips, but they can't expect to run things."

Pearl thought this made sense. Mirabelle Marilyn Meeks conducted a column of advice for teen-agers in the evening *Blaze*, the tabloid with the largest circulation in the city. Pearl herself was an avid reader of the paper's department on etiquette and human relations, edited by Mrs. Torrington Van Antwerp.

"Your father and mother can go downstairs to your Grandma Ives's apartment, so what are you fussing for?" Pearl's small, plump hand set down the iron with a thump. "Are you going to *worry?*"

Amanda's dark eyes could mirror poignant anxiety, even as she sat drinking root beer through a straw. Except for that look she was still more child than adolescent. She had a voracious appetite but was extremely thin, "built like a hairpin," her father's sister had once observed, and aside from her eyes and thick, shining mop of dark hair, did not promise to be a beauty. She had no confidence that she would ever be as pretty as her mother, but that was nothing compared to the worry that gnawed ceaselessly at her peace of mind: would boys like her?

"I guess you'd worry, too, if your last party had been a flop." Amanda, sure of Pearl's ability to follow her reasoning, began on the layer cake.

Everyone knew what it was to have a party "go dead on them," Pearl comforted her loyally. Instinctively she sensed that Amanda was never to forget the ghastly evening when the boys had stayed in a huddle at one end of the living room, obstinately refusing to join in the games suggested by their panic-stricken hostess. Advised by her closest friend, Tully Hallam, that mothers were tricky, Amanda had insisted that she be allowed to handle everything alone. The result had been that as soon as Pearl had served the food and the boys had eaten it, they departed in a body, leaving the girls infuriated and alone.

Mirabelle Marilyn Meeks, consulted, had charitably suggested that at thirteen and fourteen the boys were too young to know party behavior and had hinted that in another year their manners should be considerably improved.

"Grandma thinks I've got Uranus in the wrong house." Amanda spoke as if she might have some sort of infection. "My birthday isn't right for a party."

Pearl said, "The stars incline, but do not compel," and continued to iron placidly.

Amanda gathered up her plate, paper napkin, and silver and carried them to the sink. The empty bottle she added to the collection in the pantry; Pearl returned the "empties" to the delicatessen and collected the deposits to add to her charity fund.

"I wish I'd never told the girls I was going to have a party," Amanda said.

She had repeated this so often in the past two weeks that she suspected everyone, with the exception of Pearl, agreed with her. Other girls gave parties and apparently enjoyed the role of hostess. Her own mother entertained her bridge club without having sleepless nights before and after, as far as Amanda knew. However, her father liked to spend his evenings quietly at home. "Your daddy always had his nose in a book," her mother said.

Pearl had finished her ironing. She wanted to start dinner, and since her preparations included trying out a recipe for a new sauce, this was one of the rare times when she preferred to have the kitchen to herself.

"Why don't you do your homework early tonight? Or run down and see your grandma?" She offered these alternatives with the false brightness one uses to distract a child. "Take her the glove she left here; she may be hunting for it."

Amanda did not answer. She wandered out of the kitchen, past the dining room and the pretty living room with its white-tiled fireplace. The living room opened onto the entrance foyer which connected with the second apartment, where the main bedrooms were. The house, a co-operative, was old but well kept, and a number of families like the Carpenters had combined two apartments in the years before space had become as valuable as gold.

Contrasted with her friend Tully Hallam's room, her own appointments were rather pitiful, Amanda thought. She glared at the telephone in the foyer as she passed it. Tully had a private phone in her room and a small television set. Amanda had only her radio, a rose-and-gray room with a walk-in closet (Tully envied her that), and a bathroom that was all hers except on the rare occasions when an overnight guest had to share it with her. The guest room had been made into a study for her father and reflected his tastes, as the blue-and-silver bedroom and the bath that was also a dressing room reflected her mother's.

In her room Amanda turned on her desk light with one hand and the radio with the other. How could she be sure that she hadn't made a mistake in inviting Steve Barry? He had never asked her for a date, but she thought she remembered reading in Mirabelle Marilyn Meeks's Sunday column that a girl could invite any boy she knew to a party. It might be better to make sure. Amanda sat down at the painted pine desk

*4*

and selected a sheet of her best note paper, stamped with her name and address, a Christmas gift from her grandmother.

"Dear Mirabelle," she began, her handwriting scarcely legible, "I am in urgent need of advice. . . ."

## II

Elaine Carpenter usually cooked her husband's breakfast because Pearl, who lived with a married sister, seldom reached the apartment house before nine o'clock. An appetite for the old-fashioned hearty breakfast had never deserted Kelsey, but the little sausages and pancakes or the eggs and bacon and toast did not tempt her. Her mother worried because Amanda allowed time only for orange juice, but, as Elaine pointed out, Amanda ate steadily throughout the day. Two cups of black coffee sustained Elaine until noon and enabled her to wear the same size girdle at forty that she had worn on her wedding day.

This morning she had tried a new muffin mix with the exact creditable results pictured on the package, and she eyed the pale yellow-and-brown puffs with an artist's satisfaction. Kelsey would eat four, she calculated; Pearl and Amanda between them would finish the others.

"Isn't Amanda coming?" Kelsey asked as he poured a liberal amount of heavy cream into his coffee.

In spite of his liking for good food, he remained an exasperatingly lean man. He had a thin, rather inscrutable face, brilliant blue eyes, and heavy dark hair in which the gray was gaining over the black. Five mornings a week he sat opposite his wife at the round breakfast table and thought she looked very pretty. He was devoted to her and to their daughter and he was even markedly fond of his mother-in-law.

Amanda had gone to school half an hour early, Elaine said.

"She wants to discuss party details with Tully. I don't know why she has to get so worked up over everything she does. Mother says she wrote four letters to that Mirabelle Marilyn Meeks last week."

Kids didn't know how to eat; an orange-juice breakfast

5

was enough to give anyone a case of nerves, Kelsey said. They could take comfort in the fact that if it wasn't a birthday party, it would be something else—Amanda hadn't learned to relax.

His briefcase and one of the two copies of the morning paper lay on a nearby chair. He might glance at the headlines, but he didn't read the news until he reached his office. Elaine poured his second cup of coffee. He never hurried and was never late.

"You and Pauline have anything on for today?" Kelsey, his own day stretching out satisfactorily before him, thought it prudent to check on the domestic calendar, especially where his mother-in-law was concerned.

Elaine's brown eyes regarded him over the rim of her cup. At least they breakfasted together, but she had decided they were growing further apart every day. It was all her fault. She wasn't the type to be the wife of a successful executive. Kelsey's firm had not once asked to interview her, and she was undoubtedly holding him back from deserved promotion.

"You look worried," said Kelsey, folding his napkin. "Is it Amanda? She'll be all right—being young is rough on us all."

He came around the table to kiss her, and Elaine fancied his mind already detached and, if not at work on the problems awaiting him at the office, then at least coping with the morning traffic as he drove downtown.

She sat at the table until she heard the elevator in the hall and Albert's voice raised in greeting—the tenants were resolutely opposed to the installation of self-service elevators—and then began slowly to carry the dishes out to the kitchen sink. Pearl wanted them left there, preferring to put them in the machine herself.

The telephone rang as Elaine filled the muffin pan with water.

"Elaine, is that you, darling?" Her mother spoke too close to the mouthpiece. "I just wanted to let you know that this isn't a good day to buy shoes. Not even slippers."

6

"I wasn't planning to buy shoes," Elaine said.

"But there was a sale advertised in last night's paper." Pauline Ives loved to shop. "I need a pair of black suèdes. But this is a bad day for the feet. If you bought shoes, you'd probably have to return them."

Elaine listened patiently. She paid little attention to her mother's elaborate astrological predictions, but, if not pressed for time, rarely tried to escape. Her sense of humor was limited and she didn't find anything to laugh at in the network of portents and signs through which her mother daily threaded her harassed way. That Amanda and Kelsey were alternately amused and irritated by Grandma's chatter of horoscopes and "aspects" usually surprised Elaine.

Pearl let herself in through the back hall door during the explanation of why the afternoon would be more favorable for shopping—but not for shoes—and could be heard starting preparations for her breakfast.

"I hear Pearl banging away in the kitchen. Can't she eat breakfast before she comes?" Pauline Ives asked this question at least once a day.

Elaine's reply—that Pearl liked to sleep late—always satisfied her mother. They were all fond of Pearl and would not dream of interfering with her set routines.

"Be careful of chemicals and liquids," Pauline warned as her own door buzzer sounded. "And remember, don't buy shoes."

In the kitchen, Pearl had made instant coffee, which is without fragrance, and was beating an egg in milk for French toast. She had set a place for herself in the breakfast nook and she would enjoy a leisurely meal as the prelude to her busy day. She often stayed until nine or ten o'clock at night, if she had no date with the middle-aged bachelor with whom she insisted she was "going steady."

"Did you and Jerome have a nice evening, Pearl?" Elaine remembered that Pearl had expected to be taken to meet the bachelor's mother—always something of a crisis for the nervous, whether visitor or visited.

"Well," said Pearl reflectively, "I did and I didn't."

7

She dipped a slice of bread into the beaten-egg mixture, dropped it into the skillet, and put a plate in the oven to warm.

"The apartment's real nice. Jerome's fixed everything to save his mother steps." Pearl's round face was slightly flushed. "You can see she's a woman who's been babied all her life."

Yes, Jerome's mother was nice enough to her, Pearl admitted; she had made coffee and served a bakery cake that she tried to pretend she had made herself.

"I was so afraid that Jerome would say something about my chocolate cake—he's crazy about my chocolate cake. I bake one for him every time he comes out to the house."

Pearl transferred her toast to the plate as she talked, poured cream into her coffee, which she would not drink until it was cold, and carried her breakfast to the table.

"Jerome's scared to death of her," she said.

Elaine lingered. As she had told her mother, her interest in Pearl's affairs of the heart was never wholly unselfish. She and Kelsey had helped Pearl through the aftermath of one disastrous marriage, and it was only reasonable to hope that a woman twice married and twice divorced would question her qualifications for being joined in holy matrimony. But Pearl's appetite for romance was insatiable and she continued to "go steady" with a succession of suitors, none of whom, when it came to the test, had been economically sound. The Carpenters, breathing sighs of relief as each "engagement" fell through, tried to persuade themselves that they only wanted Pearl to be happy.

"Is it Jerome's mother who thinks divorce is so dreadful?" Elaine knew all about Jerome's mother's attitude toward divorce—Pearl had talked of nothing else for the last two weeks.

Pearl said that Jerome's mother was living in the Dark Ages.

"She doesn't even know I've been divorced. Jerome promised not to tell her, until we get really acquainted. But she's hipped on the subject. Last night she read something in the paper that started her off and she told Jerome that if he ever marries a divorced woman he can never come home."

8

Elaine's quick ear caught the faint sound of letters falling through the mail slot to the foyer floor.

"Don't worry—Jerome's old enough to manage his life." Elaine was adept at constructing sentences which sounded all right if no one examined them. "His mother can't expect to control him when he supports her."

She hurried away to pick up the mail, calling over her shoulder that she would have lunch downtown. There were two letters for Amanda, and they reminded Elaine that she had promised to meet her daughter at three o'clock to look at dresses. With her nerves already on edge because of the party, Amanda could be counted on to dislike violently any dress her mother might approve.

Elaine sighed, decided that the letter from Lucie Hendrix, Kelsey's younger sister, could wait. Nothing would induce Lucie to write if she could phone, and if the phone service was disconnected again, that meant she hoped to borrow money to pay last month's collection of bills.

### III

"Now this model is sophisticated—" The clerk's tousled ash-blond head turned toward Amanda. "But it isn't too old—" The blond head swiveled and the clerk nodded brightly to Elaine.

One entire floor of Colchester-Colossal was devoted to merchandise for the sub-teen, the junior miss, and the teen-ager. Fashion shows were staged twice a month, and models from the local schools were encouraged to compete with the professionals. The clerks were specially trained to handle parents as well as children, and the store prided itself on being one of the first to offer charge accounts to the teens.

Elaine surveyed the red velvet liberally sprayed with rhinestones.

"Utterly ridiculous!" She spoke with more positiveness than usual, since the combination had instantly irritated her.

"Why, Mrs. Carpenter, there was a photograph of that in *The Glow of Youth*," Tully Hallam protested. "A girl with Amanda's coloring would be a dream in red velvet."

9

Chronologically Tully and Amanda were the same age—their birthdays two days apart—but psychologically Tully was far older and more experienced. Her figure had developed, and she boasted that boys who had taken her out believed her to be sixteen. She was extremely pretty, a natural blond, and, as the only child of the wealthy owner of a chain of restaurants, was self-confident to a degree that perpetually dazzled and charmed Amanda.

"Amanda, don't you like the pink silk?" Elaine tried to ignore Tully, who was too much for her. "Your father loved your pink dresses last summer."

The pink was too babyish, Amanda grumbled.

"You won't let me wear black. I need something with character. Red stands out." Amanda's pretty, narrow hand stroked the velvet affectionately.

The clerk, who had lived through three similar scenes in that one afternoon, suggested that green was a good color.

"A sheath?" Amanda looked suspicious. "I'm sick of full skirts."

"You might as well put a sheath on a pencil," the clerk would say later to a sympathetic co-worker, but long training had taught her the folly of argument.

"We sell more of the full skirts," she said firmly. "They're prettier for dancing."

"But the sheath is smarter," Tully observed.

Elaine wondered whether it was too late to move to another city and break off the friendship between Tully and Amanda.

"We'll have the pink and green charged and sent," she directed the clerk. "I want my husband to see them. He'll decide quickly and I'll return one."

Amanda and Tully gazed at her with positive dislike.

"If you want to see that new movie, we have just time enough to reach the Marguise." Elaine returned their glare. "I'll treat you to a taxi. Coming?"

"Adults always win," said Amanda bitterly. "They have the money."

The Marguise was one of the luxuriously upholstered intimate little theaters that drew fairly large audiences from the handsome, modern apartment houses that lined the Boulevard. Amanda complained at intervals that "no one" lived in the old-fashioned co-operatives and intimated that she was the only girl at Miss Mary's whose family insisted on living in the South End when a North End address made a charge account impressive.

Elaine, far more devoted to the movies than Amanda, settled into her seat with a relieved sigh. She had no idea what the film would be, but she had never outgrown her ability to lose all sensation of time and place as she watched the action on the screen. Kelsey was easily bored, Amanda often scornful, but Elaine retained her childish willingness to be amused and thrilled.

"You'll love it, Mother," Amanda had said as the lights faded and the warm darkness enveloped them.

Presumably Amanda and Tully would consider the story "corny," although Tully had suggested they see it. Tully prided herself on seeing everything "new," and Amanda usually followed her lead. Elaine, conscious of the absolute silence for a brief moment, remembered that Kelsey had once asked her if she thought Tully undermined Amanda's confidence in herself.

"Not deliberately—Tully isn't that deep," Kelsey had said. "But she's always positive, she doesn't hesitate, doubt isn't in her. Amanda may think the bright, shiny surface desirable and feel inadequate."

Kelsey, Elaine reflected, was a very good father. Most of the child-guidance experts stressed the importance of the father role in a girl's life. Fortunately, they had no son, for she might have turned to him. . . . But Elaine hastily pushed her marital worries to the back of her mind and gave herself up to enjoying the difficulties of the beautiful creatures on the screen.

It might be her own life, allowing for fewer dramatic situations. Most couples, Elaine reasoned, trying not to notice that Tully was already madly feeling about for a lost pump, drifted apart slowly, almost imperceptibly. On the screen they blew up like geysers. Their precipitateness annoyed her, because the dissolution of her own marriage proceeded so slowly. It was all very well for the marriage counselor to advise objective study and analysis, but one could learn more easily by observation and comparison. She wondered how many other women were sitting around her in the safe anonymity of the dark, achingly conscious of their failure as wives and not at all sure in what direction they had failed.

"Terrible, wasn't it?" Tully yawned and began to apply fresh lipstick the instant the lights flashed on.

She had found her shoe and stood up, obviously anxious to leave.

"Mother liked it, didn't you, Mother?" Amanda's dark eyes were still resentful.

Elaine said, "The subject matter interested me," and when Amanda laughed, added, "I thought it very well done."

She would make an appointment with Mrs. Steckner for later in the week, Elaine decided, watching Amanda and Tully ordering banana splits. She hadn't consulted the marriage counselor since Thanksgiving, and it was now January. One half of her mind busied itself with the questions she meant to ask, the other marveled at the capacity of healthy young appetites. Both girls, she knew, would be ready for dinner at the regular time. Tully had a passion for drugstore fountains, and neither the trained cook in her mother's kitchen nor the chefs in her father's restaurant chain could make banana splits to please her.

"What a dope that woman was in 'Come with Me,'" Amanda said, smiling at herself in the mirror over the fountain. "She never should have married that man."

Tully let one pump dangle from her toes. She chewed thoughtfully on a maraschino cherry.

"The man was the dope," Tully said. "He married one type and then wanted another."

A blonde woman in a syrup-stained uniform, who had been washing glasses in one of the sinks, leaned across the counter.

"You been to see 'Come with Me'?" she asked. "I saw it last night with my boy friend. It's dated, I told him."

"My mother liked it," Amanda said.

"I think what ails all these parties is the stuff they have to eat." Pearl put down her tray on the folding table she had arranged across the knees of the white-haired woman in the narrow, four-poster bed.

Pauline Ives, restless and active at seventy, eyed her coffee and toast with approval. Ordinarily she was dressed and ready to go out by nine o'clock every morning, but a touch of laryngitis had alarmed her son-in-law and resulted in an order from the family's medical man that she remain in bed until he could look her over.

"Miz Carpenter's coming down soon as she makes a few phone calls," Pearl said, deftly adjusting the back rest. "Don't you try to talk."

The patient objected in a hoarse whisper that she was not ill.

"It's my voice. I had the same thing five years ago." The pretty hand that lifted the coffee cup was steady. "I was a fool to promise not to get up."

The three-room apartment was stiflingly hot. Pearl longed to open a window, but fresh air seemed to distress Miz Carpenter's mother. The smaller units of the co-operative occupied two floors of the building and were tenanted by widows and a few single women. According to information exchanged by relatives and friends, whose advice had no effect, all of them kept their windows tightly shut.

Pearl had automatically begun to "straighten up" the untidy room. She regarded Miz Ives as a member of the Carpenter family and the smaller apartment as an extension of their home, and felt responsible for maintaining it in a fair semblance of good order.

"You have more of everything than you need, that's the trouble," she grumbled as she lifted three dresses from a chair to disclose two pairs of pink feathered mules.

"Did Amanda decide what refreshments to serve?" Pauline could recall a day when even the word "refreshments" suggested a party.

In the closet a hatbox had tumbled from the shelf, hitting Pearl a glancing blow on her round nose.

"Cokes and potato chips and pizza pies." Her muffled voice jerked with irritation. "They fill up on that junk all week long. Wouldn't you think, come a party, they'd at least have fancy sandwiches? Miz Carpenter thinks a buffet supper would be nice, but Amanda says the kids would think she was trying to be ritzy."

Pauline cut her second slice of toast into small, neat squares.

"The whole month's bad for entertaining," she said. "It's the influence of Uranus."

Pearl emerged from the closet, rubbing her nose. She made a mental note to remove the astrology books and magazines from the dresser top before she left—nothing annoyed Dr. Cannon more than to be faced with these evidences of his patient's devotion to the occult.

"You want another cup of coffee?" Pearl was also wary of the planets when they threatened to interfere with her work routine. "I'll bring it to you, then I have to dust the living room before I go upstairs."

Pauline said, "The first cup wasn't half full," a fiction that enabled her to drink two cups of coffee every morning with a clear conscience in spite of her diet list.

And after Pearl had finished her dusting and gone back to the Carpenter apartment, she wondered if she could risk going out into the kitchen to make more toast. Elaine, to whom dieting was easy, thought that two pieces of dry toast should be a satisfactory breakfast.

"Avoid friction with loved ones," Pauline quoted to herself, remembering the advice given for the day in her astrological guide.

She was reading the forecast again when she heard Elaine's key in the lock. Listening, she could trace footsteps going to the kitchen, followed by the faint slam of the refrigerator door.

"More of that reducing mayonnaise," she whispered aloud.

"I heard you," she said, when her daughter appeared in the doorway.

14

Elaine kissed her, put a cool hand against one faintly lined cheek.

"Don't talk, Mama. I don't think you have a temperature, but you can't be too careful. Pearl says you ate a good breakfast."

Her mother gazed at her in some exasperation. One's children were a constant reminder of one's age but it was amazing how often their attitudes tended to annoy a parent still in possession of her mental faculties.

"Is that doctor coming?" she croaked.

The doctor had promised to come as soon as possible and that might mean not before afternoon, Elaine said. She spoke hurriedly, remembering that it was impossible to make older people understand that a busy doctor had to fit his house calls into a schedule. In her mother's day—a vague period of time unmarked by calendars—one had sent for the doctor and he had come immediately.

"I'll be well before he gets here," Pauline rasped. She prodded her throat in an effort to release her voice. "You going downtown shopping, Elaine?"

There were a few things she had to get for Amanda, Elaine said. And at noon the hospital committee met for a sample luncheon in the new coffee shop.

"But I can stay with you, Mama, if you don't want to be alone. Pearl will be busy cleaning. She'll bring you lunch, of course."

Pauline, for one wild moment, thought of attempting to explain. She often felt the need to take someone into her confidence and she saw more of Elaine than anyone else. But the impulse always died, for common sense told her that only someone of her own generation could be expected to understand.

"You run along—I'll be all right." This was her own home; she could speak with authority.

Yes, she would stay in bed until the doctor had seen her, she promised. She had given her word to Kelsey. Pearl had phoned Louis for her, breaking her hair appointment.

"I think myself it would have done me good to get my hair

15

set. Maybe later I can go down to that little girl in the corner shop. Do you know anyone who's had a rinse there?"

Elaine tried to look severe. The beauty parlor could wait.

"Try to sleep, Mama. You need rest. Dr. Cannon always tells you it's time for you to begin to slow down."

Pauline decided not to waste her voice on an opinion of Dr. Cannon. Instead, she closed her eyes to indicate compliance, smiled drowsily when Elaine kissed her good-by, and held herself rigid until the tapping of high heels died away with the closing of the outside door and the click of the latch.

She was in no danger of forgetting her age, she told herself, slipping smoothly out of the bed and reaching for the pink feather mules Pearl had arranged under a chair. No woman with a daughter and a granddaughter had any chance of being allowed to ignore the record. The modern emphasis on the cleavage between the generations made everything more difficult, too. A passion existed for classifying people according to dates and one had to be constantly alert to avoid being sealed off into specific enclosures.

In the bathroom she scrutinized her face in the mirror. No one would mistake her for a young adult, but as certainly she didn't look like a senior citizen. Elaine, who was on several charitable and civic committees for improving the condition of the aged, had once challenged her to tell how a senior citizen looked.

"Ashamed of himself," Pauline had answered promptly. "And I should think he would be."

She looked more rested this morning than usual, she decided, noting approvingly that her hair shone like polished chromium in the light of the hundred-and-fifty-watt bulb. The last rinse had kept an even color. Her skin had always been good, and she used make-up sparingly. The blue eyes that watched her in the medicine-cabinet mirror searched for evidences of collapse or decay and saw no terrifying signs.

A violent sneeze surprised her, and she looked over her shoulder guiltily. If Kelsey ever heard that! She seldom resented her son-in-law's affectionate supervision, recognizing his sincerity, but she had learned that his patience was not inexhaustible.

*16*

"You'd better get into bed and stay there," she told the woman in the mirror, for she often talked to herself. "Avoid friction with loved ones."

But after she had wrapped herself in a blue silk quilted housecoat, she padded out into the hall to pick up the mail.

Two new astrology magazines and the five-dollar horoscope she had sent for a month ago confirmed her belief in the prediction that the current day was to be favorable. If Dr. Cannon had walked in upon this literature scattered on the floor, he would have been furious enough to have walked right out again.

"What does an intelligent woman your age get out of that kind of foolishness?" he had once asked her.

She had given him some kind of conciliatory reply—the day was unfavorable, her chart had warned her, with Mars in the twelfth house promising trouble through impulsive actions— but she had no intention of telling anyone what astrology meant to her.

In bed again, she realized that she felt pleasantly drowsy. She had left the latch off; the doctor could let himself in. Once she regained her voice, she would make a new appointment with Louis and have lunch in the gypsy tearoom in the same building. She hadn't had her fortune told since Christmas. Tea-leaf readings were always hopeful, too.

## V

"I dreamt I dwelt in marble halls," sang Pearl, turning over the cake recipes in her file. "With vassals and serfs at my side . . ."

She broke off abruptly to glare at Amanda.

"Potato chips and Cokes and records!" she grumbled. "It's a wonder you kids have any digestions left."

Amanda spread peanut butter thickly on an oyster cracker. She didn't intend to have a stuffy party, she said; potato chips and Coke were what everybody else had and it was what everybody liked.

"You can make Jerome a fancy cake, Pearl. He told me his

17

mother won't let him have any cake that isn't at least two days old."

Pearl was easily diverted. Jerome's mother fussed too much about his health, she said. Fresh cake and bread never hurt a grown man. But it was all a part of the old lady's plan to keep Jerome from thinking of marriage.

"She dreamed up that warning about fresh cake as soon as she heard I am a good cake baker. And I don't believe she was set against a second wedding until she heard I've been divorced. She must have heard it somehow."

Amanda said, "This would be your third wedding."

It made no difference to Jerome's mother, Pearl retorted. One divorce or two, she intended to stress the religious angle.

"There's the sweetest outfit for a girl who's going to be married for the second time described in the etiquette column in the *Blaze* tonight," Pearl sighed. "Violet, with deep rose suède pumps and hat to match."

Amanda remembered that she had promised to call Tully Hallam and that it would be well to do it before her father reached home. Daddy, Amanda said gloomily, simply didn't understand how handicapped she was in comparison with Tully.

"If she phones me and we're at dinner, he doesn't like that; if I phone her before we eat, or afterward, he says I tie up the phone. Dozens of the girls at Miss Mary's have their own phones."

Pearl scarcely listened. She had dinner to get and, in addition, she was worried about a suitable gift for Jerome's mother, whose birthday, she had learned, was in February. Pearl regarded the point as delicate, since too elaborate a present might be misconstrued as an attempt to gain favor; on the other hand, an insignificant trifle might as easily seem too casual. She decided to ask the advice of Mrs. Torrington Van Antwerpt.

Fifteen minutes later, Amanda dashed into the kitchen, too excited to talk coherently. The most wonderful thing had happened, everything was going to be fine, she chattered, and

18

then helped herself to another cracker and more peanut butter, momentarily depriving herself of all speech.

"Tully and I . . ." She choked, but managed to swallow. "We're going to have a party together. In one of her father's restaurants. I'll be co-hostess, Tully says. But no one has to fuss. Isn't that lovely?"

"What happens to the potato chips, Coke, and records?" Pearl said.

Amanda giggled. She seldom had much color in her face, but now her skin was flushed a becoming pink.

"We don't *eat* records. I guess I can take some with me— We'll probably dance after dinner. My new dress is too plain— I wonder if Mother will let me exchange it."

Simple refreshments were all right for a home party, she explained when Pearl obstinately reminded her of earlier arguments. The kids disliked elaborate food; they felt it was the mothers' way of showing off. But a restaurant was different; people went there intending to eat. The food was ready—for one person or for a party, it didn't matter, it was there.

Pearl wanted to know "what happened to the parents," and Amanda said that Tully's father and mother would be there to see that everything started off well.

"We're to have two birthday cakes and everything." Amanda ate another cracker. "Boy, I guess I'm not cut out to be a hostess, am I?"

She thought this over for a moment, her dark eyes suddenly sober.

"It's nice not to have to worry," she said.

"I must say it's a relief to me, too," Elaine had confessed to Mrs. Hallam. "Amanda was getting almost hysterical. My husband thinks dinner in a restaurant is a little elaborate for fourteen-year-olds, but . . ."

The fact that it was Tully's father's restaurant made all the difference, Elaine said to Kelsey. Mr. and Mrs. Hallam would be there to keep an eye on the young people, who would be in a private dining room. They planned to dance to their everlasting records afterward.

"Or what they call dancing," said Pauline Ives, who forbore

to mention that the vibrations for the double birthday date were "uncertain."

Two days later, Amanda was put to bed with a well-developed case of the flu. Too wretched to care that, after hasty consultation, it was decided the party could not be postponed, she submitted to medication without protest and only mildly resented the disclosure that Tully had allotted Steve Barry to a girl she chose to consider her rival.

As she felt better, she spent hours experimenting with eye make-up, her birthday gift from Tully. The doctor's reaction to her first efforts was a startled "Good God!" but she assured him that Mirabelle Marilyn Meeks advocated a discreet use of make-up at the age of fourteen.

"You look like a barn owl," Dr. Cannon said. "You'll scare the boys off. What does your father think?"

The dark eyes, outlined in heavy black, surveyed him with pity.

"My father realizes that I have to assert myself." Amanda tried to get in her defense before the thermometer reached her lips. "I'm maturing, Dr. Cannon."

To her father, she confided her need for a dress allowance sufficient to enable her to buy her own clothes. No, she didn't want to charge things on her mother's accounts.

"We fight every time we shop together, Daddy. We don't like the same kind of clothes. I have to develop my own style; it's time I learned to express myself. After all, I'm fourteen now."

Kelsey, too, had been floored by the eye shadow and eye liner, but he comforted himself with the reminder that one interview with Miss Mary's principal would settle that.

"Does Mirabelle Marilyn Meeks advocate self-expression?" He had an idea that Elaine would want some strings tied to the dress allowance.

Amanda's sudden flare of resentment surprised him.

"You and Mother don't like her because she understands my generation," she said, and suddenly tears flooded the black-circled eyes.

20

## Chapter 2

Elaine Carpenter cradled the handset and unconsciously sighed. Lucie's telephone conversations usually depressed her, probably because her husband's younger sister demanded unqualified expressions of sympathy. Lucie felt herself blocked off from a career by a husband, two youngsters, and a house in the suburbs, and she read constantly a mass of literature that confirmed her convictions.

"She's tied down, she needs to get out more," Kelsey said, whenever Lucie borrowed money from him. "No wonder she feels frustrated."

Lucie voiced her discontent freely, sharing with other suburban matrons the belief that the American woman was unable to attain happiness. Elaine, who could scarcely escape reading along the same lines, was more secretive, more evasive, actually more confused, about her general dissatisfaction.

She had reached the age, Elaine reflected this morning, when she and her husband should be planning to resume the close, intimate companionship that had marked the early years of their marriage. All the magazines to which she subscribed warned that to avert disaster you must forestall it. Medical men and sociologists alike agreed on two issues: one, that women were increasingly unhappy, and, two, that they were confused. Acting on their advice, Elaine had sought help, but she was still confused. Mrs. Steckner, the marriage counselor recommended by several friends, had pointed out that Amanda was absorbed in the adolescent's struggle to achieve personal independence, that Pearl assumed most of the responsibility for managing the apartment, and that Pauline Ives needed, for the present at least, none of the assistance popularly extended to the aged.

"It's a golden opportunity for you to strengthen and repair the ties of your marriage to Kelsey," Mrs. Steckner had said.

She had not been surprised at Kelsey's violent reactions as subsequently reported by Elaine. Many husbands resented the idea of consultation with a counselor, Mrs. Steckner had admitted placidly. A little tact was all that was needed to persuade them of the wisdom of seeking expert advice. It had been a year since Elaine's first interview, and Kelsey had shown no sign of yielding to persuasion.

"I'll run down and see Mama for a moment, before Albert brings up the mail," Elaine said, hastily improvising a destination when Pearl found her still sitting at the phone table with the breakfast table uncleared.

Pauline Ives was one of those fastidiously neat women who always present a well-groomed appearance, but are incapable of keeping their belongings in any kind of order. Grandma's bureau drawers, clothes closet, and bedroom looked, the family agreed, as if struck by a cyclone for six days out of the seven. One day a week the patient Pearl attacked the chaos, but Elaine conceded that it was a waste of time.

She found her mother sitting on the bed, attired in a beige silk slip and a smart, tiny flowered hat. Her hat was usually the first thing Pauline put on and the last she removed. A new pair of extremely sheer stockings engaged her attention, and Elaine waited in respectful silence until they were safely adjusted and the garters fastened.

"You going out, Mama?" she asked then.

"I've an appointment with Louis for nine thirty."

Her mother's voice retained a trace of the bronchial cough, but her eyes were bright and clear. She stepped briskly about the room, finishing her toilet in deft, sure movements oddly at variance with the wild confusion surrounding her.

"I don't see how you ever find anything," Elaine said finally as she watched her mother extract a pair of pearl earrings from a small gold pillbox.

22

Pauline said that she knew where to look.

"This isn't one of your best days, is it, dear? It's a difficult morning for your sign. You're apt to be restless."

She was restless, Elaine admitted. Everyone was.

"Lucie called me this morning, Mama. She's going mad, she says. She wanted to know if I thought having another baby would do anything for her."

No, she didn't know exactly what Lucie meant by "anything," Elaine said.

"It's a feeling, Mama—I know what she means, but I can't explain it. I've been wondering if perhaps I ought to be doing something, too—like going out to help Dr. Schweitzer."

Other women had done it, she pointed out, trying to stem her mother's protests. She would never go, but it would be one way of making her life useful.

"The trouble with you," said Pauline, zipping herself neatly into a becoming black wool, "is that Mars is in your tenth house all this week. Affects your reason and intellect."

Whatever she and her mother talked about, Elaine realized, would be tied in with the stars. For Mama, astrology explained everything, solved all worries, and quieted all fears. Kelsey said that if the stars gave her any comfort or guidance, fancied or real, no one should attempt to interfere. Dr. Cannon protested when she made her appointments with him contingent on dates approved by her horoscope, and the rector of All Souls regularly suggested that it was Kelsey's Christian duty to discourage his mother-in-law's devotion to dark superstition.

The staff of All Souls would probably be surprised, Elaine thought, if she volunteered for work with Dr. Schweitzer. A woman whose husband and child were desperately seeking personal freedom, whose aging mother resented any hint of supervision, might do worse than take off for a field in which the laborers seemed perpetually to be few.

"Avoid controversial issues," mumbled Pauline, speaking around a bobby pin held in her teeth.

Elaine decided to phone Naida Steckner for an appointment. It was braver to face the failure of her marriage and try to save it than to turn her back on the problem and seek refuge in distance.

"Be sure to take a cab, Mama," she said. "Shall I come down with you? Albert may be too busy with the mail to call a taxi."

"Don't be silly," Pauline retorted. "Albert will look after me. Tell Pearl I won't be home for lunch."

Pearl liked a day with no one at home for lunch. Elaine, watching the elevator signal turn red as the car descended with her mother, thought with distaste of the only tearoom near the Thrift Shop. She was due to clerk in the shop, which was supported by a charitable foundation and staffed by volunteers, from one till four o'clock that afternoon.

The mail lay on the narrow drop-leaf table in the hall. Elaine's two favorite magazines, tightly rolled and wrapped, were on top of the letters. Mama doted on the stories, but Elaine found the marriage-counseling departments invaluable. The long, intimate disclosures made by other women had absorbed her for years, and she methodically compared their experiences with her own, only to decide that something must be wrong with her relationship with Kelsey. It was disquieting to recall no dramatic episodes in her married life to match the passionate printed outbursts.

She picked up the letters. The atrocious handwriting on one envelope addressed to Kelsey was Lucie's. (Lucie wrote to him only when she wanted money.) Amanda had a letter from the *Blaze*. (Mirabelle Marilyn Meeks must have a staff of secretaries if she answered all the letters the teen-agers sent her.)

As for Elaine, she had three letters and two appeals for contributions from national organizations, and although she was an erratic correspondent herself, she felt vaguely disappointed.

As she turned away from the table, she saw a letter on the floor. It was addressed to Kelsey, in an orderly feminine hand that slanted backward. Elaine looked for the sender's name, found it: "Mrs. Lige Cutter," with a blurred postmark and a Japanese stamp.

So, Midge Sully might be expected to turn up again! She had never, in all the years since her engagement to Kelsey had been broken, had the decency to remove herself completely from his life. True, she had not corresponded directly with him since her marriage to an Army officer, but she did write to his mother, who lived in Madrid. Elaine suspected that her husband's mother had been very fond of Midge and that she would have preferred her as a daughter-in-law.

"Did you ever make it clear to your mother that I had nothing to do with your breaking your engagement to Midge?" Elaine still asked this question at intervals.

Midge had broken the engagement, Kelsey always answered.

Elaine carefully tucked the letter out of sight under the rest of the mail and dialed Naida Steckner's number. Naida could take her at half past ten, and if she hurried, she could do the marketing first.

II

"All you need is more confidence in yourself," Naida Steckner said.

She cheerfully admitted that she told all her clients that, since most of them were women and therefore basically insecure. Everything about Naida was designed to comfort the distressed, from the atmosphere produced by her office to the impression of serenity and health she herself created.

The office was a restful room, done in blues and grays, the lamps shaded, the window draperies cleverly manipulated to screen all glare and yet avoid the effect of muffling the air and light. Deep, comfortable chairs, footrests, and handy small tables formed group patterns, and the only couches were sectionals upholstered in a quilted blue-and-gray sprigged print. Naida's desk, painted French gray and waxed to a dull finish, faced the room from a corner niche at one side of the white-bricked fireplace.

Elaine Carpenter felt better whenever she looked at the large, smiling woman seated behind the desk. This feeling she shared with Naida's other clients, none of whom could have told exactly why she insensibly relaxed the instant Mrs. Steckner's secretary ushered her into the consulting room.

"She's big, big and quiet." Elaine had once tried to describe

Naida to Kelsey. "I don't think she could hurry if she tried."

Looking at her this morning, Elaine did not think it likely that she had ever tried. A large woman, not overweight—"built like an opera singer" the husband of one client had described her—Naida radiated calmness and good will. She wore simple clothes, pulled her dark hair back into a loose knot, and freely confessed that the silver hoop earrings in her pierced ears were lucky charms.

All she did, she said, was listen to the unhappy and the afraid.

She did not profess to be a marriage counselor, although many, Elaine included, called her that. Such psychology as she practiced had been gained through experience. She had majored in home economics, and frequently expressed surprise that, after being twice widowed, she had not resumed her teaching. It was as if, she sometimes said, her consultation service had been developed without her conscious thought.

"You don't even know that this Midge Sully is coming to the United States," Naida said now.

She had a quiet, clear voice and usually made flat statements, avoiding questions.

Midge Sully was really Midge Cutter, Elaine carefully explained. She and her husband were presumably in Japan—at least the stamp was Japanese—but it was nearly time for Major Cutter to be transferred.

"I've never told Kelsey, but I've kept track of Midge—you can get the service journals at the library. She wouldn't write to Kelsey unless they are coming home. Why would she want to see him now, after all these years?"

Naida's dark eyes surveyed her client dispassionately.

"She isn't going to look the way she did when she was engaged to your husband, if that is what is troubling you." Naida had heard the story of the broken engagement before. "But you'll probably feel better if you buy some new clothes and try a new rinse for your hair."

Midge would remain an unwithered rose to Kelsey, Elaine prophesied; a man's early sweetheart was a fixed image in his mind.

26

"And Amanda will take to her at once; the way things are now, anyone I dislike has tremendous appeal for Amanda."

Naida said, "Naturally. She can't agree with you or her ego shrinks."

Elaine controlled an impulse to say, "To hell with her ego," and decided instead that she felt more resigned. Conversation with Naida was expensive—fifteen dollars an hour—but always helpful. If only she could persuade Kelsey to consent to at least one interview!

Unfortunately, as soon as she had left the soothing background of the blue-and-gray room, she began to wonder if she and Naida had settled anything at all. Before the elevator had reached the street floor, the vision of Midge, wrapped in a heavily embroidered kimono and performing the ceremonial tea service before a mesmerized Kelsey, moved into her mind. A hurried lunch in a tearoom, where breakfast was still being persistently served, failed to dispel the picture. Neither did her still more hurried dash into a dress shop, where she discovered that she had no definite idea of the style or color she wanted. She developed a dull headache, for which she took aspirin, and reached the Thrift Shop ten minutes late, but then, few of the volunteers were ever on time.

For the first hour she and Vivian Nelson, an older woman who gave three full days a week, were busy. Then, as the time came for children to reach home from school, trade slackened. Mrs. Nelson went across the street to a tearoom for hot chocolate and cake, and Elaine settled into a comfortable shabby chair with her magazine.

Her reading followed a regular pattern. She turned first to the case histories of "sick" marriages, the situations related in detail by the distressed victims and the treatment outlined more concisely by marital specialists. The letters were always written by women. In some instances they succeeded in persuading their husbands to consult a counselor, but the acknowledgment that outside help was needed came first from the wife.

The tendency of married couples, according to the testimony, to live violently puzzled Elaine. At the same time she found

27

the confessions absorbing. Faintly recognizing the dramatic appeal of hysterics, she had convinced herself that her even-tempered life, and consequently her marriage, was a failure.

It must be a failure, she reasoned, since the disharmonies in her relationship with Kelsey apparently lay buried too deep to be easily faced and analyzed. No marriage, she had gathered from her reading, could be as quietly satisfying as the years she and Kelsey had lived together seemed to be. He had hoped for more children—perhaps a son—but it had not occurred to either of them to consider their disappointment a cause for "drifting apart." Elaine, reading this afternoon the passionate flow of prose in which a husband and wife bitterly blamed each other for physical and spiritual discord, found it increasingly difficult to visualize Kelsey performing a similar self-examination. But neither could she decide whether the kindness, even tenderness, he unfailingly had for her was a sign of weakness or of strength. It simply wasn't normal not to have one's marriage "threatened."

She enjoyed her work at the Thrift Shop, and more than one grateful customer had learned to ask for her by name. Several members of the Foundation assured her regularly that she would be a great success in a smart establishment, and make money, even if she served only part time.

"With your daughter no longer needing your whole attention, you ought to begin to think about the time when she will be married and gone," these women said.

Sometimes they added, "Before your mother gets to be a problem."

She had no desire to work in a dress shop; she had never had any desire to go to business. She must be the only woman in the world who wanted to stay at home, Elaine thought. The volunteer work, performed as her contribution to church and charity, exposed her to no competition: she had no faith in her ability to stand comparisons or to work under pressure. She had thought, certainly she had absorbed the idea in her girlhood, that marriage and maternity were sufficient to fill a woman's time. And then, as she began to realize that she had no more confidence in her ability to be a successful wife and

28

mother than in her ability to achieve a career, the need for support became a necessity, a defense against intangible fears. Naida Steckner's advice, whether followed or not, offered comfort for the moment. After all, comfort was always temporary.

That night Tully Hallam was giving a pajama party, and Amanda had gone home with her from school. Elaine, waiting for Kelsey to open and read the letter from Midge, regarded his suggestion that they have her mother up for dinner as a move to distract her. Kelsey was very fond of his mother-in-law, but Elaine had suspected more than once that he relied on the presence of a third person at the dinner table to keep arguments from developing.

"All right for dinner, Pauline?" Kelsey had phoned Mrs. Ives, his hand idly turning over the mail on the small table.

And he had replaced the handset smiling.

"Pauline says the stars direct her to spend the evening with loved ones," he reported.

Light from the dining-room chandelier, in a design of half a dozen pink-shaded lamps, touched the gleaming waves of Pauline's chromium-toned hair. Her electric-blue crepe deepened the color of her eyes. The recollection that her horoscope for the day had stated definitely "You will be popular with the opposite sex" gave her an extra touch of assurance. Even if the opposite sex was only her son-in-law, she reminded herself honestly, watching Kelsey carve the steak. Sometimes she read her horoscope for a week in advance, and Kelsey accused her of getting her days and dates hopelessly mixed, which did not matter at all. The sense of continuity, of an unbroken chain of days stretching endlessly into the future, was her only objective.

Pearl usually confined her duties as waitress to bringing in the food and removing the dishes once, before bringing on dessert. Elaine waited until Kelsey had finished carving and she herself had served the vegetables to ask if he had looked at his mail.

"Saw a letter from Midge Sully—Midge Cutter, rather." Kelsey spoke cheerfully. "Wonder where she is—I didn't notice the postmark."

Elaine said that Midge was in Japan and that Pearl would probably like the stamp for her boy friend's stamp collection.

"I thought people in the armed services frank their letters," Pauline interposed. "Or at least pay domestic postage. Perhaps the letter isn't from Midge. The Fishers are traveling abroad—they could be in Japan."

"Kelsey doesn't know the Fishers," Elaine said.

He knew when he was licked, Kelsey assured them, pushing back his chair. Not only would he fetch the letter, but he'd read every damn word of it aloud if he could decipher Midge's handwriting; he hadn't been able to translate the message on the last Christmas card she had sent them.

Elaine reflected that any woman but Midge would have stopped sending Christmas cards to a couple who year after year made no return. Not that Midge remembered them every Christmas, but certainly each time her husband's new orders came through she mailed them a Christmas greeting with the corrected address. Kelsey's mother said that in this way Midge kept in touch with a long list of friends.

"You don't have to read it aloud, Kelsey," Elaine said. "It's probably rather personal—the fact that she put a stamp on it, I mean."

Kelsey, baffled, decided to let that go. He brought the letter to the table, slit the envelope with a silver knife. Pearl came in to bring hot rolls, and he read the single flimsy sheet of paper while she filled his water glass.

"Well—" He smiled across the table at Elaine as Pearl returned to the kitchen. "Midge and her husband are flying to the States, the first of February. They expect to be here for a couple of days. Here, you read it."

He handed the letter across the low bowl of dwarf tulips—Elaine thought January the most melancholy of months and insisted on having flowers on the table for every meal—and asked if anyone wished more steak.

"As I remember Midge Sully," Pauline said, "she always put her hand up to her mouth when she talked. You could hardly understand her; the words came out in a mumble."

Elaine said coldly that Midge had been terribly pigeon-toed.

30

Practically a deformity. A good orthopedic man might have been able to help her.

Kelsey laughed, and Elaine finished the letter hurriedly. It had been a mistake to consult Naida Steckner before the letter had been opened, but she had been right to trust her intuition, Elaine decided. Midge gave every evidence of planning to renew old friendships.

"I suppose we ought to have them for dinner?" Kelsey's tone was hopeful, but apparently directed toward dessert, for he immediately asked if they were having pie.

"Apple." Elaine wondered if Pearl would remember the cheese. "I don't think Midge wants to come here for dinner, Kelsey. You could take her to lunch and talk over old times."

Pearl stalked in to clear the table. She looked awkward and presumably felt uncomfortable. From time to time she reminded her employers that she was not trained to be a waitress and had no desire to acquire such training. When Elaine visualized herself as the wife of a successful executive, she worried about Pearl, who could never fit into a household given to formal entertaining.

"Didn't Midge marry a divorced man?" Pauline sensed that Pearl, bringing in the coffee, had suddenly become attentive.

Kelsey didn't know, but Elaine said there had been some difficulty. Midge, an Episcopalian, had not been able to have the wedding in her own church.

"The man was a Methodist, so she was married in his church. I heard his first wife married before he did and has since been divorced and married again."

Kelsey took a scalding sip of coffee.

"I wish I knew her sign," Pauline said. "I mean Midge's sign. You ought to remember when her birthday is, Kelsey."

He looked at her and said, "Good Lord, how should I know?"

"You were engaged to her," Elaine reminded him. "You'd better take her out to lunch or she may think I'm jealous."

"I probably wouldn't recognize her if I ran into her downtown." Kelsey eyed his pie wistfully. "We all change."

"She was always terribly pigeon-toed," Elaine said.

"So it shows I could have a church wedding even if I am divorced." Squinting at the silver cake knife, Pearl decided to give it an extra rub.

Amanda had found the bowl of cream cheese and chopped olives in the refrigerator, and with both hands full neatly kicked the door shut. As she crossed the kitchen to the breakfast nook, Pearl had a full view of her silhouette.

"That the new skirt you bought? It makes you into a perfect letter S." She gave the bottle of silver polish a violent shake. "It's too tight. I'm surprised your mother would let you wear it."

Amanda spread a thick layer of the cheese on a slice of bread and fortified herself with a long drink of Coke before she trusted herself to answer.

"I'm buying my own clothes now. Daddy gave me an adjusted allowance. I can't help it if a knit shows the lines of my figure—that's the way they're cut."

Pearl rubbed vigorously at the handle of a fork.

"It's too short. I don't know what the clerk was thinking of, to sell it to you."

"Well I like it." Amanda bit into her sandwich and discovered that she couldn't glare with her mouth full. "Mirabelle Marilyn Meeks says only the young figure can wear knits successfully."

The influence of Mirabelle Marilyn Meeks made her an opponent to be respected; if she recommended hair shirts, her youthful readers undoubtedly would find them comfortable and becoming.

"What were you saying about a church wedding, Pearl?" Amanda, recognizing that the victory was hers, could afford to be gracious. "You and Jerome engaged?"

Pearl scowled, but the temptation to discuss her affairs was stronger than her sense of resentment.

"His mother's always telling him a divorced woman can't be married in church. I still don't know for sure that she means me, but she has a thing about divorce. She dreamed Jerome married a girl who was divorced, and she woke him up crying on him."

Amanda asked with interest where Jerome had been "when he was cried on."

"In his bed, of course, asleep," Pearl snapped. "His mother went into his room to look at him. I'd like to ask that friend of your mother's—the one coming to dinner tomorrow night—some questions."

Amanda said nothing. She had slept little the night before because Tully Hallam had suggested a double date, an offer that she had intimated might be the last.

"I've tried to fix up dates for you a dozen times and you always let your family interfere," Tully had scolded. "You'll have to begin to live your own life pretty soon, or just give in and have no future."

Tully didn't write to Mirabelle Marilyn Meeks, but she did read all the advice to parents and teen-agers published in the magazines. Adolescence, Tully said, was a difficult time for young people, and if they happened to have parents who were ignorant of the modern attitude toward relaxed discipline, then the unfortunate teen-ager must fight for his independence and his right to be free.

"I haven't anything to wear," Amanda had protested, when Tully suggested the double date as a step in the right direction. "I'm buying my own clothes now and I spent the first month's allowance on sweaters."

Excuses irritated Tully, who labeled them a badge of the weak. She had plenty of clothes herself and could easily lend an evening dress.

"Your things are too babyish, anyway. I suppose you couldn't help it when your mother was picking them out, but if you're on your own now, get something striking."

To Amanda, lying awake, the double date had seemed alternately wonderful and dismaying. The impossibility of getting her father's consent, her mother's suspicious attitude toward Tully, including dislike of her manners and clothes, and the knowledge that Tully's taste in boys did not appeal to her had

33

combined to keep Amanda in a restless state until nearly morning.

"You daydreaming or something?"

Amanda realized that Pearl was staring at her, and she hastily swallowed more Coke.

"I hate meeting people who knew my parents before I was born," she said, because that was the first thing that came into her mind to say. "If Mrs. Cutter asks me to call her Aunt Midge, I'll scream."

She had been waiting for Tully to phone, but recently Tully had developed an exasperating habit of staying late at the drugstore to talk with one of the boys who had a part-time job at the fountain. Tully had no patience with telephone restrictions as imposed by Amanda's father, and she said that if Amanda was not willing to assert herself, she must take the consequences. Lately Tully had been phoning halfway through the dinner hour, and Amanda had had to say that she would call her when they had finished eating.

"I think I'll see if Tully's home yet," Amanda said. "We could talk before Daddy comes. You'd think my parents would be glad for me to have a phone of my own, wouldn't you?"

She expected no answer to this question, and Pearl had heard it so often that the words meant nothing to her. For a moment she thought of calling Amanda's attention to the debris left on her kitchen table—after-school snacks were not supposed to make extra work—but a distaste for argument made it seem not worth while. She had been depressed ever since she had learned of that Mrs. Cutter's successful compromise with canon law. If, as a divorced woman, she couldn't be married in one church, she had found one where she could be. Pearl planned to use this evidence to weaken the arguments advanced by Jerome's mother, but unfortunately they had not so far reached the point where it could be introduced. Jerome's mother was—or so he intimated—against divorce in general; she had no specific instances in mind. This, Jerome insisted, was hopeful, but Pearl's doubts constantly increased.

# Chapter 3

"I'm not forgetting the agreement was that you're to be allowed to buy your own clothes." Elaine, struggling with her hair at the dressing-table mirror, averted her eyes from her daughter, standing in the bedroom doorway.

Amanda smoothed the knitted red skirt over her round stomach and tugged it down over her thighs.

"You're making an awful fuss about me wearing it," she said.

Everything had gone wrong all day, Elaine reflected, trying to coax a wave into place. In the absence of Michael, who usually set her hair, a new operator had apparently introduced a weird pattern of his own. Pearl had complained that she was developing another bad cold, but would try to keep on her feet until after dinner. At noon Midge had phoned that her husband had been obliged to go to Washington, but that she would love to come alone, if Elaine didn't mind. And now here was Amanda, determined to look like . . . like Eliza Doolittle, but in a more ridiculous and much shorter skirt.

"You've bought the skirt," Elaine tried again. "I'm not saying you can't wear it, I'm only asking you not to come to dinner in it tonight. It's sportswear, anyway. Why won't you wear one of your dresses?"

Amanda was conscious of a flash of anger, directed not at her mother but at Mirabelle Marilyn Meeks. Mirabelle sat in a nice, comfortable office and dispensed advice, but she was never on hand to help her readers in a crisis. In the battle against parents, Mirabelle counseled teen-agers to stand firmly against injustice and warned that they must be prepared to protect their principles.

35

"I hate my dresses!" On the verge of tears, Amanda tumbled out the words rapidly. "If I can't wear this skirt, I won't come to the table at all. You'd like me to be a freak."

She rushed off, probably to call Tully Hallam and get sympathy from her, Elaine thought, regretting for a moment that she hadn't asked Tully to dinner in the interests of peace.

Her fingers worked busily with her hair, while the usual doubts and questions that followed any decisions, once made, assailed her. She had asked Kelsey if he and Midge would rather talk over old times with no other guests present. Obviously he could not have intended his answer—"the more the merrier"—to be taken seriously, but a moment's reflection had convinced her that Midge's husband might appreciate an audience for his own reminiscences. Elaine's mother, a tactful listener, had been reluctant to refuse, but the date, she explained, had so many adverse aspects that it would have been folly for her to put foot outside her own door. The guide for that date was even specific: "'Avoid social activity away from home," Pauline was warned.

Just why she had asked Lucie and Royce, Elaine still did not know. Her husband's younger sister insisted that the suburbs stifled her and welcomed every excuse to come in to the city. To all of Lucie's arguments against their way of life and the even stronger evidence of sociologists she doggedly compiled, Royce said only that they had bought the house, hadn't they?

Lucie would have to get a sitter for the two children—the lack of domestic help was another of her grievances. She frankly coveted the services of a grandmother and intimated that, since her own mother lived abroad, Elaine's mother was a logical candidate. That Pauline Ives suspected Lucie of trying to persuade her to cultivate the home-and-hearth qualities she was as stubbornly determined not to develop was a factor Elaine had not discovered.

She had asked Lucie if she remembered Midge Sully. "You must have been about five years old when she and Kelsey were engaged," Elaine had said.

Lucie thought she remembered one Sunday dinner when Midge had been present.

"But Kelsey was always bringing home girls to dinner. It saved him money, and Mother had this fixation that she ought to know her children's friends."

Kelsey's attitude toward his half-sister, more than twenty years his junior, had always been protective. He loaned her money freely, assumed her chronic discontent indicated that she was overworked, and even wondered, at intervals, whether Royce appreciated her. Lucie, Amanda frequently said, "got away with murder."

By the time she had finished dressing and had gone into the dining room to look at the table, Elaine had begun to feel that it was all unreal. Naida Steckner had explained to her that this was wishful thinking, but Elaine welcomed anything that temporarily released the tension. This was one of the reasons that she valued Pearl far above her uneven qualities as a cook. Pearl stuck to the pattern furnished her and distrusted revisions.

"The white sauce turned out right—just thick enough," she informed Elaine when she found her hovering over the yellow tulips arranged for a centerpiece.

Red tulips might have been a better choice, Elaine thought, and she was sorry she had postponed redecorating the dining room until summer.

Pearl straightened a silver knife, moved a salt dish a quarter of an inch.

"You sure this Miz Cutter was married in a church? I mean it wasn't in the rectory or the minister's study, or anything?"

Startled, Elaine was momentarily confused.

"I never said anything about her being married," she protested.

"Your mother did. She said she was divorced—no, the man was divorced. And Miz Cutter married him with a big church wedding."

Elaine recollected Pearl's worries, centering on the attitude of Jerome's mother. Kelsey had said that the question was an obsession with Pearl; he thought that she concentrated on that particular difficulty as a substitute for the far less welcome possibility that Jerome was in no hurry to be married at all.

"When you're ready to marry, we'll find you a church, Pearl." Elaine glanced at her wrist watch and abandoned the idea of doing her hair over for the third time. "You don't have to worry."

The other person's problem always seemed so simple, but you could never be sure what his problem was.

The buzzer sounded, and Amanda, who had been sulking in her room, dashed to the door.

"I didn't think she could run in that skirt," said Pearl, "and you ought to see her when she sits down in it."

Lucie's throaty voice carried into the dining room.

"Sweetie, you look darling!" she greeted Amanda. "Don't tell me we're too early—Royce nagged me to meet him at five thirty. Oh, there's Elaine!"

She kissed her sister-in-law and followed her into the bedroom, leaving Royce to Amanda, an arrangement that usually made him nervous. Lucie, tall and fair and looking impossibly young to be the mother of two children, leaned her elbows on the dressing table and dabbed at her hair with her hands. She always gave the impression of not having time to sit down, and even when actually seated seemed poised for what her husband called "a quick take-off."

"Midge and the major haven't arrived?" In the mirror her aquamarine eyes met Elaine's dark ones.

Elaine explained that the major had been called to Washington.

"And she's coming alone? Don't you think that's kind of funny?" Lucie pulled a lipstick from her handbag, started to work on her lips.

"Well, if she wants to see Kelsey and talk over old times, it's probably better this way." Elaine spoke carefully. "She's staying at the Columbia Hotel, and I don't suppose she wanted to spend an evening alone."

Lucie capped her lipstick, dropped it in the bag. As she straightened her slim figure, her beautifully fitted black velvet sheath accented her height.

"You look lovely, Elaine. All dark-haired women should wear that shade of gray—the Quakers never dreamed up that variation." Her young, restless face mirrored a flash of curiosity. "Did Kelsey go to fetch her? They're coming in together."

Kelsey and Midge Sully had recognized each other in the elevator, as Midge explained in a flat, penetrating voice. Elaine had a moment during the flurry of introductions to remember that Kelsey had said he probably would not know Midge Sully if he "ran into her downtown." Men did not forget; they couldn't tell the color of their wives' eyes (an unhappy wife had written in the last issue of Elaine's favorite magazine), but for them the face of an old flame never changed.

Her own memories of Midge, Elaine discovered, were vague. None of them seemed remotely connected with the small, thin woman wearing dark glasses and dressed in a dark brown wool that looked too heavy for overheated apartments. But she did wear orthopedic shoes.

She was also on a strict diet, she confided, when Royce followed up Kelsey's cocktails with a plate of canapés. She was allowed one Martini, Midge said, for special occasions, but was forbidden to nibble as much as a cracker.

"We had a maid in Japan who learned to make the most delicious hors d'oeuvres." Midge waved Royce and temptation aside. "It's going to be difficult for me to manage without household help. And I haven't a daughter, only boys."

Amanda, introduced, had promptly disappeared. They really needed a waitress when they had guests, but Pearl couldn't work "with strangers" and the agency was critical of permanent help. Midge's house in Japan was probably littered with servants. Every time the dark glasses turned toward Kelsey, Elaine wondered again how he had been able to recognize her. It might be that her mouth—her best feature?—had identified her for him. And when she handed her empty glass to him, he undoubtedly remembered her smile.

Elaine caught Pearl's signal with relief. Amanda reappeared like one who had just recollected an appointment, and Kelsey, walking with Midge, led the way to the dining room.

Lucie and Royce, when it was discovered that Midge's conversational efforts tended to be centered on the exploits of her three sons, worked valiantly to introduce a wider variety of topics. Lucie, in her way an extremist, disapproved of children as subjects of social conversation, and Royce was genuinely interested in firsthand accounts of life in Japan. He was twenty-seven, two years older than Lucie, good-tempered, ready to be contented with their suburban interests and prospects. As he listened to Midge's flat, persistent voice, he told himself that Kelsey could never have been interested in her —women were always dreaming up fantastic tales that had no foundation in fact.

"And Amanda's your only child?" Midge repeated at intervals. "She must be so lonely."

Amanda, the red skirt hidden beneath the table, looked vulnerable in a black jersey blouse that did not bulge at all. She scowled at the guest, but waited until the dessert to fire her bombshell.

"You may not know it, Mrs. Cutter," she said, ignoring her mother's look of alarm, "but an only child makes the best adjustments. Any psychiatrist will tell you that."

Midge's dark glasses masked her expression, but before anyone could speak, the shrill sound of the phone bell offered Amanda the perfect escape.

"It's Tully—it's the only chance she has to call me tonight— you don't care, if I talk to her now, do you, Daddy? I'm finished, Mother. . . ."

At her father's nod, she rushed from the room, and before anyone could fill in with a sentence, they heard her impassioned, "Tully, you angel, you've saved my life!" followed by the crash of the door into the hall as she presumably remembered to kick it shut behind her.

If Royce and Lucie had hoped for a game of bridge on their night off, they were quickly set right. Midge explained that she had played so much bridge the very sight of the cards irritated her.

"The art of conversation is in danger of being lost forever, don't you think?" she suggested. "Why don't we just sit and talk?"

Elaine, who had invited Lucie and Royce as possible partners for the missing major and herself, leaving Kelsey and Midge free to talk over the past, hoped that she did not look exasperated. Midge had arrived with an enormous tapestry bag which she had left on the living-room couch. She must have packed in it every picture ever taken of her three children from the moment of birth to the present day, Elaine decided as package after package of snapshots appeared.

The boys were four, six, and fifteen, Midge said; each had been born in a different country, and she was anxious now to get them started in a permanent school. Lige expected to be stationed in Washington, but she wanted to settle in a suburb farther north.

She talked (Mama had been right, Elaine thought) with the fingers of one hand held to her mouth, and eventually her confidences, explanations, and speculations became a monologue. Lucie and Royce, glassy-eyed in spite of coffee, left at eleven; they had a train to make. Kelsey, with a heavy office day ahead, declined coffee, and Midge sipped hot milk. She never went to bed before one or two in the morning, she told them; Lige was usually in bed and asleep by ten o'clock.

"My God, he probably passes out and she doesn't even know it," Kelsey said when he returned from putting Midge into a cab at half past twelve.

Elaine, emptying ash trays, yawned.

"I suppose walking pigeon-toed finally ruined her feet," she said.

II

"Oh, I got the impression, definitely, that she has about decided to live here," Lucie said into the telephone. "She says she likes our little town. It has atmosphere."

Elaine thought that a woman's place was with her husband.

"Especially when her children are boys. If Midge has lived on Army posts with Lige, why is she suddenly planning to be on her own?"

There was a chance that Lige Cutter would be able to commute weekends, Lucie said, not that a weekend husband could be of much help with the children.

"I don't know why she has to cling to me, either. She expects me to find her a house, introduce her to my friends, get her started off on the right foot. You'd think I was a Welcome Wagon."

Elaine murmured perfunctory sympathy. It evidently didn't occur to Lucie to place the blame where it belonged. Midge Sully would never have fixed on the town of Lyman as the place to "put down roots" (Midge was fond of clichés) if Lucie's mother had not constantly mentioned it in her letters. Lucie's mother was Kelsey's mother, too, of course, but for some reason she had always seemed to be bracketed with Lucie in Elaine's mind.

This morning, after Lucie had hung up, Elaine resumed her interrupted task of dusting the living room. For the last two weeks she had heard about Midge until she was sick of the subject. Her mother had proved intensely curious and, unable to reconcile Amanda's report with that furnished by Pearl, had suggested that Lucie be asked to dinner again, on a date favorable to all loved ones. Amanda was articulate in her dislike of Midge, with a bitterness so unreasonable that Elaine was compelled to admit its blatant unfairness.

"You hardly know her," she had protested once, in appeasement of an uneasy conscience.

Amanda had answered that Midge was a type.

"Pearl says she reminds her of her first mother-in-law."

To Elaine it seemed perfectly clear that the marriage tie between Midge and Lige Cutter was fraying so rapidly that strands were breaking daily, so to speak. The only explanation for the selection of Lyman as a home site was its proximity to the city where Kelsey lived. Lyman was the most ordinary of bright, thriving suburbs, overflowing with young married folk interested in producing the current fashionably large family. Midge was too old to fit in with Lucie's crowd, but then, of course, Midge didn't want to fit in. It was significant that neither Elaine nor Kelsey had yet met the major; his vague duties in Washington continued to account for his absence.

"Why do *you* suppose Midge Sully suddenly decides to settle down in Lyman?" Elaine, standing in the doorway of

42

Kelsey's study, put the question to him impulsively one night.

He looked at her across an orderly arrangement of legal papers that covered the flat-top desk. Early in their married life Elaine had learned that to be interrupted in the midst of his work evenings at home seldom irritated him. Amanda had made the discovery, too; Daddy was usually willing to listen amiably, to make good-humored decisions and offer sympathetic advice. Other husbands, Elaine knew, having compared notes, were apt to resent demands that interfered with concentration when they shut themselves up to wrestle with their office problems at home.

Elaine, in the beginning, had admired Kelsey's industry. She had regarded his documents with awe, and still did. At intervals she had worried about the possible effects of too much night work on his health. In the last few years the nagging conviction that he continued to bring a stuffed briefcase home every night because he was not "getting ahead" had tormented her. She persisted in interpreting it as a reflection of her failure as a wife, this conclusion bolstered by recollections of critical articles in her favorite magazines.

Married to one man for twenty years, she had never discovered that he was a supremely contented individual whose position—solid, unspectacular, respected—on the staff of a large law firm satisfied him completely. He specialized in the preparation of cases for appeal and never appeared in court. Secure in the knowledge that half a dozen law schools routinely suggested that he join their faculties and that when he found time to write the book impatiently awaited by as many lawbook publishers, it would be a classic reference, Kelsey Carpenter considered himself very fortunate. His apparently inexhaustible patience was based on his knowledge that no one and nothing could come permanently between him and his work.

Elaine, watching him tonight, was conscious of a feeling that was so close to envy it startled her. Of course she didn't envy a man's working half the night when he had been bent over a desk all day at the office. It was only that Kelsey so seldom looked tired, and although for the last year he had needed glasses for close work, nothing about him suggested weariness. Work didn't tire him, she reflected, but he had virtually collapsed when he had had to listen to Midge's conversation for just one evening.

"Has Midge decided to settle down in Lyman?" Kelsey sounded surprised.

"I thought Lucie had told you. Don't you think it's funny?"

Kelsey, after a moment's consideration, suggested that Midge had said something about putting the boys in a permanent school. They might find a crowded city school too drastic a contrast to the classes in which they had hitherto been enrolled.

"She and Lucie hit it off?" Kelsey struck a match to rekindle his pipe.

Lucie hadn't been consulted, Elaine said. She reminded Kelsey that Midge was years older than his sister, that their interests couldn't be the same.

"I thought perhaps Midge had talked things over with you."

Kelsey shook his head. "I can't remember what she said that night."

"I heard what she said, when she was here. Neither she nor her husband has any relatives in this part of the country. I just can't understand why she picks out Lyman—unless she's erratic."

"Do you know what I think?" Kelsey put down his pipe. "I think you'll find out she put on a blindfold and stuck a pin in a map."

There was nothing peculiar about Midge's plans to settle in Lyman, Pauline protested when Elaine confided in her at lunch the next day. A client had sent Kelsey a half-crate of fresh strawberries from Florida, and Elaine, who knew that her mother would be at home all day—the stars warned of mishaps outside the home—had suggested that Pearl make an old-fashioned strawberry shortcake for lunch. They wanted nothing with it but coffee, and it was the kind of meal to be enjoyed in the absence of Kelsey, who was indifferent, and Amanda, who was critical.

"You mark my words, Midge Sully is a Gemini type. They're

restless. At least I think so—I may have my signs mixed."
Pauline fingered an earring that pinched; the lobe of her ear
felt on fire. "This is a day full of petty irritations," she murmured so humbly that Elaine couldn't laugh.

"Darling, those earrings always do hurt you. The only
reason you wear them is because Amanda gave them to you.
I don't see that Midge is restless, either. She wants to stay put;
does that make her a Gemini?"

"Virgo, maybe," said Pauline. "Hardly anyone is a pure
type. I wish I could cast her horoscope."

Elaine waited until Pearl, lingering to hear the shortcake
praised, had been satisfied and had withdrawn, to ask rather
doubtfully if an amateur could "do" a horoscope.

"I thought it took an astrologer, Mama. Did you ever do—
cast—anyone's horoscope?"

Her mother poured a little extra heavy cream on her shortcake. She felt competent to cast a horoscope, using her own
"as a sample."

"I've about decided there's no use in my paying out money
every year for a reading. I've studied enough to know how to
interpret the cycles and the—er—adjustments."

Elaine said nothing. She was used to her mother's confusion
of astrological terms that never made sense. Often she wondered if Mama knew what she was talking about, but as a
hobby, astrology was comparatively harmless, not too expensive, and apparently a source of interest and pleasure.

"Mama, you remember Joan Bates? I've worked a lot with
her at the Thrift Shop, and she came up to the house once
for lunch, when you were here? She and her husband are
separating; he's been seeing a girl he used to be engaged to,
before he married Joan."

The words had poured out in a rush. Elaine had intended
to keep still about Joan Bates.

"You've always told me a man never forgets his first sweetheart. And this girl didn't marry; she must have been hoping
that Lester Bates would come back to her. In fact, I suppose
she encouraged him."

Pauline said, "Finish your shortcake, dear. I don't envy

45

Lester Bates, if he lets a Scorpio woman wind him around her little finger."

"I still think it's very odd that Midge should wind up in an ordinary suburb," Elaine mused. "If she wanted to live outside of Washington, there are plenty of smart suburbs with good schools for the children. And she would be near her husband and his work."

Pearl, bringing in hot coffee, managed to create a diversion and at the same time convey a hint of subtle reproach.

"I forgot!" Elaine was instantly contrite. "Mama, Amanda told Pearl that if she could get the date of Jerome's mother's birthday, you'd make her horoscope."

"The time of birth is necessary." A professional dignity descended upon Pauline. "If you know the hour when Jerome's mother was born, I can cast her horoscope, Pearl."

Jerome's mother had been very stuffy about supplying any information, Pearl said.

"Coffee, Miz Ives? She's the suspicious type and if she thought I was trying to find out her age, she wouldn't rest until she turned Jerome against me. I told him old people are always suspicious of everyone else." Jerome's mother, Pearl continued, was not as old as she had thought her to be. She was sixty-three.

"Born November seventeenth, eighteen ninety-nine. Jerome couldn't get the time; he says nobody wrote it down. That long ago I guess it wasn't considered important."

Elaine, who was to give the afternoon to the Thrift Shop, thought that the only good to be obtained from a horoscope was that it gave her housebound mother (self-confined on the days the forecast designated as unfavorable) occupation for the rest of the dreary February day.

She had planned to take a cab, but when the bus slid in beside her just as she reached the corner, her natural instinct for thrift prevailed. The interior of the bus was warm, smelly, and not too crowded. She found a seat on the aisle, and the fat woman who sat next to the window immediately offered to share her newspaper.

"There's two departments I never miss," the stranger con-

46

fided, when Elaine had thanked her and explained that she wanted to rest her eyes. "One is Mrs. Torrington Van Antwerpt's column. The other is Mirabelle Marilyn Meeks's advice to teen-agers—I guess everyone reads her."

Elaine admitted that she had heard of Mirabelle Marilyn Meeks.

"My daughter is one of her fans. I never could see that she does anything extraordinary. A girl could ask her mother the same questions and get the same answers."

Kids, the woman said, didn't think their mothers knew much.

"And lots of times a mother's tired, or worried, and she loses patience when she's expected to be listening as sweet as pie. This Mirabelle, the way she writes, butter wouldn't melt in her mouth. Maybe if mothers wrote letters and left them around—never talked at all—they'd be popular, too."

Elaine looked doubtful. Curiosity moved her to ask why Mrs. Torrington Van Antwerpt's column was admired.

"Oh, she knows what's proper and what isn't." The fat woman's cheerful face sobered. "You know you've got good manners if you've asked her what to do; keeps you from being nervous when you're asked out."

# Chapter 4

"We moved to the suburbs for the sake of the children," Lucie Hendrix said. "No one told us of the dangers."

She sat in Kelsey's law office, facing her half-brother across his desk. Hatless, her blond hair carefully set to look careless, she appeared nearer eighteen than twenty-five. Her errand this stormy February morning was, as usual, connected with money. The necessity for borrowing from Kelsey brought her to town at fairly regular intervals, and the crisis, as she outlined it, was always personal.

"Royce thinks that if he meets the payments on the house and pays the food and utility bills, he's supporting his family," Lucie had once explained to Elaine. "I have to have money."

It was distinctly jarring to have Kelsey, after having made a number of loans without question, suggest that he ought to know what she planned to do with the "couple of hundred" she had asked to borrow.

"I can't see that it makes any difference," Lucie had argued. "Sometimes I feel that a woman, once she's married, has no personal life. Royce wants to know everything I do, and now my own brother takes advantage of me, simply because I haven't any money. If I had a separate income, everything would be different."

He doubted that money would make *that* much difference, Kelsey said. The blue eyes in his thin face regarded Lucie attentively for a moment, but his voice was affectionate and warm.

"If you were rich, you might consult me as your attorney," he suggested.

When she refused to smile, he watched her grind out her cigarette in his handsome ash tray before he said, "Do you mean you are afraid?"

"Not of lions and bears," Lucie acknowledged, still ruffled. "When I mentioned 'dangers,' I had psychological hazards in mind."

His look of bafflement gratified her. Kelsey was "a brain," he was older than she, he was used to being asked for advice, but he was not a psychiatrist and couldn't be expected to understand women.

"The suburbs are all right for children," Lucie explained kindly, "but young wives, like me, are left too much alone. I'm under a constant emotional strain."

In the pale winter sunshine that brightened the lime green of the office walls, Lucie's skin was flawless and her eyes were clear and bright. Like many tall, slim women, she tended to sprawl in a comfortable chair, but at least the outline didn't suggest tension.

"Tell me some more," Kelsey said.

It was mostly the children, Lucie told him. Royce left early in the morning, didn't return until after six at night. Lucie had only the society of the children during the day, or, at best, that of neighboring wives and mothers who shared her manless world.

"The children are sweet, but they aren't very stimulating intellectually," Lucie pointed out.

Kelsey objected that the average husband absented himself from his home for the greater part of the working day.

"Elaine doesn't see much of me, from after breakfast till dinnertime."

A lawyer could always pick flaws, Lucie said angrily; Elaine could occupy her time in a dozen ways. Women in the suburbs were shut off from easy cultural contacts; if they wanted to get away to spend a day or half a day in town, they had to make it a project.

"Besides, Elaine has Pearl. Do you think Pearl would work in the suburbs? No one on our street has a maid. If I have a cleaning woman twice a month, I'm lucky—and I have to pay her fare both ways—two dollars and a quarter the round trip."

She worked too hard, of course; Kelsey thought that all young mothers were probably overworked. The lack of domestic help was a familiar problem, but no solution seemed to be in sight. Nevertheless, none of this had much bearing on his original question, which was, why was it imperative for Lucie to have two hundred dollars? The desk clock warned him to come to the point.

"Do you and Royce need money to move?"

"Move?" Lucie sounded outraged. "You couldn't pry Royce loose from that house. If I'm going to spend my life there and remain sane, I've got to see a psychiatrist. Now you know!"

Kelsey said, "Oh, good Lord!"

She didn't expect him to understand, Lucie snapped in quick resentment. Royce hadn't been sympathetic, either. Only completely stupid people waited until overtaken by a nervous breakdown before consulting a psychiatrist—and then it might easily be too late.

"A psychiatrist will help me adjust," Lucie said. "He'll relieve my mind."

There was nothing wrong with her mind, her brother assured her. Nor with the minds of hundreds of other women who were apparently willing to take every kind of exercise, except mental.

"Why don't you use your mind, Lucie? Did you ever think through one, just one, of your problems? In the name of common sense, why do you all depend on some outside agency to solve your difficulties? I wish to God I knew."

He thought for a moment of Elaine and her marriage counselor, of Amanda and her pitiful reliance on Mirabelle Marilyn Meeks, of his mother-in-law's blind faith in the wisdom of the stars. Even Pearl was guided by some unseen force functioning in the office of the tabloids. And here was Lucie asking to be added to the leaner's list.

Lucie, who had been applying fresh lipstick, closed her purse and stood up.

"Do I get the money?" she asked bluntly. "I suppose I could manage with a hundred for the start."

"Not this time," Kelsey said, surprised at his own firmness.

She might as well go uptown and have lunch with Elaine, Lucie decided, having regained a measure of her composure by the time she had reached the street. Even if Elaine wasn't home, Pearl usually prepared a meal for Grandma Ives, and the old lady would be only too pleased to have company. It was perfectly ridiculous for a girl to have the family of in-laws that she had, Lucie frequently complained to her husband, and not be able to count on them for any help. No one, for instance, ever volunteered to do any baby-sitting for her; for all they cared, she might be tied to the house and the children until the end of time.

In the taxi—since she would not have to buy lunch, a cab couldn't be labeled an extravagance—her sense of resentment and frustration increased as she watched the sidewalk crowds. She belonged in the city, she told herself; before she had married, she had worked in an office and enjoyed every hour of every day. Two other girls had shared an apartment with her, and although none of them had much money, they had managed a cultural and social life that, in retrospect, had been completely satisfying. And now she was buried in the suburbs, a slave to Royce's timetable and the children's physical routines.

"I haven't been to an art lecture since we moved to Lyman!" she said to Elaine, whom she found at home and absorbed in the task of "going through" the hall closet.

Elaine, a dustcloth tied around her head, murmured that she had to finish before lunch.

"The pickup car from the Thrift Shop is coming at two o'clock. I don't suppose you could use my light gray coat, Lucie? You could wear it to the supermarket."

Lucie declined the coat. She sat on a folding chair, which was to be sent to the Thrift Shop, and stared disapprovingly at Elaine, who was cross-legged on the closet floor.

"I hate the supermarket; it's a nightmare, trying to shop with two children. And I never escape. It isn't a normal life— and I don't know how much longer I can take it."

Elaine, exploring the pockets of a vest discarded by Kelsey, murmured that things would be easier when the children started school.

"The runabout age is the worst," she said. "Who's staying with them today?"

"Mrs. Graham—a neighbor. She offered, because she has no heat in her house; the plumber's putting in a new boiler." Lucie kicked off one pump and began to rub her slender ankle and foot. "I have to make all kinds of damn-fool arrangements to get an hour to myself."

A gentle clatter of dishes sounded in the kitchen and somewhere in the building a heavy door slammed—probably the fire door guarding the entrance to the roof, Elaine thought, conscious of the muffled tremor in the closet depths. She was only too familiar with Lucie's pet grievance, the difficulty of obtaining baby sitters who would serve without pay. Lucie made no secret of her theory that a young wife and mother should be able to depend upon her relatives for such services and she refused to call upon any of the young girls who, together with a sprinkling of older women, did a thriving business as baby sitters in the suburban town.

"I should think Amanda would be glad to get a little experience baby-sitting." Lucie let her other pump drop and began to massage her second foot. "Have you spoken to her lately, Elaine? She may have changed her mind."

Elaine backed out of the closet, dragging a cardboard box after her.

"Old rubbers and storm boots. When we clean house twice a year, how can such a mess accumulate! Lucie, I think you're sitting on my dustcloth."

Lucie retrieved the grimy length of yellow terry cloth and tossed it to Elaine. In the kitchen, Pearl began to sing "I dreamt I dwelt in marble halls," cheerfully off key.

"Does she have to sing that kind of stuff?" Lucie shuddered. "And don't you think that Amanda's at the age now when baby-sitting might appeal to her? Lots of the girls at Miss Mary's must do baby-sitting."

It was practically a profession for teen-agers, Elaine admitted. "But Lucie, they do it to earn money. You don't expect to pay anything, do you?"

She couldn't afford to pay, Lucie said. Besides, there was

52

something sordid in the idea of paying a niece; it used to be that families exchanged favors as a matter of course.

"Now the kids are brought up to expect pay for the smallest thing. I should think you'd want to train your daughter differently."

Elaine's laughter was followed by a sneeze.

"It's the dust," she apologized. "You sound like Mama. If Amanda doesn't want to baby-sit, I can't force her."

Nothing, she knew, would persuade Amanda to go out to Lyman to take charge of Lucie's children, two and three years old. Kelsey wouldn't like it, either, because it would mean that Amanda must stay overnight and sleep in the same room as the children. Amanda had not asked their advice when Lucie had first suggested the arrangement, but she had written to Mirabelle Marilyn Meeks. How much did one owe to one's relatives? Amanda had asked, and the columnist had promptly warned of exploitation.

"The relations of a teen-ager are all too prone to consider her youth and energy as an inexhaustible supply on which they may freely draw," Mirabelle had written with the effect of a fanfare. "The teen-ager has every right to protect herself from these free-loaders. In the exceptional situations where payment is offered, make sure that you are being paid the prevailing rates."

Mirabelle had added a paragraph to the effect that in emergencies, such as illness and death, it was the place of teen-agers to be as helpful as possible, acting as members of the family and without thought of remuneration.

"Don't you have any influence with your own child?" Lucie, cramming her foot back into the shoe, sounded cross.

Elaine said, "No, have you?" and at that moment the buzzer sounded twice, her mother's signal.

Pauline Ives looked so little like a grandmother that Lucie's irritation increased. A really generous woman, Lucie reasoned, would remember that every child was entitled to a grandmother in his background. Her own mother being too far away —a situation that irked Lucie still further—the need for a substitute was obvious.

"Nana, how glad I am to see you!" Lucie made a mental note to ask for the name of Pauline's perfume—spicy, probably carnation.

Pauline Ives disliked being called "Nana," especially by the sister of her son-in-law, a relationship that could not possibly be twisted to cast her in a grandmother's role. Her bright eyes surveyed Lucie warily; the girl never came to town unless she wanted something from Kelsey or Elaine.

"I didn't know you were going to clear out that closet, dear." Pauline recoiled delicately as her dusty daughter scrambled to her feet. "Why don't you have Pearl help you?"

"She makes better waffles than I do, and you thought waffles would be nice for lunch, Mama," Elaine reminded her. "You and Lucie go into the living room, and I'll wash my hands and tell Pearl we're ready."

Her mother called after her, "Take that cloth off your head, for pity's sake," and as she led the way into the living room she confided to Lucie that no woman should ever allow herself to be seen with her head tied up "like a boiled pudding."

"Are you going somewhere, Nana?" Lucie limped across the rug to the small love seat between the two windows.

Pauline examined her reflection in a mirror above the fireplace. Her black silk suit was new—a little early to wear it, but she had her fur jacket—and her close-fitting flowered hat was really lovely. She looked the way she wanted to look— not overdressed, but as certainly not dowdy.

"I'm going to a matinee with a friend," she said. "Did you come in for the day?"

Lucie removed her pump, an automatic gesture with her whenever she could sit down. It had been simply ages since she had seen a matinee, she sighed.

"The doctor is always telling me I need to get out more, that I'm too tense. But how . . ."

"Doctors are always telling women they're too tense," Pauline interrupted quickly. "You don't have to go out; there are exercises you can do. I read a book about it—or did Pearl tell me?"

54

Elaine's announcement that lunch was ready served as a truce. But Lucie, smarting under the morning's earlier defeat, was determined to be heard.

"Don't you think you'd like to come out and see the children, Nana?" She buttered her waffle sparingly, mindful of the current cholesterol warnings. "The lawns are really green now, out with us."

Pauline, a city woman, was more than content with the grass in the parks, but she murmured politely that the suburbs were always lovely in the spring.

"Are you taking coffee, Mama?" Elaine wondered whether, if she kept still, Lucie would mention Midge Sully.

"With cream," said Pauline. "Is this the new syrup? It's very good."

"We'd love to have you come out and spend the night. Royce could bring you out with him," Lucie persisted. "The children are growing so fast, you won't know them."

Pearl's service might not be that of a trained waitress, but she made excellent waffles. She had never learned to move quietly about the kitchen and she had a tendency to lunge when she entered the dining room, but Elaine, reflecting that Amanda was given to comparing Pearl with the trained waitress Tully Hallam's mother employed to supplement the trained cook, told herself that at least Pearl never complained about guests. Mrs. Hallam didn't dare have unexpected company and she was bound by an agreement to pay a stipulated bonus for each invited guest.

"Don't you ever feel shut in, living in an apartment the year round?" Lucie, accepting a second waffle, decided that perhaps butter was unsaturated fat.

"Well, I don't," said Elaine, who recognized that her mother was beginning to lose patience. "We've never had a house. And Mama's lived most of her life in apartments, too."

Lucie's aquamarine-blue eyes turned reproachfully to Pauline.

"Don't you *want* to come and see me, Nana? Be honest— after all, we're related, you know. I like people to be perfectly frank with me."

Pauline Ives glanced composedly at her wrist watch, a Christmas gift from Kelsey.

"I'll have to be running along; I had no idea it was so late," she said. "You're sweet to ask me, Lucie, but this month is bad for journeys. My horoscope warns me to be careful, in fact, until some time in the summer. And I've been meaning to tell you this, but I always forget: your children are born under signs that clash with mine. We're incompatible—I mean it. Children are extremely sensitive, and they'd know at once that I could never understand them. If people only took the trouble to consult the stars, they could avoid so many difficulties."

She smiled impartially at Elaine and Lucie, who were both speechless, pushed back her chair, and stood up.

"I hate to hurry off, but I'm meeting Carolyn Mills and I have both tickets. Tell Pearl I'm still working on the chart for Jerome, won't you, Elaine? And thank you for the lunch, darling."

She disappeared in the direction of the bathroom; in the silence, Pearl managed to drop a plate, with shattering effect.

"Have some more coffee." Elaine, as hostess, suddenly felt inadequate.

"I don't believe a word of that horoscope nonsense," Lucie said. "Nana's so afraid I might ask her to baby-sit that she dreamed it all up."

From the hall Pauline's voice interrupted her gaily.

"Good-by, dears, I'm off! Give my love to Royce and the children, Lucie."

A lock of Lucie's blond hair fell across her forehead, making her look like a sulky child.

"I suppose Nana's forgotten how children tie a woman down," she said as the door latch clicked.

Elaine remembered that she had an appointment for three o'clock, but it would seem heartless to abandon Lucie in her present unhappy state of mind. Besides, what about Midge Sully?

"We'll go in to my room—I have to dress—and let Pearl clear the table." Elaine was conscious of a brief flash of grati-

56

tude that she didn't have to listen to her sister-in-law every day.

Lucie felt on the rug for her shoe and stood up, her face flushed.

"I wonder if Pearl wouldn't come out once or twice a week," she said as she followed Elaine across the hall and into the large, comfortable bedroom.

The idea evidently pleased her. Pearl was at a settled age, Lucie pointed out; she could watch television with her boy friend—what was his name?

Neither Pearl nor Jerome would be tempted, Elaine returned with unusual firmness. Pearl had a horror of "the country," which for her began at the city limits. As for Jerome, he was the active type; if he didn't bowl, he had to play shuffleboard or dance. Yes, certainly he and Pearl went dancing; an evening just sitting still presumably exhausted them.

Lucie, seated on the bed opposite the dresser mirror, began absently to pat her hair into shape with the tender, caressing movements that so many women reserve for their hair. She worked deftly, even expertly, her long, slim fingers restoring the pristine lines of her good foundation cut.

"I don't want to hurry you," Elaine said, pulling on the skirt of her suit, "but I'm due at a Forum lecture. Can't you go to a movie? Are you meeting Royce to go home with him?"

She had no time to waste on movies, Lucie retorted, without shifting her gaze from the mirror. What she really should do was buy several books, but she didn't have the money.

"I suppose it would be all right if I charged them to Kelsey's account at his bookstore?"

Elaine hesitated. Kelsey, protective and sympathetic toward Lucie and her many complaints, had recently criticized her tendency to be extravagant. Elaine also recalled Lucie's habit of charging items on her, Elaine's, store accounts and forgetting to mention either merchandise or money.

Books, however, were not clothes or luxuries; Elaine shared a rather common impression that buying books mysteriously elevated the shopper to a higher plane. It was a commendable and even a faintly virtuous act, and should not be discouraged.

"It will be all right, but be sure you tell him." Elaine flicked a powder puff across her nose and picked up her purse. "What book do you want?"

Lucie said she had a list. "There are four I want especially. They're all on psychiatry. Midge Cutter wants to borrow them, when I get them."

Elaine waited until they were in the elevator to ask if Midge had moved to the suburbs.

"Oh, nothing's settled—she's trying to make up her mind. I've given her the names of two real-estate agents. She went down to Washington for a week to be with her husband, and I don't know whether she's back."

She wasn't looking forward to having Midge as a possible neighbor, Lucie revealed, but every cloud had a silver lining.

"She's years older than I am, and privately I think she's an awful bore."

The elevator swayed to a stop at the ground floor, and Elaine gently pushed Lucie out. She had a habit of holding the gate open while she finished a conversation, a practice Albert discouraged.

"You're in an awful hurry, aren't you?" Lucie commented, her heels clicking on the tiles as she tried to keep up with Elaine's swift pace. "My feet are killing me today; these shoes are new."

Elaine said, "They're lovely shoes. Have you ever noticed Midge's feet? She's pigeon-toed."

Out on the street, Lucie decided to take a cab to the bookshop.

"What did you mean by the silver lining?" Elaine had not lost the thread.

Lucie looked puzzled for a moment, then her face cleared.

"Oh! Why, Midge told me that Army wives often exchange baby-sitting. I'm going to suggest that we arrange something like that. If she moves to Lyman, I mean. I want a couple of afternoons a week free—if I'm to be analyzed. No psychiatrist takes people at night."

"What on earth . . ." Elaine began, but she remembered that she was already late. "You'd better not tell Kelsey," she advised hurriedly, and signaled a passing taxi.

When she looked back, Lucie was stepping into another cab. The bookshop was in the business district, the Forum hall at the other end of the city.

Elaine wondered if books on psychiatry were expensive; she decided that they probably were.

# Chapter 5

The intermission was the most valuable part of these lectures on understanding teen-agers, most of the mothers who attended agreed. They listened respectfully to the teachers, doctors, lawyers, sociologists, scientists, psychiatrists, and psychologists who addressed them, and they took voluminous notes. But it was in the intermission—when they relaxed and consulted each other, shared impressions and experiences, and confessed their anxieties—that they felt they might be making progress.

All about her, Elaine saw women who, like herself, had faithfully sat through the fall semester and would dutifully finish out the spring term. And next year they would presumably sign for another series, since child guidance continued to offer a measure of hope.

"I don't feel that I've learned very much," one woman had said to Elaine just before the Christmas holidays, "but I don't know what else to do."

Elaine didn't know what else to do, either. Teen-agers, the majority of lecturers assured their hearers, were confused and confusing. The likelihood of parents being able to understand their young was growing fainter with each generation.

This afternoon, at the announcement of a ten-minute interval to be followed by the question period, the crescendo of women's voices started almost before the speaker had left the platform.

"Do you know the topic assigned to my daughter's class for weekend homework?" the woman on Elaine's left fairly sputtered.

On the other side of Elaine, a thinner, younger-looking woman leaned forward.

"Don't ask her, I'll tell you," she said. "It's 'How I Think My Parents Can Improve the Feeble Minds God Gave Them.'"

Elaine laughed, but the first speaker almost choked in her eagerness to answer.

"You haven't got it quite right, but the idea is the same. Joan's topic is 'What I Dislike About My Parents.' I don't think they should encourage children to pick their parents apart like that. Joan says it's time parents learned they are not on pedestals."

"Does she know what a pedestal is?" The other woman put a hand up to her hair, and the sunlight flashed on her diamond rings.

Elaine said that so far her daughter's school had been conservative; as far as she knew, criticism of parents was not invited.

"My husband thinks this, this passion for finding fault with parents is a reaction from the mother-knows-best theory that we were taught. But he doesn't approve; at least the mother, as older and more experienced, has a better chance of being right than a child with no experience at all."

A voice behind them suddenly boomed. "Will you kindly tell me why we now have a generation of parents and children so exquisitely complicated that neither can communicate with the other? We have to have experts to explain us to the children, explain the children to us, and then remain in control for evermore to see that no one runs off the track. What happened to turn the parent-child relationship into a deadly hazard, as it were, overnight?"

In the confusion that followed the attempt of several listeners to answer simultaneously, Elaine remembered that Amanda had asked Tully Hallam for dinner that night. Pearl would be off—for a moment Elaine considered Pearl's future and whether it was likely to contain Jerome—but the dinner would be easy to get. It was regrettable that neither she nor Kelsey liked Tully, Elaine admitted to herself, but she had the feeling that this was one reason Amanda clung so fiercely to the friendship. Tully, Elaine suspected, had standards more flexible than Amanda's code approved, but nothing would ever induce Amanda to acknowledge it.

The speaker returned—a blonde, beautifully dressed woman somewhere in her early forties. Elaine remembered that her mother, who had attended one lecture with her, had described Mrs. Cobalt as "sprightly."

"She acts as if she had just swallowed a whole bottle of B-twelve," one exhausted listener had observed.

There was, in fact, something not quite natural about Mrs. Cobalt's boundless energy and the perpetual brightness of her eyes and smile. Her audience, almost to a woman, suspected that she hoped to encourage them to follow her example; teenagers, she had instructed them on several occasions, appreciated mothers in whom they could take pride.

A low white leather chair had been placed near the edge of the platform, providing a foil for her trim black suit, her smart blue hat, her alligator bag, and her golden hair. She knew how to sit so that her short skirt made a nice line. Elaine wished that Amanda could benefit by this example of how to be graceful under difficulties.

Mrs. Cobalt's practice was to recognize the raised hands in her audience.

"First, the third from the right, in the back row," she said cordially. "Try to make your question brief and of general interest."

No one paid any attention to this cliché, which was presumably automatic.

"What I'd like to know," said a high, nervous voice, the tone of a woman bracing herself to speak in public, "is your honest opinion of Mirabelle Marilyn Meeks."

Elaine glanced briefly over her shoulder, but the speaker had already resumed her seat. The advertisements had assured her, in large type and in small, that Mirabelle Marilyn Meeks was known to thousands, so it was rather silly to be startled by the mention of her name.

"What I'd really like to know . . ." the nervous voice began again, wavered, then seemed to gain confidence. "What I'd *really* like to know is how to combat her."

Mrs. Cobalt said, "You mean her influence?"

"I mean just that. She tells my two girls what to say to me. I'm so sick of her I could scream."

"Amen!" boomed the woman behind Elaine.

Mrs. Cobalt's level glance conveyed a reproof.

"All right, let's consider Mirabelle Marilyn Meeks and the other columnists who write for teen-agers." She smiled at Elaine without actually seeing her. "Teen-agers feel that these columnists are their friends."

Forestalling the natural question, "Why?" she added hurriedly that Mirabelle was an excellent listener. She communicated only by letter or in print.

"The teen-ager feels that she's allowed to state her grievance, or her need for advice, uninterrupted. She's treated as an equal. The ego, you must remember, is very sensitive at this age."

At the back of the hall, the high-pitched nervous voice tried once more.

"Do you think she ought to take the place of parents?"

"Certainly not." Mrs. Cobalt was properly indignant. "I think, if you're honest, you'll find that nine times out of ten, the columnists uphold the parents. At their worst, these writers are harmless, but at their best they can be a source of security and comfort."

Impulsively and to her own astonishment, Elaine raised her hand.

"But why should these children pour out their hearts to strangers?" she asked. "If it's privacy they want—and you are always reminding us that the adolescent must have privacy—a mother, or a father, would be . . . well, safer."

"Perhaps," Mrs. Cobalt conceded. "Not, however, if there is anything to conceal. Most teen-agers seem to feel that confidences, given to a parent, only arm authority."

The audience stared silently for a moment, not actively hostile, but with visible resentment.

"I'd like you to know," said a stout woman at the end of

63

Elaine's row, "that I am about fed up on Mirabelle Marilyn Meeks and her ilk. If she confined her advice to telling the kids how to get along on dates and what to say when a boy has to borrow money from a girl before he can take her to the movies—well, that may be all right. Does she stop there?"

Mirabelle Marilyn Meeks did not stop there. The audience rustled in acquiescence; Mirabelle went much further.

"She told my daughter I'm hopelessly old-fashioned because I won't let her wear lipstick at thirteen." The stout woman's indignation was mounting. "She tells her that her father is too critical of her boy friends. And on top of everything else, she tells her to be patient—that parents mean well!"

The question period was beginning to get out of hand. The mention of Mirabelle Marilyn Meeks was an irritant to the mothers present. Elaine was glad to discover that her dislike of the columnist was shared by other women. If, as Amanda claimed, she was narrow-minded, hers was not an isolated case.

Mrs. Cobalt had risen, but before she could assume control, the booming voice behind Elaine exploded into words.

"My two girls wouldn't dream of changing their hairdos, or buying a pair of shoes, without consulting Evelyn Empress; she's on the *Evening Star*. She's never seen the girls, but she tells them what to wear, says it's important for them to establish their identities, even if it means fighting their parents, who want to hold them back."

"Our time," said Mrs. Cobalt with the firmness born of desperation, "is about up. I'll try to take up this subject of columnists and their advice next week. It's a matter of vital importance to adolescents, and parents should make every effort to understand. For the present, I'll say just this: Almost without exception these writers do a good job of counseling and will, whenever possible, uphold the authority of the parents."

She hastily gathered up her papers from the table behind her, raised her hand in the familiar farewell salute, and withdrew through the curtained doorway which delivered speakers to a private exit at the back of the hall.

The reaction of the audience, crowding into the aisles, was expressed in the comment of a brisk young woman who looked like a teen-ager herself and who was improving the enforced delay by touching up her mouth with a tortoise-shell lipstick.

"I'll bet she has her own column. Wish I could start one," the girl said.

She responded to Elaine's sympathetic glance with the information that once you had a column "going," with the backing of a good syndicate, you were on the road to riches.

"The kids have lost their heads completely. They'll buy anything, do anything, if they read it in their favorite column. Seeing their letters in print does something to them—don't ask me what. I've got two young nieces and I swear that if this Mirabelle mess told them to go jump off a cliff, they'd be looking for a cliff the next morning. It's uncanny."

They had reached the vestibule, but Elaine lingered.

"And yet you want to write a column like hers?" she asked. "Or do you mean you'd exercise better judgment and uphold the parents' views? After all, the responsibility is ours, you know; these outsiders don't take hold when anything happens."

"Well, you have a point there," the girl said, pulling a scarf from the pocket of her tweed coat.

She tied it over her pretty bright hair, oblivious to the fact that the effect was hideously unbecoming, and murmured that she must be on her way.

"A column that accepted parents would be a flop," she told Elaine. "You have to take sides with the kids. It doesn't matter what they beef about. Half of them will complain that their parents are too strict and another half will moan that their parents don't care what they do, when they come in, or when they go out. You can't please kids at a certain age—you could save yourself an awful lot of misery if you'd just admit that."

Elaine experienced confusion and a curious mounting respect.

"You're not . . . you haven't children . . ." she was beginning to loathe the word "parent."

She had two youngsters, the girl said, both boys and not old enough to worry about their mother's divorce.

"They won't be uneasy until they read somewhere that they're the product of a broken home. You can't bring up a child today without having him learn that he's a problem. He gets the idea early that he isn't normal unless he is a problem."

Elaine had time to wonder, as her taxi crawled through the late-afternoon traffic, what attraction Mrs. Cobalt could have had for the mother of preschool children. If she ever saw her again, she would ask her. Not that the afternoon had been particularly helpful to the mothers of adolescents. When you came right down to it, Elaine reflected, she was sick of advice. Everyone advising everyone else, and was anything ever settled? Naida Steckner had a way of making you believe whatever she said, as long as you could hear her. Once you were out of her office, the old specters rose up to confront you—Midge Sully, for example. And Amanda, who leaned on Mirabelle Marilyn Meeks for comfort, was never fortified for the next worry; if anything, the more advice she received, the more helpless she seemed to be.

Her mother let herself be guided by the stars, and it might be, to quote her new acquaintance, that she had a point there.

"But you have to have faith," Elaine said aloud, to the astonishment of the cab driver. "I wish I believed in astrology. You don't have to think at all. It's worked out for you. Mama simply follows her charts."

"I'm Sagittarius myself," the cab driver said.

## II

The first thing Elaine noticed about Tully Hallam when she found her sitting on a floor cushion before the television set was her hair. The blonde girl's tousled head was undoubtedly an example of the artichoke cut enthusiastically promoted by the beauty salons, but it was a coiffure much too old for her. She had been experimenting with eyeshadow, too. Elaine, remembering her own teen-age days, when lipstick was the coveted symbol of maturity, decided that her birthdays were showing.

"Hi, Mrs. Carpenter," said Tully civilly. "Amanda and I are doing our homework before dinner."

Amanda, she explained, was in the kitchen, putting food

66

back in the refrigerator. They had had a snack, but the Pulse-Finder program went on at five thirty and to be eligible for the contest, you had to listen from the beginning to the end.

Elaine murmured that she had to see about dinner. A steady stream of chatter from the voluble young woman on the screen followed her to the kitchen door. Tully would have to tone down the volume when Kelsey reached home.

"For pity's sake!" said Elaine when she saw her kitchen.

Amanda, transferring dishes from the machine to a tray on the table, looked disapproving.

"I hope you girls haven't spoiled your appetites for dinner," Elaine said, worried. "And you certainly could leave the dishes —Tully's all alone."

Tully could stay alone, Amanda said crossly; she would rather put away dishes than listen to that fool Kathryn Kirby on the Pulse-Finder.

"But I'd better go in now—we have a lot of homework to do. Did I tell you that Tully's going to have her ears pierced? She says it won't hurt much. There's a man uptown who does it. One of the girls she met on a double date told her."

If they didn't do their homework in front of the TV set, they turned on the radio, or put on a long-playing record. Elaine had never been able to decide whether Amanda's generation possessed superior powers of concentration, or whether the homework assigned to her made no demands upon her mind. The school appeared to be satisfied with her progress, and Kelsey took it for granted that she would go to college. The subject had not been mentioned for a year at least, following Amanda's correspondence with Mirabelle Marilyn Meeks, who had advised a coeducational college.

"I lack self-confidence," Amanda had told her father. "At a girls' college I might not have any dates."

A tenor voice singing one of the popular songs penetrated into the bedroom where Elaine was changing from a suit to a brown-and-white silk print. Kelsey was not going to be pleased to see Tully. He didn't understand that no one, adult or child, submitted willingly to having his friends selected for him. They had done the best they could, Elaine reminded him, in sending Amanda to Miss Mary's, a school with high standards and staffed by exceptionally well-trained teachers.

Elaine powdered her nose. Mama had said that Amanda's stars were to blame for her choice of Tully Hallam as her best friend. Amanda's birth sign was the reason she found life difficult to cope with.

"Of course, at fourteen she hasn't had much life," Mama had admitted, because Kelsey, as usual, had laughed at her. "But Amanda's sign doesn't encourage her to make any positive effort. Tully Hallam is more than willing to make the effort for both; she carries Amanda along."

Well, there were times when *she* would like to be carried along, Elaine decided, heading for the kitchen. Mrs. Cobalt's lecture had left her confused, it was impossible to accept her mother's theories, and it was disquieting (to say the least) to realize that two of the most baffling products of modern civilization would presently be seated at her dinner table. The phrase was Mrs. Cobalt's, and at this moment it was one of her few generalizations that made sense.

Mercifully, the girls had retreated to Amanda's bedroom before Kelsey came in. He liked to make the salad on Pearl's night off, and she had left everything ready for him. His favorite dinner was one of the easiest to cook—the classic plan of steak, baked potatoes, and peas. At the beginning of Amanda's friendship with Tully, the thought of the Hallam chain of smart, expensive restaurants had made Elaine slightly uneasy whenever Tully dined with them. She soon discovered that the girl was not interested in food beyond satisfying her healthy appetite.

"Amanda's having company?" Kelsey shook his bottle of French dressing violently. "Why didn't you ask Pearl to stay? She wouldn't mind."

Pearl didn't mind changing her day off when she wasn't "going steady," Elaine said. Now that she and Jerome were having dates, it wouldn't be fair to ask her to give up her regular day.

"Besides, Tully Hallam isn't exactly company. She and

Amanda have been doing their homework. I wonder if they've finished."

He had shut the television off, Kelsey said, and he hoped they would be too busy after dinner to turn it on again. He had brought work home, and in spite of closing his study door, the noisier programs came through in a jumble of sound.

"I'll speak to them," Elaine promised. "Kelsey, Lucie dropped in for lunch today. I suppose she stopped at the office?"

Lucie had been depressed, Kelsey said as he cut a tomato into quarters. Not that the hothouse tomatoes had any flavor, he grumbled; they contributed nothing to a salad but color.

"It's hard on a woman to live so far out. If Lucie could persuade Royce to sell the house, I know they'd move back to the city." Kelsey broke off as the phone rang. "I'll get it."

The call was for Tully, and she was still giggling at the instrument when Elaine announced that dinner was ready. Tully, reluctantly terminating her conversation, suggested that "Gene" call her later. She gave the number and strolled dreamily into the dining room, her pretty face preoccupied.

"We were talking about phones, just before dinner," she said, watching Kelsey carve the steak. "Daddy says he's sorry he didn't have the phone put in for me two years ago."

"It's pale blue." Amanda spoke with curious reverence.

Kelsey continued to fix his attention on the steak, and Elaine picked up the conversational ball.

"Did you two get your homework done?" She spooned hot, buttered peas from the bowl in front of her onto the plates as Amanda passed them to her.

Amanda said, "Oh, Mother! You never realize the amount of homework we have to do. I may have to phone one of the girls about an assignment, too."

That was another reason why she found her individual phone so useful, Tully said, eying the hefty chunk of butter on her baked potato with evident approval. A girl who had a phone in her own room could get advice and assistance from her classmates at the exact time she needed it—when doing homework.

"Without tying up the family phone," Amanda suggested.

Kelsey smiled across the table at Elaine.

"I should think you'd be tempted to talk, instead of work, Tully," he said. "Isn't it a little difficult to limit your phone call to how many pages and in what book?"

Tully flashed him a dazzling look, lifting her chin and half closing her eyes. It was so obviously something that had been practiced before a mirror that Kelsey found himself interested in appraising the public display. Tully, he decided, had been seventy-five per cent successful.

"I can control the conversations, Mr. Carpenter," she assured him. "Very few minutes are wasted." Before anyone could reply to that, the phone rang with explosive force. Tully was halfway out of her chair when Kelsey's quiet, "I'll get it, Tully" stopped her.

Tully resumed her seat, murmuring an apology. She was expecting a call. She had told Fish Milate where to reach her.

"But this is dinnertime for nearly everyone," Elaine objected. "I doubt if . . ." She broke off, for Kelsey stood in the doorway.

"A lad named Fisher Milate would like to speak to you, Tully," he said impassively.

Tully overturned her chair in her haste to reach the phone and gave no sign that she heard Amanda, who called after her to take the number and give Fish a ring later.

"If I'd had a phone of my own, he could have called her in the bedroom and you wouldn't have to hear it," Amanda said. "When do you think I can have my own phone, Daddy?"

"The logical answer would be, 'When you can afford to pay for it.'" Kelsey winced as Tully's giggle ascended the scale.

Feminine creatures didn't care for logical answers, he had learned, Kelsey went on. They wanted everything looked at from their point of view, and their point of view was invariably cluttered up with unessentials that obscured their vision.

"Like our windows. Your mother and grandmother would have three layers of curtains at every window if I didn't interfere. That's the chief value of a husband and father. He . . . For the love of Pete, is she going to keep that boy on the wire all night?"

70

Amanda laughed. Tully always talked too loudly into the mouthpiece and openly envied Amanda, who could whisper and yet be heard at the other end. Tully was trying to impress Fish Milate.

Elaine said, "I wonder if it will be all right to serve dessert. Do you know the boy she's talking to, Amanda?"

All expression died out of Amanda's face, leaving it a mask. "I know him a little," she said.

Tully liked him to fill out a double date. She was probably arranging one now, for Liz Abbott, who was worried because she didn't have dates. Tully was so well supplied with dates herself that she could outfit other less-fortunate girls on short notice. Amanda had heard one of the teachers on the school staff say so. Liz Abbott wasn't the only girl who worried because she didn't seem to please the boys, but she was the most outspoken. All she wanted, Liz told anyone who would listen, was to get married, and she would marry practically the first boy who asked her.

"Well, really, this is a little too much." Kelsey glared at his generous portion of apple pie. "Pearl make this? I wonder if I hadn't better go and shut them up. Perhaps Tully doesn't know how to wind up a conversation."

"Oh, *no*, Daddy!" Amanda's wail of anguish startled him. "You can't tell her to hang up. She's our guest."

Tully's shriek of laughter cut across the second of silence, and Kelsey pushed back his chair.

"Do you want to tell her to come back here and finish her dinner, or shall I?" he said.

Amanda's pathetic look of entreaty made him hesitate. After all, the girl must eventually run out of words.

"I think she's finished," Amanda whispered.

Tully, her face pink, eyes shining, hurriedly circled the table and slipped into her chair. Her hair looked as if she might have been tugging at it in nervous tension as she chattered.

"I didn't think it would take so long," she apologized. "I didn't hold you up, did I? What lovely dessert—coffee and pie."

She liked her coffee black, she answered Elaine's query.

"I drink it three times a day, but most of the girls at Miss Mary's have it only for breakfast, if at all. Amanda always says she likes milk. I simply can't endure milk."

She couldn't endure Tully, Elaine confided to Kelsey, who helped her clear the table after the two girls had been excused to finish their homework. Homework, Kelsey had observed, was like Pauline's horoscope—a handy excuse for avoiding whatever threatened to be unpleasant.

"Why don't you break up the friendship?" Kelsey yawned; housework, he complained, made him sleepy.

It would be a terrible mistake to try to separate Amanda and Tully, Elaine told him. Amanda would begin immediately to idolize Tully and build up an image of her that could lead to unhealthy results.

"Sounds pretty silly to me," Kelsey said.

But he agreed that as long as the two girls attended the same school, it would be difficult to separate them.

"They might have a violent quarrel," Elaine suggested hopefully, "that is, if Amanda ever decided to assert herself. Tully is the dominant one now. She acts more like seventeen than fourteen."

Elaine started the dishwasher after Kelsey had shut himself into his study. Years ago, before the birth of Amanda, he had dried the dishes for her, as part of their household routine. He had been anxious, even then, to have his evenings for study, and their social life, or, rather, the lack of it, had worried her mother.

She herself had not worried, Elaine reflected. Kelsey was ambitious and was climbing the ladder to success. What did worry her was whether she could keep pace with him. She had secretly tried to "use her mind," a phrase that alternately nagged and depressed her. The courses for which she enrolled in the Adult Education Center, she dropped one by one. The subjects, she admitted frankly, were over her head, and, besides, she had read several articles which declared that brainy wives were not an altogether popular type.

Elaine had watched her husband's progress, baffled by the quietness of his achievements. They had reached their comfortable, unspectacular standard of living in a series of steps that marked, she knew, promotion in his firm, but the procedure had baffled her. A wife, she had supposed, was considered a social asset, and certainly in the movies she saw and the novels and magazines she read, a man's business success depended to a great extent on the ability of his wife to meet his superiors and impress them favorably. It was bewildering and exasperating to have one's husband advance steadily in his work, apparently appreciated and rewarded, with no questions asked about his home life.

"Of course they know he's married—we get wedding invitations," Elaine had once said to Naida Steckner. "There are three partners and they all have children. I go to funerals with Kelsey, too. But that's about all."

Tonight she found herself thinking about the Hallams. Tully's mother, she knew, entertained elaborately for her husband's business associates. She accompanied him to conventions, too, and Tully had told Amanda that her mother seldom wore the same evening gown twice. This bit of information had emboldened Elaine to telephone and ask if the castoffs might be sent to the Thrift Shop. Mrs. Hallam had revealed that she sold her discarded clothes to various friends, and had added with embarrassing frankness that she depended on the proceeds for pin money. Mr. Hallam was generous with charge accounts, not with cash.

Elaine felt that she might have "helped" Kelsey at the conventions—lawyers as well as restaurateurs held conventions, she had learned—but it was not a question of having him go alone. He never went at all. Every year Elaine read the newspaper accounts of the elaborate programs, dwelling enviously on the efforts of the entertainment committees and the special attention given to the delegates' wives.

But when she had suggested to Amanda that a little daughterly persuasion might waken Kelsey's interest in this end of his profession, Amanda's blunt reply had been a shock.

"They've been trying to get him to go for years," Amanda had said. "He doesn't want to make a speech, so he keeps saying no."

## Chapter 6

Pauline Ives reached under her bed for her feathered mules, but her fingers encountered only empty space. She straightened up and saw the slippers on a small table across the room. How they got there, when she knew positively that she had taken them off the last minute before getting into bed, perplexed her. However, she had no time for mysteries this morning.

Yesterday had been a disturbing day, according to what she remembered of her horoscope. Today carried the unqualified label of "good." The utter absence of any of the familiar cautions, such as, "Keep your emotions under control," gave her a feeling of exhilaration. Since the next day was ominously forecast "difficult," it behooved her to make every minute count.

She decided on a program of immediate action, to include eating breakfast in the nearest restaurant, shopping for a new hat, and possibly consulting Dr. Cannon about the pain in her knee. If she didn't get to the doctor, it wouldn't really matter, because the sixteenth was specifically designated an excellent time to seek medical advice.

Pauline, propped high on her pillows, let her gaze rove about the familiar, cluttered room without actually seeing the disorder. She had read so many astrology books dealing with her birth sign that her mind was a rag bag of predictions, warnings, promises, and veiled allusions, unrelated and impossible to sort out. For weeks she had been trying to find the month and the day when she might expect "an increase in income," a prediction she had read and ever after had been unable to trace.

74

This was surely the day to have her fortune read in tea leaves in the gypsy tearoom. Unfortunately, the food wasn't good, and she did enjoy a nice lunch downtown. Still, the money she saved on lunch could go into her hat. At the thought of that shopping spree, Pauline flung back the covers and, ignoring her troublesome knee, jumped out of bed as nimbly as a girl.

She dressed quickly with characteristic precision. Her clothes were apt to be strewn about on the chairs, but she always had one ensemble in order, ready to be worn. A sudden impulse that she translated as a warning halted her slim fingers as they applied the powder puff.

The list of her lucky and unlucky days—the monthly list she had obtained from her astrologer—had there been something peculiar about the paper as she recalled it now?

Before she began to tumble the contents of her purse on the bed, she knew with disheartening certainty that the paper had been blue, the February list had been typed on blue paper. Lucky and unlucky days for March had been listed on canary yellow paper. In a laudable intention to tidy her purse— so many silly jokes were printed about the contents of women's handbags—she must have thrown away the yellow paper.

Pauline stared at the silver-framed perpetual calendar on her night table. March second—a whole month to go and she had no idea which were her good and bad days, let alone the disturbing or critical. Today, which she had assumed to be perfect for her projects, might be, for all she knew, the most hazardous in the month. She didn't feel like spending another ten dollars to consult her astrologer and, although she might be able to compile a list herself, the thought of searching through her accumulation of books and papers wearied her. Besides, she had no strong faith in her ability to read the stars; she was often confused and she suspected that Kelsey had a conviction that half the time she didn't know what she was talking about. Not that he would ever hold her up to ridicule. Kelsey was loyal, she loved him, and she hoped that he loved her.

Her discovery had so shaken her that she felt the need of

75

a cup of coffee before starting out—if she did start out. She had no heart for a restaurant breakfast, but over coffee and toast she decided that she might look at hats. Her shopping expeditions were always solitary. She found the presence of a second person, even Elaine, distracting and preferred her own judgment to all well-meant advice. She hoped now that she could get out of the apartment house without meeting Elaine.

She acknowledged Albert's "Good morning" so absently that he was immediately concerned.

"Is it one of those critical days, Mis' Ives?" His round, placid face creased in anxious lines and he put a hand under her elbow to steady her.

Albert had a great respect for her astrological experience, and Pauline had no intention of risking any loss of prestige. She said that the day was a "little difficult" for her sign, but reminded him that she was forewarned.

"Well, I sure had me a difficult day yesterday." Albert brought the elevator to a stop on the street floor, but did not open the gates. "I guess there was trouble in my ninth house."

He had an exasperating habit of keeping the gates closed to insure himself a captive audience. From time to time the tenants complained, but their irritation was temporary and counterbalanced by the memory of Albert's twenty-five years of service, his patience with their children, and his absolute honesty.

"A car ran into me and wrecked my lights." Albert referred to his car, a ten-year-old model on which he spent all his free time and most of his money.

Pauline listened sympathetically while he berated careless drivers, the traffic police, and the law that allowed double parking. His horoscope had hinted that he might be involved in an accident, he said, but he had just "got clear of Saturn" and believed he was in a lucky stretch.

Albert's interest in astrology was haphazard in the extreme. A peculiar angle was that his calculations were a year behind the calendar because of his reliance on the books and magazines that Pauline discarded at the end of each December. She had explained to Albert that past dates were worthless in working out predictions, but Albert's argument was that a year wasn't much out of the way and that he saw no reason for spending good money for books when those Pauline threw away were in such excellent condition.

"I'm in rather a hurry, Albert," she suggested now. "You may have made a mistake in reading your chart."

He didn't think so, he said, but he opened the gate and followed her to the entrance door.

"What I really like is a day that says 'Proceed with your plans,'" he confided.

She liked that kind of a day herself, Pauline realized as she stepped out into the bright, cold March sunshine. If she could only be sure about her luck this morning; the uncertainty made her nervous and imposed a necessity for caution that hampered her in carrying out the program she had arranged. For all she knew, this might be the worst time in the month for buying a hat. As for Dr. Cannon, it would be sheerest folly to consult him until she was assured of an appointment under a favorable sign. Doctors were all too ready to emphasize the worst, and she had no intention of being examined by Bruce Cannon on one of her disturbing days.

The bus slipped up so quietly beside her as she waited at the corner that she was startled. Fortunately, it was one of the new models with a low step that gave her knee no trouble at all. Kelsey thought that she should always take a taxi, but she found them difficult to get in and out of—not that she ever said so—and, besides, it did seem like such a waste of money.

All the window seats in the bus were occupied, but she selected an aisle seat beside a plump woman folded into a dark purple coat. The color wasn't too happy a choice with her red hair and pale blue eyes, but when she glanced up from her paperbound book, her smile was friendly.

"Got room enough?" She squeezed her body tightly against the window ledge and took a firmer hold on her enormous purple handbag, which threatened to slide to the floor.

Pauline thanked her and, to discourage conversation, opened her newspaper. She had bought a tabloid for the horoscope readings. The general prediction was "Variable," a word that Pauline privately considered slipshod. She was advised to remain cheerful and to co-operate with her mate.

"You reading the horoscope?" The plump woman pressed against her shoulder. "Scorpio's supposed to be my sign."

Pauline glanced at her rather coldly.

"If you know when you were born, you know your sign," she said.

She was interested in astrology, the stranger said, but she had read just enough about it to realize how ignorant of the subject she was.

"Some of the stuff I read kinda scares me," she confessed.

Pauline relented. There were, she said, good factors to ameliorate the bad.

"Scorpio people go to extremes; you're either enthusiastic or depressed. One thing or the other."

In the next fifteen minutes they had compared birth signs and discovered themselves to be "compatible," and the stranger had introduced herself as Lena Hannister. Pauline could not analyze the reluctance to be identified that made her hesitate to reveal her name. Her new acquaintance apparently did not notice the omission. She talked steadily, her interest in horoscopes the main topic. She had intended for years to write to an astrologer and have a horoscope prepared, she said, but she kept putting it off. Yes, she could understand that she had probably lost years of valuable guidance.

"Say, why don't you come home with me and have a cup of tea. You can tell me what I ought to have to work out a horoscope myself." Lena Hannister dropped her book into the capacious purple bag. "The next stop but one is mine."

Pauline hesitated. She was thoroughly disconcerted by the tardy realization that she had taken the bus line that served the Rosewood section of the city, instead of following the route to the downtown business center. Dr. Cannon's office was within a block or two of the next stop. She didn't intend to see him, but if she had ever doubted that this was one of her unlucky days, this was all the confirmation she needed.

"I don't think I can do that," she heard herself saying, again assailed by a reluctance she could not have explained. "I . . . I have an appointment."

Yes, she admitted, she intended to get off at the next stop.

"I'll get off with you," the other woman offered. "There's a nice little park where we can sit for a minute while you write down some addresses for me. I'm so glad I met you—why, today may change my whole life!"

The park was small and gritty, and even when they were seated on a bench, the tangle of tall bushes behind it failed to break the force of the wind.

"I've made up my mind to consult your astrologer," Lena Hannister said. "Have you a pencil, so you can jot down her name and the address?"

She was pressing so closely against Pauline that she could hardly escape seeing the contents of the older woman's opened purse.

"What a pretty lining . . ." Mrs. Hannister did not finish her sentence.

Pauline had a glimpse of a dirty hand and a sweater sleeve and then her purse was snatched from her lap and she saw a figure dart around the bushes and disappear.

"My bag!" She sprang to her feet and started running after the boy—the runner streaking across the still brown grass looked like a boy.

Mrs. Hannister tugged at her arm.

"You stay here! You can't run, you'll have a heart attack. I'll get him—the dirty little sneak!"

She set off in the direction the thief had taken, at a lumbering gait a lame dog could have bettered, Pauline muttered to herself in scorn. Evidently Mrs. Hannister had no faith in herself as a runner, for she turned and shouted, "I'll get a policeman."

Pauline sat down on the bench to wait. When she thought of the keys and papers in her bag, and her new fountain pen, she foresaw a good deal of annoyance, but the money loss would be comparatively small. She must have about twenty dollars in the zipper compartment—she had intended to charge her hat—and of course her charge coin was included in the loot.

"That boy must have been hiding in the bushes, back of the bench," she said to Dr. Cannon, almost an hour later. "Probably specializes in purse snatching. These teen-agers!"

She had waited in the chill wind for Mrs. Hannister to return accompanied by a policeman, but at the end of half an hour she had begun to have doubts. When another fifteen minutes had passed, she had concluded charitably that "something" had prevented Mrs. Hannister's return. Very possibly she had been attacked by the robber and was now lying unconscious in a hospital ward.

This gloomy picture had reminded her that she was without bus or taxi fare, stranded in a neighborhood where she knew no one—but, of course, Dr. Cannon.

"So I thought you could lend me some money and I suppose you might as well look at my knee," she had greeted him, but gratefully, for his nurse had slipped her in between appointments.

"Looks like a put-up job to me," the doctor commented promptly. "It's never safe to get chummy with strangers; the next time you might not be so lucky."

Pauline said that she was not a perfect fool.

"I didn't accept her invitation to go home with her and have a cup of tea. You think she keeps someone hiding in those bushes and steers people to that park bench?"

A quick grin smoothed out the doctor's anxious frown.

"One of the Lorelei, eh? No, I don't think her game works quite that way. My guess is that she had a confederate in the bus, within hearing distance of your conversation. If you had gone on to her house, your purse would have been snatched somewhere along the way. The park made everything easy."

He insisted on phoning the police, who were, in Pauline's opinion, extremely blasé and agreed only too readily with Dr. Cannon that "Mrs. Hannister" was an old hand, playing old tricks.

"You want to go downtown and see if you can identify

her photograph in the rogues' gallery?" The doctor's question was evidently prompted by the person at the other end of the wire.

"My heavens, no!" Pauline backed away from the desk in her chair.

"Don't you want to see justice done? You don't?" Dr. Cannon shook his head.

"No dice," he said into the phone. "Yes, I know the public's like that. Well, you have the name and address, if the purse is turned in. And thanks . . . eh? Oh, co-operation—doctors have the same difficulty."

"How are the police supposed to catch vandals if women like you refuse to even attempt to identify them?" he demanded irritably of his patient.

Pauline said, "You don't know how funny it feels, not to have a purse. Or a handkerchief . . . or lipstick. My gloves were in it, too."

"Haven't you any sense of civic duty?" he persisted.

"Not much," she admitted. "And—well, you see, she didn't hurt me. Conk me, I believe the term is. She didn't conk me. Also this was daylight; if anyone snatched my purse at night, on a dark street, I'm sure I'd have a heart attack. What I'm trying to tell you is that I don't feel Mrs. Hannister is a vicious person."

Certainly she would be willing to help the police track down any person who conked her, Pauline said. That would indicate brutality, as distinguished from the merely weak. The more she thought of Mrs. Hannister, the more certain she was that the poor woman was mentally retarded.

Dr. Cannon said that he was rapidly becoming unhinged and that he would like to examine the ailing knee before he was finally committed. As his skillful fingers probed and manipulated, Pauline wished that she had the courage to ask him not to mention the episode to Kelsey. She had his word that he did not discuss her physical condition with either Elaine or Kelsey without her permission—he respected each patient's privacy—but his overdeveloped sense of responsibility might result in a betrayal of her confidence.

"For it is confidential," she said aloud. "I hope you'll say nothing to Kelsey. When you come right down to brass tacks, this is all my fault and I'm perfectly willing to take the blame."

He adjusted the pad on her knee, sat back in his chair.

"You mean *you* engineered this holdup?"

"I mean I took a chance on coming out when I didn't know whether it was a lucky or an unlucky day. Well, I found out, and look at what happened. I'm not going to stir from the house again until I get a duplicate of my list."

After a moment of complete silence, the doctor said, "Do you suppose it was Mrs. Hannister's lucky day?"

II

"And, of course, I stepped out of the cab and there was Amanda barging off . . ." Pauline hesitated a moment, decided she had the right word. "Barging off, to spend the night with that Tully Hallam."

Pearl, on what she called "a picking-up tour" of the bedroom, made a sympathetic sound in her throat.

"You'd think it was the first time she'd ever seen me come home in a taxi." Pauline propped herself higher on her pillows. "I still don't know what made me burst into tears when I saw her," she said crossly.

Pearl had brought down a tray dinner. (Elaine had remained downtown to have dinner with Kelsey and attend the annual theater party for the benefit of the Thrift Shop.) She had also phoned the doctor for advice.

"Dr. Cannon says it's delayed shock. You take one of your pills tonight, and you'll wake up fine in the morning. Could you eat another éclair?"

It was a household legend that when anyone in the family was ill, Pearl urged second helpings of dessert as a therapeutic measure.

Pauline declined the éclair, but she had discovered an odd reluctance to be left alone. She prided herself on being able to fill in her time, enjoyed her privacy, and was inclined to be critical of friends who confessed to a desire for constant companionship. Tonight she had no intention of examining her sudden weakness—put it down to an attack of nerves.

"Stay and talk to me, Pearl." She gestured toward her favorite rocking chair. "Jerome isn't coming tonight, is he?"

Jerome was bowling with his club tonight, Pearl said. "I've been meaning to tell you about that horoscope for his mother, Miz Ives . . ."

Pauline interrupted. She had intended to have the horoscope ready two weeks ago, but there had been so many interruptions she did not feel obligated to confess that the attempt to cast a horoscope left her hopelessly confused.

"I've gone far enough, Pearl, to be able to tell you that Jerome's mother is jealous and possessive and her approach to life is austere." Pauline broke off abruptly. "What's the matter?"

Pearl sat down in the rocker, jumped up to straighten the tilting lamp shade on the dresser, sat down again.

"I only found out yesterday and haven't had a chance to tell you. Would you believe it, Miz Ives, Jerome's mother told him everything wrong? She's ten years older than she says; she wasn't born in July, she was born in March. Last night Jerome phones me to say the information his mother gave him is a pack of lies and to invite me to her birthday party. It's tomorrow night. What'll I take her for a present? A potted plant?"

It wasn't Mother's Day, Pauline reminded her. It might be tactful to avoid any extravagant display of spending. A woman like Jerome's mother would be likely to ascribe bribery motives to a showy offering.

"But that's judging her from the horoscope I started, and I may be all wrong." Pauline suddenly pulled herself upright. "I know—I'll make you one of my fancy aprons, Pearl."

The suggestion delighted Pearl. She specified pink organdy and offered to get the materials from the neighborhood needlework shop in the morning.

"If you're sure you're going to be well enough, Miz Ives. The doctor said you may feel shaky in the morning."

She had no intention of feeling shaky in the morning, Pauline retorted. Dr. Cannon had put her in the cab as if she had been a basket of eggs and had given the driver directions as if she had lost her mind.

"He meant well, I know that. Remind me to send him a check for the five dollars he loaned me, Pearl. You're the only one, except him, who knows what happened. There's no sense in upsetting my daughter or son-in-law."

Pearl agreed not to "tell," if Miz Ives would try to go to sleep early and not read half the night.

"Sometimes having people fuss over you is worse than having them neglect you." Pearl rose awkwardly from the low rocker. "You sure you'll be all right tomorrow?" she asked.

Pauline smiled and sank back on the pillows in relief.

"Tomorrow's fine—I looked it up. 'Loved ones sympathetic,'" she quoted.

And in the morning, after a restful night, she was composedly eating toast and drinking coffee when Elaine let herself in. Pearl could be trusted to keep her word, but it would be like Amanda to have asked questions about a grandmother's unexplained tears.

Elaine said, "Hi, darling, how do you feel?" which was her normal, daughterly greeting.

She declined coffee, put down the package she was carrying, and puckered her attractive eyebrows in a worried frown.

"Mama, are you sure you feel up to making an apron for Pearl, a rush job, I mean? She says you offered to make a cover-all, and it will take you most of the day. Kelsey doesn't like the idea of you killing yourself for Jerome's mother, either."

Her sympathetic loved ones were living up to the day's prediction, Pauline thought, and a secret warmth enfolded her like the best-quality eiderdown.

"I feel just like staying home today," she said. "The apron will be what Amanda would call my project. Is it pink?"

Pearl had selected shocking-pink organdy, and Elaine was inclined to think the color too violent, considering the age of Jerome's mother.

Not that they knew her age, she admitted; they didn't even

know her name. Now and then, Elaine said, she had been led to question whether Pearl knew it. Jerome's mother, a widow, had married for the second time when he was about fifteen.

"You're sweet to make an apron for Pearl to give her, Mama. I only hope the woman likes it and doesn't snub Pearl. She's been upset for the last week, and twice I've found her crying in the kitchen. She'll be singing 'I dreamt I dwelt in marble halls' now that you've cheered her up."

And Pearl, when she "looked in" to bring the morning paper and later when she arrived to cook and serve lunch, apparently looked forward to a pleasant evening.

"Your eyes get tired, Miz Carpenter says, and she told me to make your lunch, so that you would have time to take a little nap." Pearl glanced at the mass of organdy that reminded her of a pink cloud. "It sure is going to be pretty," she said.

She insisted that Pauline take a nap after her lunch, but came down twice in the afternoon to ask if there was anything she could do and to check on the progress of the apron. Pauline had it finished by half past five, and Pearl's delight and gratitude were reflected in her round, shining eyes and even to some degree in her round, shining nose.

"It's beautiful," she said over and over. "Just beautiful. Amanda's promised to gift-wrap it for me—I bought a white box."

As she backed out of the apartment, the apron laid reverently across her arms, she smiled radiantly at Pauline.

"Miz Carpenter said we'd have a very simple dinner. I'm too excited to cook."

The very simple dinner nearly collapsed when Jerome phoned just before it was time to turn the chops. Elaine took the long fork from her with a sense of foreboding. Pearl had brought her dress from home and had planned to have Jerome pick her up at eight o'clock.

"That was Jerome." Pearl drooped in the kitchen doorway. "He can't come get me. I said I wouldn't mind if he was a little late, but he can't come."

Elaine slid the chops back under the flame.

"Was it . . . is it . . ."

"It's his mother." Pearl's eyes were dull, and, mysteriously, her nose had also lost its shine. "She wants him to help her receive her guests."

Elaine said, "Damn!" but a new anxiety beset her.

"You didn't tell him you're not coming, did you?" she asked.

Pearl had not trusted her voice to say much of anything, and if Jerome had wondered how she was to get to the party in her green satin pumps and burdened with the elaborately wrapped and ribboned apron box, he had made no suggestions.

"I'll put you in a cab," Kelsey promised after dinner, and while Elaine cleared the table, Pearl disappeared into Amanda's room to dress.

When, half an hour later, she swept self-consciously into the room, there was a glow, an expectancy, about her that, despite her age and the doubtful "gold tips" she had added inexpertly to her hair, suggested inexperienced youth.

Kelsey carried the box down for her and put her in a cab with instructions that if Jerome didn't offer to take her home, she was to have him call a taxi for her.

At eleven o'clock Elaine, watching a television program, heard the hall door open and close, the movement betrayed by one faint click. Before she realized her fear, Pearl walked silently into the living room. One hand held her coat clutched around her shoulders, the other grasped her small green satin evening bag. She was crying, her face blotched and red, make-up ruined.

"Why, Pearl!" Elaine sprang up in dismay. "What happened?"

Instinctively she guided Pearl to the sofa, for the poor woman wobbled badly on her high heels.

"What happened?" Elaine repeated. "Didn't you have a good time?"

She knew, of course, that Pearl had not had a good time. It was too early for the party to be over, for one thing, and, for another, no happy guest returns dissolved in tears.

Elaine tried again.

86

"Did Jerome bring you home? Did he make a pass at you?"

Pearl mopped her face with a lace-edged handkerchief. Between sniffs she said that she had brought herself home and that she was sorry to have upset anyone.

"I didn't want to have my sister see me until I know what to tell her," Pearl said. "I talked so much about this party, she's going to think it's queer if I get home too soon."

Jerome's mother, she said, had insulted her.

"She's picked out a wife for him and she had the nerve to invite her there tonight and talk about her to me."

Elaine listened, slightly bewildered, to the long, incoherent story—Jerome was not to blame, Pearl insisted—and finally persuaded Pearl to phone her sister and say that she was staying overnight at the apartment. In an emergency, usually in the case of a heavy storm, she slept in the small guest room.

A night's sleep apparently did much to mend Pearl's disappointment, but Amanda, to whom she had poured out her story at the first opportunity, doubted that she had forgiven Jerome.

"I don't suppose you read the *Blaze* very often, do you, Daddy?" she asked her father a few evenings later.

"Well, it isn't my favorite newspaper," he admitted. "Have I been missing something?"

There was a letter in Mrs. Torrington Van Antwerpt's column that she wanted to read to him, Amanda said.

"It's an etiquette column, Daddy—you wouldn't know that. Someone writes and asks, 'Is a white hat suitable to wear to the funeral of my fiancé's mother?' and it's signed, 'Troubled'."

Pearl was a faithful correspondent of the etiquette column's editor, Amanda explained. She always signed her letters "Troubled."

"It's probably a popular signature," Kelsey objected. "What makes you think this has to be a letter from Pearl? Jerome isn't her fiancé, is he?"

Pearl thought of herself as engaged to Jerome, Amanda said.

"But what makes me really sure is that she has a new white hat."

Kelsey laughed and refused to be impressed. But when Amanda read the letter to her mother, Elaine was rather shocked.

"You make it sound as though Pearl would be willing to do away with Jerome's mother," she said.

Elaine was having a private attack of nerves, following a telephone conversation with Lucie that morning.

"Midge Sully has decided to settle in Lyman." Lucie had not sounded pleased. "I hope she isn't going to depend on me for everything."

By "everything," Lucie meant, presumably, the establishing of a social life for the Cutters. The children, Lucie said, were to be entered in the public school. "I reminded Midge that it's pretty late in the term, but she says Army children are used to being transferred—the boys can take it."

Midge's oldest son, Marsh, was the right age for Amanda, Lucie had suggested.

"For Amanda?" Elaine's astonishment exploded in her normally even voice.

Marsh was a nice boy with lovely manners; Amanda's boy friends were decidedly short on manners, Lucie said. At fifteen Marsh had a great deal of poise and could easily pass for seventeen.

Elaine had terminated the conversation rather abruptly. If Lucie had an ounce of tact, she would know that Midge Sully and her children were not subjects of enthralling interest to the woman Kelsey had married. There was a possibility, too, that Lucie was being deliberately experimental. Elaine remembered that she was, in her own words, "mad for psychology," and she might be filling a casebook with her, Elaine's, reactions.

Something, perhaps one of her stars passing through one of her houses—Elaine was hopelessly lost whenever she tried to think in astrological terms—urged her to consult Naida Steckner. As usual, she hated to spend the money, but whenever she thought of Midge Sully she felt helpless and at the mercy of Fate. Midge in the suburbs was infinitely better than Midge in a town apartment, but Lucie was apparently destined to be a link or a bridge, and Midge was an expert on using people to her advantage.

The phone rang before Elaine had definitely decided whether to rely on tranquilizers or spend fifteen dollars, and it was her mother.

"Darling, I wanted to catch you before you went out." Pauline breathed a little quickly. "This is a difficult day for your sign. A domestic matter can cause disputes."

Elaine said, "I wish you wouldn't tell me, Mama. You know it upsets me."

She could avoid disputes, her mother pointed out.

"Your sun is adverse and so is Venus. Is any domestic matter troubling you?"

Elaine gulped and insisted that nothing troubled her.

"And, Mama, don't tell Pearl if this isn't one of her best days. We've just got her calmed down after all that trouble at the party. Jerome is taking her to the movies tonight, so she's happy."

She wouldn't dream of unsettling Pearl, Pauline said. Intelligent people preferred to be prepared for difficulties, but she always used her judgment and seldom revealed the complete warning. Just enough to put her loved ones on guard.

"Mama, are you hiding something from me? What else does the book say about my sign for today?" Elaine's elbow knocked the bottle of tranquilizers to the floor.

Pauline said, "I heard something fall. You're not nervous, are you? I suppose I might as well tell you: 'A forgotten person may return to complicate your life.' I know you don't believe in astrology, but it's enough to make you think, isn't it?"

Elaine agreed. She promised to "be careful," a phrase her mother used constantly in an effort to propitiate the stars, and immediately phoned Naida Steckner's secretary for an emergency appointment. It was understood among Mrs. Steckner's clients that she held several half-hours each day open for emergency counseling. She charged for the full hour, but that, she explained, was to make sure that the term "emergency" was not abused.

"There's nothing I can put my finger on," said Elaine, making a conscientious effort to relax in the blue-gray lamp-shaded room. "Nothing has happened. It's only that I have a feeling Midge is going to be more and more a figure in my life—in our lives."

The large, dark-eyed woman on the other side of the desk studied her for a silent moment.

"The worst mistake you can make is to avoid all mention of this Mrs. Cutter—Midge. Try to speak often of her, mention her naturally to your husband. Don't, in effect, sweep her under the rug," she said.

What made everything so difficult, Elaine confided as tears filled her eyes, was that Midge's husband would be in Washington most of the time. That left Midge in something of the position of a widow, appealing and helpless, a woman without a man.

"Kelsey is the protective type. And I don't suppose he has ever forgotten they were once engaged."

She wiped her eyes and peered at her face in the mirror of her compact. Most women cried when they talked to Naida Steckner, who accepted tears with a placid indifference that was more soothing than a torrent of sympathetic words. She regarded solitary crying as a bad, even dangerous, habit, and she advised that tears shed in the presence of husbands and children accomplished nothing. But she firmly believed in weeping as an emotional release and had been known to remain detached throughout demonstrations of hysterics.

"All you need is confidence in yourself," Naida Steckner said.

Confidence in herself was precisely what she did not have, Elaine reflected dismally, but she had asked for advice—and paid for it—and now she had to put it into practice. Her first attempt, at dinner that night, to mention Midge "naturally" to Kelsey was discouraging.

"I heard from Lucie this morning; Midge Sully is going to settle down in Lyman," Elaine said.

"I'll bet her children are brats." Amanda frowned, remembering that she had been labeled an only child. "Tully knows a girl whose father is a captain and she went to the same school as Midge's oldest boy."

Elaine said, "I was speaking to your father. And please say 'Mrs. Cutter,' not Midge."

"I don't believe I heard what you said," Kelsey apologized.

"Midge Sully has decided to live in Lyman. Lucie told me." Elaine hoped that Pearl would stay in the kitchen. "I suppose she's tired of traveling."

Kelsey said, "Oh."

"This girl had a fight with Marsh Cutter and two weeks afterwards she wrote to Mirabelle Marilyn Meeks to ask how she could get him back." Amanda smiled at her father. "That's what makes boys so conceited."

Elaine allowed herself to be momentarily diverted.

"Midge is just back from Japan. How could her son have been going with a girl in the United States?"

Amanda's "Oh, Mother!" coupled with an exaggeratedly patient explanation adapted to the understanding of the mentally retarded never failed to irritate Elaine.

Mirabelle Marilyn Meeks's column drew mail from all over the world, Amanda said reverently.

"She's in more than two hundred newspapers in the United States. This girl's father was stationed in Japan, but I suppose they had an American paper sent to them. You could ask Midge."

"Your mother doesn't wish you to speak of Mrs. Cutter as 'Midge,'" Kelsey reproved.

Elaine thought that possibly she ought to "begin over," as the children said.

"I suppose we'll be seeing a good deal of Midge now, in one way or another," she suggested. "We can't expect Lucie to give her much time."

Kelsey, plainly bewildered, brightened as Pearl entered the room.

"Will you bring me the little glass pepper mill, Pearl?" he said.

It showed, Elaine told herself in the stretches of a restless night, that he was anxious to avoid the topic. She spent several unprofitable hours wondering how much emphasis Lucie might be putting upon the old relationship between Kelsey and Midge. Twenty years ago, Lucie had been far too young to realize the significance of an engagement. Kelsey's widowed mother had married the cousin of her first husband, so that Kelsey and Lucie had the same surname and comparatively few people knew that she was his half-sister,

Breakfast the next morning was hardly the place to speak naturally of Midge, especially after a wretched night, and Elaine watched Kelsey eat bacon and eggs and Amanda drink a glass of orange juice, in a kind of speechless daze. The only reason she didn't have breakfast in bed, she had once told her mother, was that Kelsey would be sure to think she was dying.

"No matter how wrapped up he is in a case, he knows whether I'm there or not. I think a vacant chair makes him nervous," she had explained.

It was annoying to have Lucie telephone a few minutes after nine o'clock. Midge, Lucie said without preliminaries, was going to be hard to take.

"She wants the name of a doctor and dentist in town— doesn't trust suburban professional men, she says. Our supermarkets, schools, and churches are all right, but the best medical men stay in the city, according to her light."

Midge wasn't putting down roots, she was laying concrete foundations, Lucie said. She was prepared to join the P.-T.A. and had made Lucie promise to take her to St. Simon's eleven o'clock service the next Sunday.

"I think she's going to join the orchestra, too; she plays the violin." Lucie added vaguely that she guessed Army women fought homesickness by keeping busy.

"You better give her Dr. Cannon's name. And who's your dentist? I told Midge you'd be glad to help her."

Three nights later, when Amanda was having dinner with the Hallams, Elaine brought up the subject of Midge at her own table.

"Her husband can't do a thing to help her, he's in Washington so much of the time. Midge has to do everything herself."

"Someone said Lucie was helping her." Kelsey gave his pepper mill a vigorous twist.

She had told him that, Elaine reminded him.

"Why don't you ask Midge to come in and have lunch with you someday?"

"Good Lord!" said Kelsey, and added, "What for?"

Midge could find her way around without assistance from him, he grumbled when he had finally sorted out Elaine's explanations.

"How do you suppose she managed in Japan? Or in Germany? They were stationed in Germany, weren't they? Acording to Mother, Army wives can take care of themselves in any situation."

Kelsey accepted his second cup of coffee, tasted it with evident appreciation.

"I'll tell you what to do," he said, like a man relaxing in a kindly glow, "you have Midge in. Take her to a couple of matinees and lunch at the Melodeon. It will be nice for you to have someone new to talk to—and you seem to think she needs friends."


## III

"Fix up a double date with Tully?" Amanda was outraged at the suggestion. "Why, I wouldn't go out with Marsh Cutter if he was the last boy left on the face of the earth."

"You don't know anything about him." Elaine, who had been prompted by Midge to make inquiries, tried to be severe.

Amanda said darkly that she wasn't going to ruin her friendship with Tully by appearing with Marsh as her date.

"Aunt Lucie's told me about him," she went on. "And if you want to know what I think of Midge, I think she's a total loss."

Because she had to, Elaine said, "Your opinion hasn't been asked and you're to call her Mrs. Cutter."

But for the first time in her life she felt a conviction that it might be comforting to have a daughter.

## Chapter 7

"Mama, you're going to church this morning, aren't you?"
Elaine had brought her mother one of the Sunday papers.
"It's a lovely, clear day."

Pauline Ives, in an azure-blue silk housecoat, was enjoying
her second cup of coffee, a luxury she liked to think she allowed herself only on Sundays. She had brought her breakfast
tray into the living room and she had a feeling that if only
Elaine would go away, she might have a third cup, really half
a cup, while she read the editorials, and the advertisements.

"You haven't been to church more than twice since Christmas," Elaine said, "and now Lent is almost over."

Pauline adjusted the turnback cuffs of the housecoat; the
sleeves were a little too long.

"Dr. Ferguson asked me last Sunday if you were ill, Mama.
He'll be coming to see you." Elaine caught sight of an astrology magazine under the couch. "The stars don't tell you anything about church, do they?"

The rector of All Souls knew exactly why she had been
staying away from church, Pauline said coldly.

"I told Dr. Ferguson and both curates. I told you and
Kelsey, although you don't pay attention to anything I say. I
have a good reason for everything I do."

The silver coffeepot—part of the Sunday breakfast ritual—
had kept the third cup of coffee hot. Elaine, watching her
mother pour it and add sugar and cream, sighed, remembering
the restrictions of her diet.

"Tell me again, Mama," she coaxed. "You used to love to
go to church."

94

Pauline said rapidly in a nerve-racking falsetto, "Hi yah, Jesus, what's cooking?"

"*Mama!*" Elaine stared at her in alarm. "What on earth is that?"

"The Bible," said Pauline in her normal voice. "Revised Version."

The Revised Version was nothing like that, Elaine protested.

"Lots of people can't understand the King James Bible, and Dr. Ferguson says the Revised Version is simpler. But there's nothing in it like . . . like slang. It's simply more informal."

It was too informal for her, Pauline retorted, pushing up her sleeves as if going into battle. Manners were informal, morals were informal, poetry was informal—so informal no one with sense could understand a word of it—meals were informal—people would be back to eating with their fingers soon—and now even the Bible had to be informal.

"I'm staying at home with my King James Bible and my prayer book—they'll go to work on that next, I suppose—and you can tell Dr. Ferguson why."

Elaine, rather stunned by this outburst, abandoned further argument. Mama was very thorough in her dislikes. It was to be hoped that if Dr. Ferguson called on her she would not feel impelled to repeat her original translation, but she could be counted upon to be emphatic. Well, the rector, a specialist, you might say, in theology, could handle his side of the debate, but, Elaine reflected, neither she nor Mama was exactly qualified to analyze her reasons for attending church or for staying away.

Murmuring that she must dress, she turned at the door to find her mother's blue eyes watching her soberly.

"You can say some prayers for me," Pauline said.

"Oh, I do—always," Elaine assured her. "For you and for Amanda. But you depend so much on the stars, and lately Amanda has been talking about Zen."

"What does a child her age know about Zen?" Pauline demanded, the image of the outraged grandmother.

Amanda knew little or nothing about Zen, Elaine said, but she had decided to investigate all the religions of the world.

"Kelsey says it's a phase."

She might do better to study the stars, Pauline said with great firmness.

"The clergy are narrow-minded about astrology, but the Bible is full of references to signs and portents. Maybe not the Revised Version. King James."


II


"Pearl's had another fight with Jerome," Amanda said. "I can tell, because she's mopping the kitchen linoleum and making it too wet for me to get anything to eat." She looked hopefully at her grandmother. "Have you any food, dear?" she asked.

Pauline, making sandwiches, setting out bottles of Coke, wondered why Pearl should discourage a loyal listener.

"She tells all her troubles to you, Amanda, and it's far better than to have her brood in silence. Did you try to talk to her?"

Amanda had not outgrown her love for peanut butter and jelly. She eyed her sandwich appreciatively.

"You sure put enough in, Grandma. I just asked her how come she was mopping the kitchen floor at three in the afternoon and she said I ought to know she was overworked and never had a minute to herself."

Whenever Pearl was "mad" at Jerome, she transferred her irritation to the whole Carpenter family, Amanda said. It was psychological.

"I like to study people's psychological reactions. Especially if they have complicated characters. Tully Hallam is very complicated."

Pauline indicated a cream-cheese-and-olive sandwich, uncapped a second bottle of Coke.

"I saved a piece of chocolate cake for you, too. Amanda, you won't like me to say this, but Tully isn't a friend you can trust."

Amanda said crossly, "Her sign and mine are incompatible,

96

I suppose?" She pronounced the word carefully. "Well, I don't happen to believe in your astrology."

She had not based her warning wholly on the stars, Pauline admitted reluctantly, but on personal observation and numerous "little things" Amanda herself let drop in conversation.

"She's too sophisticated for her age, too—that's another drawback. You can't possibly have the same interests."

"Oh, we both like boys and dates." Amanda drew an imaginary arc in the air with her sandwich, to indicate the width of her horizons. "But Tully gets lots more dates than I do."

This was because Tully had no difficulty with her parents, Amanda explained. They were interested in helping her to develop all "faucets" of her character. Strict parents were an awful handicap to a girl.

"The word is 'facets,'" Pauline supplied absently. "What makes you think your parents are strict?"

Amanda was prepared for the question. She couldn't go out on school nights. Tully could. She was forbidden to accept dates with older boys who could drive cars. Tully wouldn't date a boy unless he had a driver's license.

"I can't even double date with Tully unless Mother and Daddy know who the boys are and where we're going and when we'll be home. Honest, Grandma, no boy is going to put up with that sort of thing. Tully says they all laugh at me."

The familiar look of anxiety flooded her dark eyes as she surveyed her grandmother over the rim of the Coke glass. The child must drink several gallons of the stuff a month, Pauline calculated, trying not to shudder as Amanda began on the chocolate cake. It would be a waste of time to mention the dating customs of even Elaine's generation—mention of her mother's girlhood invariably bored Amanda—and of course no teen-ager believed that her grandmother had ever had boy problems.

"It's enough to make me go out on a double date without telling." Amanda licked icing from one pointed finger. "Too-strict parents develop the rebellious spirit in a child."

Pauline said, "I suppose you read that somewhere. All those columnists copy each other."

She read everything she could find, in newspapers and magazines, about teen-agers, Amanda admitted, partly in an effort to understand herself and partly because it was her duty to try to understand her parents.

"Mirabelle Marilyn Meeks is the best writer, but some of the others are pretty good. Parents are reluctant to have a child develop."

"Well there's no law against developing in the right direction, and it isn't the way Tully Hallam is going." Pauline knew she sounded like a grandmother.

Amanda carefully replaced the cover on the peanut-butter jar and tidily carried the empty Coke bottles to the sink.

"You don't have to worry about me." She delivered the classic response unconscious of a smear of chocolate on one cheek. "I can take care of myself."

But, listening to Albert's monologue on the weather as the elevator creaked its way up to the eleventh floor, she realized that a host of delayed doubts and fears were closing in upon her. There was no one in whom she could wholly confide, although she could say more to Pearl than to her grandmother, and Mirabelle Marilyn Meeks was unavailable for emergencies.

"There's a full moon tonight—it affects some people's minds," Albert said, opening the elevator gates. "Makes them crazy."

Amanda found Pearl cheerfully starting dinner and singing "I dreamt I dwelt in marble halls," with her radio tuned to a news broadcast. All she ever really heard was the weather report at the end, but it could be taken as a sign that she was recovering from what the family called the "Jerome Blues."

Amanda, invited to stay and talk, pleaded that she had to get ready for dinner. But in her own room, she made no move to brush her hair and she stared at herself in the mirror without seeing the chocolate smear.

It was all very well to stand up for Tully when the family picked her apart; she hoped Tully would do as much for her. Amanda whispered to the girl in the mirror that she was so nervous she could scream!

She picked up the hairbrush and seated herself on the bed. Something—perhaps the influence of the moon—had tempted her to tell her grandmother about Tully and Fisher Milate. Now she was thankful that something else—perhaps the stars—had kept her from blurting out any part of the secret.

Tully said that she was mad about Fisher Milate. He was old—eighteen—and his father had just given him a handsome new sports car. It was unfortunate that Mr. Hallam, ordinarily so "reasonable," had taken a dislike to Fisher, who was the most popular boy Tully had ever dated.

"All my father has against him," she had grumbled to a sympathetic Amanda, "is that he drinks a little and likes to speed. And oh, yes, Daddy says he's too old for me."

There was nothing to do, Tully had said, but to assert herself. Sooner or later she would have to free herself from her parents' crushing restrictions, and it was better to risk a little unpleasantness now than a total break later.

"But if your father won't let you date Fisher, what can you do?" Amanda had asked, and Tully's reply had thrilled her.

"I can date him, period."

But Amanda had been jolted when Tully outlined an intricate plan that demanded loyalty and co-operation. The very least a true friend could do, Tully said, was to be ready to take necessary risks.

"I'll tell my parents that I am doing my homework with you and that I'll be home about ten thirty—that your father will put me in a cab. All you'll have to do is be ready with some kind of an answer if my mother should happen to telephone."

Jitters had immediately gripped Amanda.

"What can I say to her? What makes you think she might phone?"

It was a tiresome habit of parents to do their checking by phone, Tully had explained. Not that she expected her mother to call the Carpenters—with any luck at all things would go smoothly—but it would be fatal if she did phone and anyone but Amanda should talk to her.

"You can tell her I just went down to your grandmother's apartment to borrow a book, or something. Whatever you do, don't panic."

She was panicking now, Amanda thought, and the phantom Tully wasn't due until after seven. Tully could think quickly, she didn't mind taking chances; faced with a . . . a crisis, she always knew what to do. In contrast, Amanda felt herself to be a plodding thinker—"practically a moron," she concluded when acutely depressed—and hopelessly behind Tully in her ability to handle a situation.

Amanda heard voices—the quick, light tones of her mother and the deeper murmur of her father's responses—which warned her that dinner was only minutes away. Her mother called to her, and she answered, proving her remarkable presence of mind, because she had just remembered that she would have to spend the evening within easy reach of the telephone.

She had not taken into consideration—nor had Tully—her habit of shutting herself into her bedroom to do her homework, soothed by background music from her records or the radio and occasionally from both. Her father was going to think it strange when he saw her huddled over her homework in the living room, close to the entrance into the hall and the telephone stand.

"Dinner, Amanda!"

Amanda stood up, feeling her worries to be as heavy as stone weights tied to her hands and feet. She ran a comb through her hair, dabbed at the streak of chocolate with a tissue, and applied powder.

The conviction that she had been left "holding the bag," and not for the first time, and that if anything went wrong Tully would be too busy extricating herself to be able to offer assistance to a fellow-conspirator, exerted a relentless pressure on her chest. The evening stretched before her, an endless march of hours through which she must drag herself until Tully chose to release her.

*I must be an awful dope,* Amanda thought.

But she took a melancholy pleasure in staring into the

mirror and fixing a smile upon her face that she hoped would look natural to her parents.

## III

The phone could be reached more quickly from the dining room than from the living room, Amanda decided after Pearl had cleared the table and been assured that her white hat was "suitable" for the wedding of Jerome's second cousin. She had read that wedding guests who wore white might be accused of competing with the bride.

Amanda had assured her—"Not a *hat*, Pearl"—and had spread out her books and papers at the end of the table nearest to the hall door. Her mother said merely, "It gives you more room, doesn't it?" but her father had suggested that she might be distracted by the television in the living room.

"There are a couple of programs I want to catch," he had said. "It's quieter in your own room—why, what's the matter?"

Amanda, unaware that she was gazing at him in mild horror, stuttered in confusion. She was tired of studying in her room; she needed more space in which to spread out. And television wouldn't interfere: at Miss Mary's they taught you to concentrate.

But when her mother had gone downstairs, "for a few moments," which might easily be the entire evening, Amanda nervously considered the new predicament. Ordinarily her father shut himself up in his study and worked on his papers. He made no attempt to answer phone calls then and almost no one called him at night.

Her grandmother would say that the stars were responsible for his inexplicable decision to remain in the living room. He cared nothing for television; Amanda couldn't remember how long it had been since her father had expressed an interest in any program. And now here he was, sitting glued to the screen on the one night when she had counted on having him safely out of the way.

A growing resentment against Tully possessed her when she opened her notebook. How could she study if she had to be prepared to leap for the phone at the first sound of its bell? Tully was probably having a wonderful time snuggled into Fisher Milate's dazzling sports car, and Tully would have some clever excuse to offer the teachers for her unprepared assignments.

Amanda crumpled a sheet of paper, numbered a fresh page.

The telephone rang, and she leaped convulsively, feeling something—a brick, at least—crash into the pit of her stomach.

"I'll get it, Daddy." She almost groaned aloud as she recognized the voice of Mrs. Hallam.

Amanda sat down gingerly in the straight-backed chair. She was determined to keep her caller anonymous, a feat that required mental dexterity, especially since it was also necessary to keep Tully's name out of the conversation.

Mrs. Hallam, Amanda perceived at once, was committed to lying smoothly.

"Amanda, dear, I'm not sure just when Tully said she'd be home. Do you mind asking her?"

"Ten thirty," Amanda said. "I'm sure."

"You two girls are working hard, I suppose? Tully thought she was getting a sore throat and I'm wondering if she ought not to come home earlier. She mustn't get too tired."

Ten thirty wasn't late, Amanda said. Her father had lowered the volume of the television set, presumably to avoid confusion, and he must be hearing every word.

"Well, perhaps I'd better speak to her." Mrs. Hallam coughed gently. "Will you call her, dear? I'm interrupting a bridge game."

"She's downstairs, getting a book from my grandmother." Amanda rattled off the sentence at top speed, staking her all on the use of the pronoun. "I'll tell her you called."

Tully didn't have to call back, Mrs. Hallam said, apparently satisfied. If she could be persuaded to come home early, take some aspirin and go to bed, her cold might not develop. Someone—probably her bridge partner—shouted impatiently, and to Amanda's intense relief Mrs. Hallam hung up hastily.

The odd sensation that all her bones had collapsed inside her skin urged Amanda to lie down on the floor at least long enough to recover the use of her backbone. This, however, might attract her father's attention, and she dared not run the risk. She began to walk quietly and rigidly back to the dining room, wondering how much he had overheard and trying to imagine how her part of the conversation had sounded to him.

Daddy, she admitted to herself as she typed a few words blindly, was no dope. She tried to remember whether she had spoken Tully's name, even once, and decided that on that point she was safe. But could she be certain that her father had accepted the pronoun "she" to mean her mother? At the time it had seemed like an inspiration, but now miserable doubts were unsettling her complacency.

Amanda's imagination began to supply a dialogue that interfered with her typing.

"I don't remember your mother saying she wanted to borrow a book from your grandmother," her father *might* say.

To which she could reply, "You probably didn't hear her when she said it."

At this point a new complication presented itself to add to the turmoil in her mind.

What would be more natural than for her father to say, when her mother returned, "Someone phoned you; Amanda took the message."

Daddy was too polite to ask outright who had phoned, but it wouldn't be strange if he should mention the incident. It was not, Amanda realized drearily, a matter of life or death with him.

And suppose Mrs. Hallam phoned a second time!

The miserable evening crawled by. Amanda, hopeful that her mother's continuous absence meant that she had been captured to serve as a fourth at bridge, found her father's actions increasingly significant. For months he had ignored the television set, yet this evening he appeared to be fascinated by a succession of programs. It was also alarming that he made no attempt to talk to her, although this might indicate an exaggerated respect for her display of energy and concentration.

At ten o'clock, Amanda permitted herself to hope. Tully, due at home by half past ten, could no longer be subject to a phone call from her mother. The horrid chance that the Hallams might send the car to pick up their daughter was a new thought and too awful to be considered.

Amanda began to gather up her papers and books. If she could get to bed before her mother came in, the telephone call might be forgotten.

"Maybe you need food," her father suggested when she announced that she had finished homework and was "dead."

The thought of even a glass of milk nauseated her and the fear that he might try to persuade her to sit in the kitchen and talk to him, while he rummaged in the refrigerator for the delicatessen specialties Pearl stored for him, gave her a hollow feeling under her ribs.

"I'm too tired—we have tests tomorrow," she said.

And when she had kissed him good night and had closed the door of her bedroom, she thought for a moment that she was going to be sick. Her head throbbed, but her hands and feet were cold and she shivered as if she might be coming down with flu.

The physical discomfort terrified her because she was alone, but she sat down on the bed and the disagreeable symptoms soon passed. A great weariness, in its way as alarming as the bodily coldness, fell upon her like a blanket, and she was tempted for the first time in her life to lie down and sleep without removing her clothes. She did skip all the rites that made up her usual elaborate routine and had no recollection of getting into bed or putting out the light on her night table.

"Amanda? Amanda, dear, wake up. Don't be frightened—it's Mother, dear."

Sleep, deep and black and heavy, smothered Amanda. She struggled against the weight, became aware of someone bending over her, smelled her mother's perfume. The room was dimly lighted, but it couldn't be morning.

"Amanda, wake up. I have to talk to you," her mother urged.

"Uh huh," muttered Amanda drowsily. "What time is it?"

"Half past eleven." Her mother sounded short of breath. "Mrs. Hallam just called me. She wants to know why Tully isn't home yet."

Amanda jerked herself to a sitting position. *Tully!*

Elaine's hurried, urgent voice betrayed her own anxiety. Mrs. Hallam was all mixed up; she had the odd idea that Tully had been doing homework with Amanda.

"I told her that Tully hadn't been here tonight and she insists that she telephoned and you told her Tully had gone to borrow a book from your grandmother. It just doesn't make sense."

Amanda felt again the sick, hollow sensation under her ribs.

"Tully hasn't been here, has she, dear?" Elaine probed.

"No." Amanda gulped.

"Mrs. Hallam seems to think you know where she is. You don't, do you?"

It was like Tully to stay out till midnight, when she had promised to be home by half past ten. She didn't care how many friends she involved in her escapades. Amanda, torn between loyalty and the sickening conviction that she was in a terrible mess, made a dogged attempt to pick up the pieces.

"Tully's all right," she said.

But Elaine had recognized in Mrs. Hallam's frantic appeal the outline of the terror, a form without shape, that haunted her and, she sometimes thought, all the mothers in the world.

"*Do* you know where Tully is, Amanda? Is she out with a boy?"

If Tully was out with a boy, she was in a car, and who could tell what might happen?

"I don't know where she is," Amanda repeated, but she shivered.

"Then her mother is right and she's with Fisher Milate, who doesn't know how to drive. She must have told her mother that she was coming here to study with you."

Amanda couldn't tell whether it was her mind or her stomach that heaved and tossed.

"Fisher knows how to drive; he has his license," she argued, thankful to be able to avoid Tully's name. "He's been driving for at least six months."

Elaine, still shaken by the phone call, pressed her child gently back against the pillows. In her first moment of understanding that Tully's whereabouts were unknown to her family, a great fear had gripped Elaine and she had opened the bedroom door half expecting to find an empty bed. Fool, she had berated herself a moment later, of course Kelsey had been home all evening; Amanda could not have left the apartment without her father's knowledge.

"You're shivering, dear." Elaine drew the sheet and light blanket up and bent down to kiss Amanda, who had no way of knowing that guilt, contrition, and gratitude flavored the caress. "Try not to worry about Tully. She may be home by now. Go to sleep, darling."

To Amanda's distress, her teeth began to chatter. Her effort to hold them still resulted in spasms that shook her whole body.

"How about a sleeping pill?" she managed to say.

"You don't need a sleeping pill." Elaine was horrified at the suggestion. "I'll heat some milk for you. Yes, I know you don't like it hot—I'll put cinnamon in it."

Amanda pulled the sheet over her head and waited apprehensively for the milk. Her new terror was that her father might bring it. She had a shrewd idea that he would remember the phone call she had managed to keep anonymous, and it would be like him to march in and question her. Amanda tried to remember her answers to her mother's questions. She had not, she assured herself, told any lies, except to Mrs. Hallam. That fib had been necessary to protect Tully, who depended on her as a loyal friend.

"Drink this and you'll go right to sleep." Elaine, in her stocking feet, had entered the room silently. "I'll call Mrs. Hallam the first thing in the morning. Sip it slowly," she added. "I'll come back and make sure you've turned off the light." Elaine closed the door gently behind her.

Amanda, drinking milk, watched her shadow on the wall. Fisher Milate preferred parking to driving, the girls said. Tully had no business dating him on a school night. Mrs. Hallam might not have checked up at all on a Friday or Saturday date. Even Mirabelle Marilyn Meeks didn't think much of dating through the week.

"If you turn Fisher down once, he's through," Tully had once explained. "He boasts he never gives a girl a second chance. He doesn't have to."

"Personally, I can't stand Fisher Milate," Amanda whispered hardily, but she could not visualize herself refusing any boy a date.

She finished the milk, put the glass on the table, and snapped off the light. The droning of an airplane started in the distance, and as she listened for it to pass over the house, she fell asleep.

When she woke in the morning, a path of sunlight fell like a band of insertion across the bed. She turned to look at the little clock ticking on the night table and immediately sat up. It couldn't be half past nine!

"You awake?" Pearl must have been talking through the keyhole.

Amanda called "Come in," and slid to the floor as the door opened.

"Why didn't someone call me? How can I go to school as late as this? Where's Mother? What time is it?" The clock, Amanda thought, couldn't possibly be right.

Miz Carpenter, Pearl said, had gone down to her mama's apartment. Yes, Mr. Carpenter had left for the office.

"Your mother wants you to sleep, but she'll come back and have breakfast with you—I'm to let her know soon as you get up." Pearl seemed to be reciting a message committed to memory. "She called up the school and said you wouldn't be in."

Amanda found herself staring at a closed door. Pearl liked to talk, and it wasn't like her to barge off, without asking even one question.

Amanda wondered, as she dressed, whether Tully would be in school. She liked to talk about "cutting classes," but Miss Mary's staff believed in strict discipline, and attendance rules were firmly enforced. The other girls would hear about Tully's date with Fisher Milate before Amanda could see her. Because of the lack of telephone privacy in the Carpenter home it was not likely that Tully would phone until after she had

107

had time to soothe her parents. In one way or another, Amanda reflected, children had to spend a great deal of effort in keeping their parents good-tempered and serene.

"I'm starving!" she announced, her dark eyes mirroring depths of anguish, as she slid deftly into the breakfast nook. "Look how long it's been since I've had anything to eat."

Pearl placed a tall glass of orange juice before her and said, "There's your mother," at the sound of the front door closing.

Elaine came into the kitchen with such an air of determined cheerfulness that her "Good morning, darling" sounded rehearsed.

Amanda surveyed her across the narrow table.

"You've been crying, Mother. Is Grandma sick again?"

Elaine dabbed at her eyes with a handkerchief. The tears became a flood, and she picked up a paper napkin.

"I wanted you to eat your breakfast; don't let me upset you," she sobbed. "Pearl's made h-hot muffins for you."

Pearl brought a second glass of orange juice and put it down before Elaine.

"You might as well tell her now," she said.

Amanda wanted to put her hands over her ears, to refuse to hear whatever her mother had to tell her. She wanted to close her eyes and shut out the picture of her mother's face, with its blotched, tear-stained make-up. Instead, she sat silently, her eyes enormous pools of fear.

"It's Tully," Elaine said. "She's badly injured—the Hallams didn't hear until two o'clock this morning."

It happened to other girls. Amanda, her throat dry, tried to swallow a mysterious lump at the back of her tongue. Kids were always getting themselves hurt in accidents; such stories were in the newspapers every day. But not—until now—anyone she knew. Tully Hallam was her best friend, not a name and address in print.

"What—what happened?" Amanda asked in a hoarse whisper.

"That wretched, ghastly, horrible boy!" Elaine's shattered nerves exploded in a shower of epithets. "He lost control of the car and crossed over into the wrong lane. Drink your orange juice."

Pearl, bringing hot coffee and chocolate, realized that anger was a relief to Elaine, but Amanda listened to her mother in dismay. Elaine's dislike of Fisher Milate was apparently intensified by his lack of injuries. His car was completely wrecked, and he was to be charged with reckless driving, but he had escaped without a scratch.

"Tully was thrown through the windshield and landed on the concrete highway, her father says." Elaine helped herself to a muffin from the plate Pearl offered, but did not seem to know what to do with it.

Amanda gulped. Not even scalding-hot chocolate had any effect on the dry throat. She hesitated to voice questions without knowing that it was because she dreaded to hear the answers.

It was Pearl who asked if Tully had been taken to one of the city hospitals and if visitors would be allowed to see her.

"She's in St. Andrew's." Elaine named one of the large private hospitals serving the downtown section. "Her father was calling all the hospitals. I don't know when they would have let him know if he hadn't happened to ring them. He's still at the hospital, and Mrs. Hallam with him. One of the maids told me what happened when I called around eight this morning."

Amanda had the curious sensation of having shriveled into a small, hard knot within her skin. Her vivid imagination had pictured Tully's slender body going through the car's windshield and falling with cruel impact on the hard concrete road. What had Fisher Milate been doing—sitting still, perhaps, with his eyes shut against the glare of the oncoming headlights?

"If she had only kept her word, about coming here to study with you!" Elaine drank cold coffee which she had sweetened three times. "She must have met this horrible boy on the sly."

If she tried to explain, it might seem like trying to put the blame on Tully, but if she kept still, could she be sure that her motive was not to escape a family row? Amanda stopped listening to her mother and brooded on this complicated, ethical question.

"As long as she's on the critical list, I don't suppose there is anything we can take her?" Elaine spoke to Pearl. "Flowers won't mean a thing, either, but her mother might like to know we're thinking of her."

Hospital nurses loathed flowers, Pearl said, and she had known several patients who couldn't stand the fragrance in the early days of convalescence.

"Better wait, Miz Carpenter. That little girl's going to be smothered with attention. Wait till you can ask her what she wants."

That was probably sensible, Elaine agreed. She intended to call the hospital at noon, not that any hospital ever released a crumb of real information.

"I'll phone from downtown. Lucie is coming in to see her psychiatrist and we'll lunch together. What are you going to do, Amanda? Wouldn't you like to come, too? We might look at the new bathing suits."

The image of Tully, pitching forward through the windshield, then lying crumpled on the roadway, persistently repeated itself in Amanda's mind. The thought of listening to Lucie, who would be sure to harp on the topic of baby sitters, revolted her. And certainly she had no heart for looking at bathing suits—especially since she wouldn't be allowed to get a bikini.

Then, inexplicably, she remembered that she was not alone. Sympathy, compassion, above all understanding, were hers for the asking. She straightened her shoulders; she sat erect.

"You needn't worry about me, I have something to do," she said.

When her mother had gone and Pearl had disappeared to wash "a few things" in the basement laundry, Amanda sat down at her painted pine desk and selected a sheet of her best note paper.

"Dear Mirabelle," she began, a little frown of concentration creasing her smooth forehead, "I am in urgent need of advice. . . ."

"I don't even know whether she will go to see Tully when they finally allow visitors." Elaine, a week later, had stopped in at her mother's apartment to deliver a coffee ring.

Amanda, Elaine continued, refused to discuss the hospital reports, never asked what progress Tully was making, shut herself up in her room every night to do her homework and to write letters.

"She must have written a dozen letters to that Mirabelle Marilyn Meeks. Kelsey won't buy the papers, but I did. I wanted to see what on earth she can find to tell a perfect stranger."

Mirabelle's column had not been very revealing, Elaine admitted. Mirabelle was evidently more interested in giving advice than in publishing the letters of her correspondents.

"She quotes a line or two, then she's off. I can't imagine Amanda or any of her friends listening to all that guff. Why does it fascinate them in print?"

"They put fewer and fewer pecans on their coffee rings," Pauline Ives said. "Mirabelle's chief charm is that she represents her readers' choice. No parent recommends her."

Elaine said, "I should hope not," but added that she could take Mirabelle or leave her.

"It's Amanda who worries me, Mama. Mrs. Hallam tells me that Tully has been talking of her, and the doctor thinks that perhaps by tomorrow Amanda can see her for a few moments. Suppose Amanda won't go?"

"Oh, for pity's sake!" Pauline felt around in the toe of a brown suede pump and produced a pair of silver earrings. "I put them there last night so I'd know where to find them," she explained. "Really, Elaine, I do think that mothers today are not quite right in their heads. Is there any reason why you shouldn't tell Amanda that she is to go to the hospital and then see to it that she gets there?"

Amanda was too old to spank, Elaine pointed out. "And I can't see myself dragging her into the hospital by the hair of her head. Amanda wouldn't mind screaming every step of the way, and I'd probably wind up in jail."

Pauline lifted a heap of clothing from a chair and retrieved an ivory-backed mirror.

"You used to mind me," she said. "And I didn't find it necessary to drag you around by your hair."

Amanda's generation was different, Elaine reflected, but the difference was not easy to define. It seemed to her, in retrospect, that she had been a little afraid of her mother, and Amanda certainly did not fear her parents. Not that Mama had been a despot, Elaine thought, watching the slight, active figure stepping briskly around the cluttered room.

"My spirit was probably crushed when I was a child," Elaine said in a tone of sweet reasonableness.

Pauline hooked the silver hoops to her pretty ears and stepped back from the dresser to admire the effect in the glass.

"Who crushed it?" she demanded.

All mothers crushed the spirits of their children, Elaine said, unless they understood psychology. She had grown up believing that "Mother knows best" because in her teen-age years that slogan had carried the weight of a Bible text.

"I used to think it was from the Bible myself. Now, people like Mirabelle Marilyn Meeks preach that Mother doesn't know anything."

A spark of laughter glinted in Pauline's blue eyes.

"There are always shocks," she observed cheerfully. "All the time *I* was growing up I was trained to believe that the young owed a great deal to the old. My parents took care of their parents, I took care of mine. But when I reach eighty or ninety, I expect to go into a Home."

Elaine looked stricken.

"You've always said that you didn't want to live with us, Mama. And Kelsey's mother wants to die and be buried in France."

She was merely using an illustration, Pauline insisted. Times changed, the concept of duty altered.

"By the time Amanda has children, the Lord only knows what will be expected. Right now my advice to you is to have Kelsey drive Amanda to the hospital."

For a moment Pauline stood silent, the motion of her hands

rummaging in a dresser drawer stilled. Then gently, almost as if speaking to herself, "He might tell her that we cannot refuse the dying," she said.

The old-fashioned Victorian phrase startled Elaine as much by its wording as by its import.

"Oh *no!*" she protested. "Mama, what have you heard? Or is it the stars? You haven't been looking up Tully's birth signs, have you?"

This was one time when she preferred not to look into the future, Pauline admitted reluctantly. No, she had not phoned St. Andrew's—she had some regard for the overworked switchboard operators—but Pearl had given her a detailed report of Tully Hallam's injuries.

"Elaine, I hope the doctors will be frank with her parents. I don't see how the girl can possibly recover."

Tully was young, modern surgery performed miracles, the accident was already a week old, and Tully was supposed to be holding her own. Elaine, frantically listing her fragile hopes, wondered how any woman could lose a child and go on living.

To her surprise—but then, her daughter was unpredictable —Amanda readily accepted the suggestion that they visit Tully the next day. Elaine, who never drove the family car in the city, arranged to pick up Amanda at the school in a cab.

She was waiting on the pavement in front of the school when Elaine's taxi stopped at the curb the next afternoon. A group of girls stood on the school steps, and Amanda said that they would have liked to go in a group to visit Tully.

"Miss Mary told them Tully can't have more than two visitors a day, not counting her father and mother." Amanda felt in the pocket of her polo coat. "I bought her some new eye liner," she said.

Tully would be smothered in flowers and she didn't eat much candy because she wanted to keep her figure, but it wasn't likely that anyone else would think to give her eye liner, Amanda said with perfect seriousness. Tully was mad about cosmetics; she would try anything.

"If she isn't interested today, you mustn't feel disappointed," Elaine warned. "She's still on the critical list."

She had been afraid to say too much, but the moment the nurse took them into the clean, bright, impersonal room, Elaine knew that she had said too little. But how, under any circumstances, could she have prepared Amanda for the sight of the figure on the bed? Tully's face was covered in bandages that left slits for her eyes and a gash for her mouth. Both legs were in traction.

A radio blared what Pauline Ives would have called the "thump-thump" type of music, and the nurse hastily closed the door to keep the noise sealed in. She was a middle-aged woman with an intelligent face and quick, light-gray eyes. Her name, she said, was Miss Hatry.

"Yes, she can talk—a little," she said in answer to Elaine's imploring look. "It's difficult. She lost all her front teeth, you know."

Amanda's face was colorless, her eyes dark pools of anguish and horror. She moved stiffly to the bed, but her voice when she spoke was warm and did not falter.

"Hi, Tully! It's me—Amanda. I'm so sorry you got banged up."

Tully mumbled something, but the radio drowned out her voice.

"She has it going every waking moment," the nurse said to Elaine. "You'd think it would drive her mad, but her mother says she keeps it on all day at home."

"The girls at school are all asking about you." Amanda spoke loudly and distinctly.

The nurse said, "Don't touch her. Don't touch the bed."

Elaine remembered the box of eye liner, and the feeling that she ought not to be listening drove her toward the door.

But before she could open the door, Tully said two words that carried above the dreadful metallic beat of the radio orchestra.

"Fisher Milate?" It was impossible to miss the interrogation.

Elaine, plunging into the corridor, caught the beginning of Amanda's reply.

"I haven't seen him—"

"Do you feel faint?" A passing nurse paused to give her a professional glance.

Elaine shook her head, said hurriedly that she was waiting to see Mrs. Hallam.

"I'm not on the case, but I believe she's trying to get a little sleep." The gray-haired nurse was already moving on. "She has a room here in the hospital," she added, over her shoulder.

The door behind Elaine opened, and Amanda came out, followed by Tully's nurse.

"I thought you and Tully might like to talk privately," Elaine said, answering the question in Amanda's eyes.

Tully ought not to try to talk, the nurse was saying briskly; she hoped that Amanda would pass the word along to her friends. If they would be content to drop in, one at a time, speak a few words to assure Tully that she wasn't forgotten, and leave quickly, the effect might be good.

"It will give her mother a chance to get a little rest, too." The slender uniformed figure turned to go back to Tully. "It's more for the Hallams than for the patient," she said with a direct look at Elaine.

In the elevator the need to establish communication drove Elaine to ask Amanda what she had done with the box of eye liner.

"I put it on the table. Miss Hatry said she would tell her about it." Amanda hesitated. "I asked her if her head hurt and she said no."

# V

Tully Hallam died suddenly the next night, with only her distracted mother in the room. Elaine could be thankful that she, and not Amanda, had phoned the hospital at ten o'clock. Amanda was already in bed and the news could be kept from her till morning.

"She's been so odd, ever since the accident," Elaine fretted. "I'm half afraid to tell her. But she couldn't have expected Tully to recover—not after seeing her yesterday."

Kelsey, sorting papers at his desk, pushed a bulging briefcase to one side. Amanda, he said, was suffering from a case of nerves brought on by a feeling of guilt.

"I can't be sure, of course, but I think I'm right. She let Mrs.

Hallam think Tully was here that night she went riding with Fisher Milate. No, she didn't tell me, but Mrs. Hallam phoned and I heard the conversation."

Elaine protested. "But I didn't know anything about it. Why didn't you tell me, Kelsey?"

"What could you have done? What could any parent have done—then?" He smiled a little sadly. "Amanda is going to shift the blame to us now," he said.

"But I'm afraid," Elaine said. "I look at Amanda and I think, Suppose she goes out in cars when we don't know it, with boys who can't drive, or who drink. The nights she's spent with Tully—how do we know, Kelsey, what Tully may have coaxed her to do?"

They would never know now, he said, but later he would try to talk to Amanda, discover, if possible, the root of her fierce resentments.

"For the present our daughter is a hostile witness, who cannot be forced to testify."

The trouble with her, Elaine told herself wearily during the days before Tully's funeral, was that she expected people to be *reasonable*. Neither her husband nor her daughter was reasonable. Kelsey talked in riddles, and Amanda hardly talked at all. The girls in Tully's class at school planned to attend the services in a body, and Amanda was to go with them. She was quiet and withdrawn and so coldly polite that, as Kelsey said, it was more insulting than if she had been defiant. When Mrs. Hallam, who denied herself to all callers, sent word that she would like to see Amanda "for just a few moments," Amanda flatly refused.

"She wasn't decent to Tully" was the explanation she gave to Pearl. "Of course she's making a big fuss now, but she doesn't fool me."

Gradually, and only to Pearl, Amanda revealed that she considered the behavior of her own parents to be hypocritical.

"They never liked Tully when she was alive, and it makes me sick to see them pretend to be sorry that she died. I don't have any respect for people who put on an act."

"You don't have to like people to be sorry when they die,"

Pearl objected. "I'm sorry for anybody who dies. It's worse, too, when you're young."

Amanda said coldly, "Would you be sorry for Jerome's mother if she died?" but she relented when Pearl looked vexed and changed the subject by asking her to take the vanilla pudding down to her grandmother.

"You can't avoid your family forever," Pearl sensibly pointed out, but at Amanda's refusal she took the pudding and endured Pauline Ives's questions with her customary patience.

"Of course I didn't admire Tully Hallam and she couldn't have been a good influence for Amanda, but what makes the child think I'm a monster?" Pauline demanded with accumulated irritation. "Can't I be sorry for Amanda and for Mrs. Hallam—that poor soul—without being accused of being two-faced?"

The days before a funeral were the worst, Pearl reminded her. Once that was over, Amanda would be able to relax.

"She needs more friends. It isn't a good thing to be so wrapped up in one girl," Pauline said.

But an uneasy feeling persisted that Amanda thought of herself as totally bereft, a ridiculous situation when you considered that the girl had a grandmother and her father and mother at hand.

It was also ridiculous for Amanda to pour her heart out to Mirabelle Marilyn Meeks, Elaine said. She was never to know exactly what went into the long letters that Amanda wrote night after night, following Tully's funeral. The excerpts published in the *Blaze* were difficult to identify, since Mirabelle was frankly committed to protecting her correspondents. She warned that initials were misleading and that she edited figures and facts.

Amanda mailed her letter each morning on the way to school and brought home a copy of the *Blaze* each afternoon when she returned. Even to Pearl the letter writing seemed excessive, and she ventured a mild remonstrance.

"I never knew anyone who wrote a letter to a newspaper every day," she said.

Amanda's reply silenced her.

"I never knew anyone who died before."

Very gradually, because silence and secrecy have limitations for the young, Amanda confided to Pearl that she was planning a memorial for Tully, with the help and advice of the columnist.

"Mirabelle's going to give a prize to the reader who sends in the best suggestion—that is, the one I like best," Amanda explained. "I want something that will have Tully's name on it."

And when the final decision had been reached, a longing for a larger audience than Pearl impelled Amanda to reveal the plan to her father. The prize-winning suggestion for Tully's memorial was to be the annual contributions of her friends to the paper's camp for underprivileged children.

"It's to be called the Tully Hallam Fund," Amanda said. "I'll send some money every year on Tully's birthday."

"May anyone contribute?" Kelsey asked gravely.

Amanda hesitated, struggling with conflicting emotions. He watched the desire to hurt him fade in her expressive eyes.

"Why, yes—I guess so," Amanda said.

She stood with her back braced against his closed study door, ready for instant escape. Like a bird, or young rabbit, whose fear of the trap was instinctive, Kelsey thought. But what should a man's own child know of captivity? He debated rising to pull a chair forward for her, but decided the action might startle her into flight.

"Sit down for a moment, dear." He indicated a handy chair with a careless wave of his hand.

"Why?" Amanda said.

"You haven't dropped in to see me for a long time. We could talk to each other," Kelsey suggested.

Amanda said, "I haven't anything to talk about."

But she lingered, an odd little figure in a purple sweater that came halfway to her knees, silhouetted against the gray door.

"Is that something new?" Kelsey asked doubtfully. "It's a sweater, isn't it? It looks a little long."

118

"They're wearing them longer," Amanda said.

Kelsey opened a drawer of the desk, took out his checkbook. "You'll accept a check?" He uncapped his pen.

"Oh—why, yes." Amanda took a step toward him.

But when he had filled out and signed the check, Kelsey let it lie on his desk.

"Amanda, once, years ago when I was away at school, the boy who sat next to me in class was killed in an accident. We were friends and I've never forgotten him. So perhaps I know something of how you feel about Tully."

Amanda was silent for a moment. Then she said, "What kind of accident?"

The boy had been hit by a pitched ball in a baseball game, Kelsey said.

"His father and mother set up a fund in his memory, to buy books for the school library."

Amanda had reached a chair. She sat down warily on the edge of the seat.

"Parents are like that—show-offs," she said.

The contempt in her voice stung him, but Kelsey kept his temper.

"Don't you believe that fathers and mothers are grieved when they lose a child, Amanda?"

They might grieve, Amanda admitted, but she was not impressed.

"The time for parents to show they love their children is while the kids are alive. Making a fuss, the way the Hallams are doing, is just cheap publicity. They didn't try to understand Tully when she was living."

Kelsey was aware of increasing irritation. The constant use of the word "parents," pronounced with Amanda's peculiar inflection, rubbed him the wrong way, as it did Elaine. And the phrase, "cheap publicity," grated on him, too.

"I suppose you feel we don't understand you, either," he said.

"Oh, I suppose you think you do," Amanda conceded with a hint of graciousness, "but naturally you can't expect to actually understand me. Your generation and mine are too far apart.

Mirabelle Marilyn Meeks says that the most we can expect of parents is that they will *try* to understand us."

Kelsey stifled an impulse to damn Mirabelle Marilyn Meeks.

Instead, he asked, "Why do you have such implicit confidence in that woman?" and instantly realized his mistake.

Amanda's face tightened into a familiar mask. "You wouldn't understand," she said.

"Couldn't you explain?" Kelsey was humble.

"Well, you see, she understands us," Amanda said. "Mirabelle Marilyn Meeks knows how difficult it is to get along with parents. Kids ought to be allowed to lead their own lives, she says. No kid ought to be a rubber stamp."

"But does that mean everything a parent asks should be disregarded?" Kelsey could see her mind closing against him, even as he spoke the words. "Is disobedience the only way to demonstrate your growing independence?"

Amanda hesitated, patently groping. Then she brightened.

"We have to rebel," she explained. "Growing away from parents is a healthy sign, Mirabelle Marilyn Meeks says."

"What about responsibility?" Kelsey said carefully. "Does Mirabelle Marilyn know that parents are legally responsible for their children's actions until they're of age?"

The heavy-handed parent was out of date, Amanda assured him. Kids should be responsible for their own actions. Times had changed.

"You don't know it, Daddy, but kids my age are much further advanced than your generation was. We're much better able to take care of ourselves. We're more mature in every way."

"But you keep asking for advice," Kelsey pointed out. "You write steadily to Mirabelle Marilyn Meeks."

Out of pity his daughter managed a small, forgiving smile for the general obtuseness of fathers.

"Of course I write to her. She understands me," Amanda said.

## Chapter 8

"It's all a part of the rat race we call living," Elaine said. "We don't even have time to be neighborly until something awful happens."

"You read that in a book." Lucie spoke without animosity and helped herself to a second sandwich. "If you want to know what a rat race really is, ask me. And if you think no one has time to be neighborly, move right out to Lyman—the neighbors will smother you."

She and Elaine were having tea and sandwiches in the living room because the dining room was being repapered and Pearl was washing the china, which filled all available space in the kitchen. Lucie had arrived without warning, a trick that infuriated her when she happened to be the victim, but she felt justified in surprising Elaine because she had a full-time maid.

"Pearl cooks lunch whether Elaine is home or not," Lucie had said to her husband.

It was a little pathetic, Elaine told herself, pushing the cheese crackers toward her guest, that Lucie, once she had a day off, didn't seem to have anything planned. She complained that she had no money to spend. If she went shopping, she used Elaine's charge accounts, and if she didn't ask Kelsey to take her to lunch, invariably she "dropped in" at the apartment between twelve and one.

Today Elaine had a slight cold that accented her depression —the death of Tully Hallam had been a severe shock to her —and she had intended to phone Naida Steckner for an emergency appointment. It was one of those days when it seemed worth fifteen dollars to have someone willing to listen to her, or, better yet, throw her a life line of words that would rescue her from her private slough of despair.

"I feel so . . . so inadequate," she would say to Naida, and in less than half an hour—the "blues" dissolved, replaced by an intangible hopefulness—she would find herself cheerful and composed.

"When I leave Mrs. Steckner's office, it's like walking on air," she had once confided to another client, an elderly woman waiting in the reception room.

The beaming response, "Well, do you know that's the way I feel too, when I've been to my chiropodist," was disheartening, but Elaine blamed herself for the impulse to trust a stranger.

"My psychiatrist knows exactly what living in the suburbs is doing to me." Lucie had been fortified with two cups of strong tea. "And of course I was married too young."

The only reason she had been able to get away from the house and the children this morning, Lucie said, was because the girl across the street had her mother visiting her.

"She left her three with her mother and I took my two over there. Vi wants me to help her get up a psychiatry group, so she's ready to do favors for me. I hope her mother stays a month."

The group would be less expensive than private appointments, Lucie rattled on. Why, of course there were enough women who needed treatment; she and Vi Tyler expected to be snowed under by applications.

"You live here in the city with everything near you, Amanda is old enough to be no trouble at all, you have a maid, your mother isn't a dependent—why, look at your hair!" Lucie's burst of resentment culminated on a high note. "You can get your hair done without having to take two kids with you."

Elaine said, "Pearl didn't make any dessert. I have some chocolates put away."

When she returned with the candy, Lucie had lighted a cigarette and looked more relaxed.

"I suppose Amanda was all broken up about the Hallam girl. They were quite close friends, weren't they?" The only emotion in her voice was curiosity.

Elaine tried not to speak coldly. Lucie had not known Tully, so she couldn't be expected to feel more than a conventional sympathy.

"It's Amanda's first experience with death. She won't get over it for a long time. They were great friends."

"Amanda's being difficult, of course." Lucie had flashes of shrewdness. "Oh, don't try to deny it, Elaine. She's at the age where she loves being a problem. There's nothing you can do about it."

There didn't seem to be anything she could do about her own problems, she complained, as she selected a fat chocolate from the box. The psychiatrist made no constructive suggestions. Apparently he considered himself paid to listen, but nothing beyond that.

"The more difficult it is for me to get away from Lyman, simply to breathe, the more deeply I get involved," Lucie said. "As if I hadn't enough troubles, I've got Midge Cutter on my hands."

Elaine waited. She had not been deceived by the tactics of Midge Sully Cutter, who had apparently dropped out of sight. Kelsey had not mentioned her name, and Elaine had been too proud to question him. But the sixth sense possessed by every wife told her that they communicated through his office. Midge could write to him, telephone him, casually drop in for a consultation—women were always consulting lawyers—and get herself invited out to lunch. Studying Lucie covertly, Elaine decided that she was unaware of the intrigue. She looked irritated and discontented, but certainly not in the least excited.

"Midge is the type of woman who never solves her own problems," Lucie said. "I always thought Army wives were resourceful—used to coping with this and that, you know. My God, if a fuse blows out, Midge comes over and gets Royce to put in a new one. She doesn't even phone—she's afraid to stay in the dark."

She wasn't the only one who found Midge a first-class nuisance, Lucie went on; the other neighbors were beginning to weary of her constant demands on their time. Midge expected them to share her worries about her children, her choice of draperies, and the difficulty of finding a part-time maid.

"Anyway, as Vi says, it will be the last straw if Midge tries to join our psychiatric group. No one wants her listening to private discussions. For one thing, she's too old."

Too old for their group, she meant, Lucie interpreted, conscious of Elaine's involuntary wince. Midge was past forty, if she was a day, and she simply didn't fit.

"Why don't you take hold and give your old pal a helping hand?" Lucie suggested. "Integrate her. Or let her talk to your Mrs. What's-her-name—Mrs. Steckner."

Elaine said that Midge Sully—well, Midge Sully Cutter, then—could do her own integrating, and that she was not, and never had been, a pal.

"And why should I introduce her to Naida Steckner, especially since the idea seems to be yours alone?"

"I only thought it would be a kind deed," Lucie said modestly. "Something tells me the woman is having husband trouble."

The sound of china shattering in the kitchen made Elaine jump. In a movie, she told herself, she would have been the one to let a cup drop to the floor.

"That was only a kitchen bowl, Miz Carpenter," Pearl's cheerful voice called.

"How do you mean, husband trouble?" Elaine recognized the expression borrowed from Amanda.

There was nothing specific, Lucie admitted; no one knew whether the Cutters were actually living apart or not. But the major had never been seen in Lyman, and although Midge went down to Washington, "off and on," that proved nothing. She took the children, since there was no one to leave in charge of them, and Vi had pointed out that Midge could be visiting friends. Army people were always on visiting terms with someone in Washington. The major had the car, Lucie added; that was one of Midge's grievances and also an extra reason why she got in everyone's hair. She was always begging transportation.

"Your Mrs. Steckner might straighten her out," Lucie said.

124

"Take that candy away—I'll bet I've gained two pounds."

Elaine watched her light a cigarette. She had no intention of providing Midge Sully with a marriage counselor, much less of attempting to "integrate" her with her circle of friends. Kelsey must have mentioned Naida Steckner to Lucie, or perhaps Mama had made the disclosure innocently. Lucie could ask leading questions with great finesse.

"Don't commit the folly of bringing an old flame into the home," Naida Steckner had warned Elaine in their last interview.

Husbands, she had said, were apt to visualize wives as taking delight in sticking pins, figuratively speaking, into the old girl friend invited to join the family circle. His protective instincts aroused, a husband would go to any length to shield the woman who had trusted him enough to become his wife's guest.

"At the same time," Naida had urged smoothly, "and for the same reason, you must be careful not to speak ill of a designing woman, whether she is under your roof or not. The thing to remember is not to give your husband cause to put on the armor of a shining knight."

Kelsey already had a tendency to be sorry for Lucie—who, of all women, least needed his support—and Elaine had no difficulty in picturing his sympathies easily kindled by the recitals of Midge's worries. Lawyers heard as many feminine confidences as doctors, and Midge could talk to Kelsey for hours on the pretext of consulting him.

"Well—" Lucie took one more chocolate, ground out her cigarette, put on one shoe. "I don't suppose we could go downtown and look around?"

Shopping with Lucie was an exhausting performance that Elaine dreaded, but the wistful eagerness in her sister-in-law's face touched her. After all, if Lucie had come up to the city to "breathe," it was natural for her to covet a tangible result of her freedom.

"I'll go with you to look at Italian knits; Mangloves has a sale," Elaine said.

"Pearl says that Amanda has known it for a week." Elaine looked from her needlepoint to Kelsey standing in the doorway of the living room. "It was in the *Blaze*."

"Then all the tabloids have had it." Kelsey glanced at the evening paper in his hand. "There's a small paragraph in the *Lantern*. Strange Amanda hasn't talked about it."

Amanda, Elaine reminded him, avoided all mention of the Hallams.

"I think she feels that Judith and Gil Hallam didn't understand Tully—any more than we understand her."

Kelsey half turned to go back to his study, changed his mind, and crossed the rug to the armchair facing Elaine on the other side of the fireplace. A small, gentle fire of chemically treated wood burned quietly, the heat welcome on a damp, cool night in early May.

"So Judith Hallam finally got around to suing for a divorce," Kelsey said. "She may not have understood her daughter, but she put up with Gil Hallam for years, to avoid a scandal."

Elaine looked at him with astonishment. Pearl had insisted on giving her the details of the court battle looming between the Hallams, and had confided that Jerome had referred to Mrs. Hallam as a "cold-blooded bitch."

"She's going to bleed him of every last cent he has. Jerome says she's the type to enjoy ruining a man's good name."

Pearl had confessed to having reservations. For one thing, it had been her experience that all men stuck together. Mrs. Hallam undoubtedly had her faults, but she doubted that Mr. Hallam was any whited sepulcher.

Amanda had not called her attention to the story and photographs in the *Blaze*, Pearl said, but Amanda never skipped her daily copy of the paper and no reader could have missed the headlines.

Tonight Amanda had gone down to her grandmother's for dinner and, since it was Friday, they were going to the movies together. It was really sweet of Mama to go, Elaine reflected, since she loathed the label "Senior Citizen" with which Amanda had recently tagged her. Mirabelle Marilyn Meeks was advocating missionary work by the young in behalf of senior citizens and Golden Age Clubs, and Amanda regarded her grandmother as a fruitful field.

"How do you know Judith Hallam put up with anything for years?" Elaine took a careful stitch. "For all we know, she may be a hard woman to live with."

*Never speak ill of a designing woman.* Instinctively Elaine felt it safe to identify the wife as the culprit.

Judith had put up with a philandering husband for longer than should be expected of any woman, Kelsey said with what Amanda would have called his judicial manner. The corespondent named in the suit could have been picked at random; presumably the evidence revealed a wide choice from which to choose.

"But you don't *know,*" Elaine argued. "He may actually be in love with this woman. Of course it's hard on Judith, but I think she's making a mistake to be so openly bitter. What is that Chinese proverb? 'Love goes where it is sent'."

"Are you trying to tell me that this thing may be bigger than either of them—Gil and his redhead?" Kelsey's sardonic glance was lost on Elaine, who was rethreading her needle.

She said, "Has she red hair? And I suppose she's young—at least, younger than Judith."

Midge Sully was at least six months older than herself, possibly even a year older, Elaine thought. Men were never very clever at estimating a woman's age; they depended too much on the color of *hair.* Pearl boasted that Jerome could guess a woman's age by the way she danced; after twenty, Jerome insisted, her bones began to stiffen. Gil Hallam adored dancing, so perhaps he placed a high value on young, supple muscles and bones.

"I wish Amanda wouldn't read the stories about the divorce," Kelsey was saying, "but that's too much to hope for. Probably Miss Mary's is all agog, with 'adultery' the word on every tongue, providing a thrilling taste of sin."

"Well, you didn't like it when Amanda dragged 'buttocks'

into the dinner-table conversation every night for a week," Elaine, tense and irritable, flinched when Kelsey laughed.

He might be an old fogy, he apologized, but anatomy, especially the school-girl version, didn't appeal to him as a topic for dinner conversation.

"Anatomy soon bored her, and perhaps adultery will, too, although unfortunately it's capable of greater variations." Kelsey folded up his paper.

"What does surprise me is to find that you sympathize with Gil Hallam, Elaine," he said. "The man's personal life has been a scandal for years, and this what's-her-name—'Jelly Jam'—has figured in a couple of night-club riots for which he's had to pay damages."

It sounded dreadful, Elaine agreed, unwilling to show her distaste. She must be careful, too, not to reveal the reasoning behind her support of the disreputable Gil. Undoubtedly she was managing clumsily, but she must try to establish in Kelsey's mind the picture of herself as a broad-minded wife who could understand that he might find another woman, say an old flame, indelibly attractive. The broad-minded, tolerant woman was the ideal of the magazine marriage counselors. It was a masculine, not a feminine ideal, but Elaine and her fellow-readers regarded it respectfully. She had no intention, however, of being broad-minded or tolerant enough to yield sweetly to a demand for a divorce, but she wanted Kelsey to feel free to talk the whole miserable business out, not with a fellow-lawyer, but with her.

She said, "I don't exactly sympathize with Gil Hallam. I could, if he was a decent man who had found himself in love with a woman not his wife. Civilized people ought to be able to remain calm in such a situation."

"My God, what have you been reading?" Kelsey got to his feet. "Maybe you'd better switch to the tabloids—at least they cling to a vestige of reality."

He could shut himself up in his study and in less than five minutes forget her. Elaine, left to her needlepoint, reflected that he would also forget Midge and Amanda and the fact that his mother's birthday was next week.

128

A dentist's appointment took her downtown the next morning and since the question of a gift for Kelsey's mother remained undecided, she might as well plan to spend the rest of the morning shopping. She was reluctant to consult Lucie, who would certainly think she must come in and be taken to lunch and who would choose something expensive and too heavy to be sent by airmail. For years Elaine had had only a vague, pleasant letter friendship with her mother-in-law. When she could forget the older woman's fondess for Midge Sully, she found her determination to live abroad, and her frugal management of her annuity, cause for gratitude. Kelsey, of course, supplemented the income with gifts of cash, but Elaine knew that his mother made no demands upon him.

It was absurdly easy to shop for her own mother; give Mama something to wear and she was delighted. Costume jewelry, too, especially the zodiac designs, pleased her. Kelsey's mother spent most of her time in Spain and wore nothing but smocks. She had taken up painting and apparently alternated between art classes and long sessions in which she painted without instruction. None of her family had ever seen any of her work, but Lucie talked of persuading her to hold a one-man show some day in New York.

The walls of the tearoom in which Elaine ate a lunch that looked lovely and had no flavor of any kind displayed a collection of small oil paintings, and two young women at the table next to hers compared notes on the expense of certain colors in oil paints. They were completing the spring term of a night class in painting, and Elaine listened with interest to their chatter. And when she had left them trying to divide the check, she had made up her mind to buy oil paints for Kelsey's mother. They would be a flattering gift in a way, an acknowledgment that her son and his wife appreciated an artist in the family.

But out in the bright, busy street, the idea appeared a little fantastic. Kelsey ought to take some of the responsibility for selecting gifts, Elaine thought with sudden irritation. For all she knew, Spain's oil paints were superior to American brands —if there were brands of paint. It might be better to stop in at Kelsey's office and ask him; he could at least sign the card to be enclosed.

The building in which Kelsey's firm had offices was on a corner, and Elaine, on the opposite side of the street, had to wait for the light to change. She had a clear view of the wide entrance as she stood on the curb; to her astonishment, Midge Sully emerged from one of the revolving doors, and stood hesitantly, a solitary figure, in the flow of pedestrians who obviously had fixed destinations.

Elaine dashed forward as the traffic signal flashed green. She had some vague idea of intercepting Midge, but before she could reach her, the slight figure turned suddenly and re-entered the lobby.

Midge had remembered something more she wished to tell Kelsey. Or she had left her glasses in his office; she had not been wearing her dark glasses and might have realized that she was without a disguise. Elaine, conscious of her heart beating rapidly and of the blood rushing to her face, was vaguely alarmed by an odd tremor in her knees. She continued to walk, grateful that she had not acted upon her first impulse, to catch up with Midge and question her. A scene, her tired brain repeated endlessly, was to be avoided at all cost.

Presently the feeling of breathing too quickly left her and the hinges of her knees behaved with normal firmness. She still would have liked to sit down, but aside from bars and railroad stations, there are few places in an American city where the public may collect its thoughts. Elaine noticed that her hands were clenched and she began to straighten her stiff fingers in her gloves.

It was just as she had thought, but there was no satisfaction in having been proved right. Midge met Kelsey in his office, an arrangement that could go on for a long time with no danger of building up a scandal. She would give Midge the benefit of the doubt, Elaine thought bitterly, and assume that it had all started innocently. Say that Midge, needing the services of a lawyer, had turned to Kelsey, presumably with the expectation that he would not charge her for his help. What she would need a lawyer for wasn't important and it would never occur to her that Kelsey didn't handle individual cases.

If he had turned her over to someone else—as he would have to do—Midge would still expect him to advise her. Helpless, in distress, dependent upon a friendship that might easily have been so much more, Midge would be a pathetic figure—in spite of being pigeon-toed.

Elaine halted at one of the street telephone booths. She had passed a number of the glassed-in shelters without even seeing them, but now she wondered whether it would be best to phone Naida Steckner immediately or wait until she had had time to think things over. It was Naida's theory that no constructive thinking could be done by a woman while she was emotionally disturbed. Lucie had received similar advice from her psychiatrist.

"Personally, I feel that I do my best thinking when I'm emotionally disturbed," Lucie had confided.

Elaine was also secretly convinced that to be in the state so glibly described as "emotionally disturbed" stimulated her brain. The objective attitude extolled by Naida seemed to her merely cold and remote.

But when she tried to work out in her mind an opening sentence with which to impress the marriage counselor, Elaine was dismayed to feel the pressure of a torrent of tears too long repressed. She managed to signal a cab and to reach the apartment without breaking down, but once in her bedroom with the door locked, she could let the flood of anger and self-pity and despair have its way. It had been years since she had wept with such abandon, but the salt tide erased the sunny past with an evil magic, leaving her convinced that she had always been unhappy.

The necessity for pulling herself together and for hiding the ravages of grief at least to some extent only emphasized the weight of her burden. Until she could have an interview with Naida Steckner, she did not trust herself to discuss Midge with Kelsey, and in the interim she must go through the motions of normal living. Perhaps if they ate dinner by candlelight, Amanda might not notice that she had been crying. Kelsey, of course, if he noticed her puffed eyes at all, would think she had developed a cold.

# Chapter 9

At the dinner table, Amanda appeared to have what Pearl called one of her "talking fits." Elaine, grateful to have Kelsey's attention engaged, listened for the most part silently. She hoped to achieve a deliberate state of numbness in which the mental image of Midge could not exist.

The annual school play interested Amanda, but she did not say that the proceeds, donated each year to a charity selected by the senior class, were to be given to the Tully Hallam Fund. Elaine had learned of this through a telephone call from Mrs. Hallam, an awkward and strained conversation in which neither woman had mentioned the pending divorce suit.

"I think Pearl is boning up on secret marriages," Amanda observed, dropping the discussion of the school play abruptly.

Some book, or it might have been a movie, had put the idea into Pearl's mind, Amanda said, but so far Jerome had not been enthusiastic.

"I'm trying to make Pearl see that she ought to go to work on the mother of Jerome; she's an old lady with nothing to do and naturally she lets herself get all wrapped up in Jerome."

Amanda thought that Pearl should persuade Jerome's mother to join a Golden Age Club. Next year the girls at Miss Mary's were going to plan entertainments for the aged, and Mirabelle Marilyn Meeks had promised to offer mimeographed sheets of suggestions on how to form teen-age committees to assist the senior citizens.

"I don't think your grandmother is exactly mad, as you'd say, about this sort of thing," Kelsey protested mildly. "A little tact will go a long way, if I may venture to make a suggestion."

Mirabelle Marilyn Meeks had said that the field had great possibilities, Amanda assured him.

"I have to write a letter to her tonight. She wants to know how many of her readers have close contacts with their grandparents, or any other old person."

When she had been excused after dessert, Kelsey asked for a second cup of coffee.

"About this Mirabelle girl—do you suppose details of our personal lives are being passed along to her?" He saw Pearl circling the table to remove his cup, and waited until she had disappeared into the kitchen.

"I'm wondering if reticence is one of our daughter's traits," he said.

Pearl brought him fresh coffee, and Elaine thought she saw an opening. A tactful approach was absolutely necessary if she was to get their conversation focused on Midge.

"I don't believe Amanda tells Mirabelle Marilyn Meeks *everything*," she said, unconsciously imitating the bright, brittle manner of a television commentator, so that Kelsey eyed her curiously.

"I mean she knows that certain things are not discussed outside the family," Elaine floundered on. "Of course you can't expect her to have your ethics. She isn't a lawyer and the only personal affairs she hears are ours."

Kelsey stopped stirring his coffee and stared at his wife in genuine astonishment.

"You mean you think it's all right for her to blab her family's personal affairs to a perfect stranger? Not that I suppose she has much to tell—it's the idea of Mirabelle Marilyn being offered a teen-age version of Amanda's home life that revolts me."

Amanda wasn't as hipped on the word "confidential" as he was, Elaine said, mystifying him still further.

"Your mind is probably crammed full of things women . . . people, I mean, have told you and you have promised them not to tell."

Kelsey suggested that she might be confusing him with a priest.

"The firm doesn't do divorce work, you know. I'm the receptacle for very few clients' confidences."

Elaine said, "But people do consult you. On personal matters. Mama does."

Kelsey put down his coffee cup to laugh. He didn't pretend to compete with the stars, he said. Her mother's visit to the office had been for the purpose of asking him whether she could be sued.

"Sued?" Elaine was alarmed. "What for?"

"She didn't say. I understood that she was exploring the future."

This could go on indefinitely. In a few moments Pearl would have finished her dinner and be anxious to clear the table. Kelsey, his coffee gone, would shut himself up in his study for the evening.

"I suppose what Midge Sully had to tell you was in confidence," she said.

"Midge?" Kelsey's thin face expressed only bewilderment. "What about Midge?"

She had seen Midge Sully downtown that afternoon, Elaine said. Not to speak to, but she could not have been mistaken.

"No one else walks so pigeon-toed. Besides, she didn't have on her dark glasses. She was coming out of your building."

"Why didn't you speak to her?" Kelsey was folding his napkin.

"Because she went back in," Elaine explained.

She wasn't making much sense, even to herself, but she was doggedly determined to find out something about Midge's visit to the office.

"I don't want to know anything she said to you; you're her lawyer and I realize you can't discuss her case." The words rushed off her tongue, and Elaine tried to force herself to speak more calmly. "But it would seem only natural for you to mention that you had seen her."

Kelsey pushed back his chair but made no motion to rise.

"You're all mixed up, Pussy," he said. "I haven't seen Midge. I'm not her lawyer. If she has deep, dark secrets, she never told them to me."

134

"Pussy" had been her family pet name in childhood, and Kelsey had often called her that before Amanda had been born.

"But I saw her—she was coming out of your building," Elaine repeated. "Where had she been, if she didn't see you?"

There were several hundred offices in his building, Kelsey pointed out. Midge Sully had a wide range from which to choose. The lobby directory offered her not only lawyers, but engineers, brokers, architects, advertising men, public-relations firms—Midge might even find a doctor or two, if she had been seeking medical attention.

Elaine said that she thought it extremely odd that Midge should come up to town and wander around Kelsey's building without dropping in to see him. It didn't seem natural.

"I'm sure no one would think it strange for an old, old friend to want to see you at the office—" Elaine stopped because Pearl had pushed the swinging door open and was asking if they wanted more coffee.

A guilty feeling that Naida Steckner would say she had handled the situation badly nagged Elaine for the rest of the evening. She had been unable to drop the subject, and that, Naida had emphasized, was a wife's cardinal mistake. But it was comforting to recall Kelsey's reminder that his firm did not handle divorce cases; if Midge wanted a separation or a divorce from her husband, she could not hope to have Kelsey handle her case.

Amanda, having finished her letter, and presumably her homework, by ten o'clock, emerged from her room to announce that she was hungry. A mixture of sounds poured through her opened door, and when Elaine protested, Amanda said that she couldn't think in a void. But she went back and shut off the record player and the radio.

"All that needlepoint makes you nervous, I guess. Shall I heat some milk for you, Mother?"

"I'm not tottering," said Elaine with dignity. "And I loathe hot milk."

"You've reached the age when you should take better care

135

of yourself," Amanda said. "I'm going to have a sandwich and Coke."

Elaine put down her sewing and followed Amanda into the kitchen.

"You're going to make coffee? It'll keep you awake," Amanda warned.

The exasperated Elaine forgot her dignity.

"Are you suggesting that I join a Golden Age Club? Coffee hardly ever keeps me awake."

"You could count on hot milk putting you to sleep," said Amanda, who was not easily deflected.

Elaine put on the kettle for instant coffee and waited silently beside the gas range, while Amanda made herself a cheese-and-tomato sandwich on raisin bread. As an afterthought she added a layer of peanut butter.

"I guess Pearl ate all the olives." Amanda looked disappointed. "Or maybe she fed them to Jerome. She's trying to sell him the idea of a secret marriage and she'll give him anything he wants to eat."

The kettle began to rock gently, and Elaine filled her cup. She decided to drink it black, recollecting that Amanda and Mirabelle Marilyn Meeks believed that a woman began to lose her figure in middle age.

Seated opposite her daughter in the breakfast nook, Elaine tried not to think of the mixture Amanda apparently considered delicious, eaten alternately with sweet pickles and swallows of Coke. Amanda's dark eyes surveyed her solemnly, and Elaine wondered, not for the first time, whether a child ever thought of a parent as a human being with an inner, secret life.

"I hope Pearl has too much sense to mention a secret marriage to Jerome," Elaine said. "What earthly advantage would there be in it for her? She's of age; no one can interfere if she and Jerome decided to be married."

Jerome had a thing about his mother, Amanda sighed. Pearl knew it and admitted that he didn't have much backbone.

"But she says her other two husbands had worse faults. One was so bossy she couldn't call her soul her own and the other spent all his money in bars. You don't see Pearl's point of view, Mother, but I do."

Elaine disliked black coffee and she had a suspicion that she had made it too strong tonight. It probably accounted for the irritated condition of her nerves as she asked what Pearl's point of view might be.

"Oh, she's all for getting married. You may not know it, but you hope she won't marry again. She might not go on working for us."

A *constructive* solution, Amanda added kindly, might be for Jerome and Pearl to marry openly and continue to live under separate roofs. That had been Mrs. Torrington Van Antwerpt's idea, Amanda explained—a temporary measure to allow Jerome's mother time to adjust to the inevitable.

"I wish Pearl wouldn't talk such nonsense to you." Elaine let weariness wash out tact. "You're too young to be listening to problems that are years beyond your experience."

Amanda flushed. She raised her chin in a gesture remembered from some outraged heroine on the screen.

"My generation is far more advanced than yours was at my age, Mother," she said. "That is one of the things parents find difficult to understand. We mature earlier, but parents don't seem able to grasp this fact."

She used a peculiar tone for the word "parents" that set Elaine's teeth on edge. It suggested that to Amanda, and to her friends in the same age bracket, parents were not so much mentally retarded as undeveloped and presumably not responsible for their handicaps.

Long after Amanda was asleep, and after Kelsey, in spite of the troubled conscience with which Elaine endowed him, had gone to sleep in the middle of a mumbled sentence, Elaine lay staring into the gray darkness. She could see Kelsey in his bed; the outlines of the furniture remained fairly distinct. When, years ago, they had spent a summer on a farm, the intense blackness that filled their bedroom night after night had impressed her by its contrast to the radiance of the light when the moon was full. The throbbing pressure of the dark, the brilliance of the moonlight, and the intensity of the stillness that kept her listening half the night—these she had always remembered. The city's reflected glow kept the apartment bedroom in a perpetual twilight that linked with the night noises, and reassured her that there was nothing to see and nothing to hear.

Tonight the coffee was to blame for her inability to sleep. That and the nagging image of Midge coming out of Kelsey's building. The only explanation—that Kelsey had lied to her—might as well be examined now.

But an out-and-out lie, a flat denial, was too painful to be connected with Kelsey in her mind, so she tried to work out something more acceptable. The one lie that even the clergy had been known to condone was the falsehood offered to protect another. Someone weaker. Preferably a woman. Men had died on the scaffold—for a few moments Elaine's thoughts wandered to the scaffold rigged on a building across the street where painters were at work—men had died on the scaffold to protect a woman's honor.

Kelsey had lied to protect that hussy, Midge. If she had no more discretion than to go to his office and embarrass him by pouring out the story behind the failure of her marriage, Kelsey at least had had more sense. By refusing to admit she had been there and by not repeating her silly disclosures, he had made it possible for her to attempt a reconciliation with her husband.

Having tested this theory from several angles, Elaine decided that it satisfied her. To be sure that she wasn't practicing self-deceit, she would make an appointment with Naida Steckner and get an objective opinion. Naida frequently warned of the danger of persuading oneself to believe only what one wished to believe.

It would be a great relief if Kelsey would make even one visit to the marriage counselor with her. Or to another counselor—anyone. He might have more respect for a psychiatrist, although the expense would be greater. Elaine doubted that he would consult Lucie's psychiatrist—he might wonder what Lucie had already told him—but Naida could recommend a good man.

Meanwhile, who was it who had mentioned the power of suggestion, applied while the "patient" was unconscious or asleep? Elaine glanced at the outline of Kelsey and tried to recall the formula. How did it go?

"You will be willing to go with me and see Naida Steckner," Elaine whispered. "Or a good psychiatrist."

At the fourth whisper, Kelsey suddenly sat up.

"Don't you feel well?" He snapped on the light. "Want me to get you some hot milk?"

## II

The Hallam divorce case, or, more accurately, the publicity accorded to it, was to be deplored, the teaching staff of Miss Mary's agreed. They could forbid the sensational tabloids' being brought into the school but there was nothing they could do to control the rush for newspapers after school or the exchange of lurid details among the groups who huddled together in recreation periods or at noon in the lunchroom.

Amanda, at first reluctant to be reminded of Tully in any way, gradually yielded to the flattering realization that her status had improved. Even the seniors asked her questions about the Hallam household and consulted her to learn whether the published photographs were real or "faked."

The general attitude of teachers and parents was considered to be extremely silly by the student body as a whole.

"Plenty of us have parents who are divorced," said Edith Andrews, a pretty junior. "Mine have both remarried. Does Miss Mary think I believe my father is dead or something?"

Amanda, eager to contribute to the conference, suggested that some divorces were managed quietly.

"Mr. Hallam wants to marry someone else," she explained.

The group at the little table in a corner of the lunchroom shrieked with laughter, and Amanda flushed.

"What other reason is there for a divorce?" Edith demanded. "My father fell in love with his secretary. But my mother wouldn't make a fuss. Tully's mother is determined to make a stink."

The Hallams had no children to consider, said one of the seniors, a tall girl at the next table who planned to do social-service work when she had finished college.

"Only completely selfish parents would play up their divorce in the newspapers—their children should always come first."

Amanda, finishing her lemon snow pudding, scarcely heard the animated comment on the duty of parents. She was trying to decide whether her father was in love with Midge and, if the affair had not gone too far, what a devoted daughter could do to spare her mother humiliation and a broken heart.

She walked home from school that afternoon to have more time to think. The one fact of which she was sure was that her mother disliked Midge Sully. This was natural and nothing to be held against her. Amanda had seen enough movies and television plays to know the pattern: a man was engaged to a girl; they broke it off and each married someone else. Years later they came together and—pouf! Once Amanda had found her mother crying over a letter from Grandmother Carpenter, who lived in Spain. The letter, her mother had said, depressed her, but she had let a faded snapshot drop to the rug, and when Amanda had picked it up, her mother had snatched it almost angrily from her fingers. But not before Amanda had glimpsed a young man and woman hand in hand—her father and Midge Sully.

Granted that her mother was jealous of Midge—Amanda liked the phrase "insanely jealous"—what about her father? Daddy would never give himself away. It was a weakness of parents, too, to assume that their children were deaf and blind and would accept without question any picture of marriage that the father and mother chose to paint. She had tried to say something like this to Grandmother Ives a long time ago, and Grandma had been outraged.

"Your father and mother are very happily married and always have been," Grandma had said.

Amanda turned in at a drugstore, ordered a Coke, and sat down to consider Midge. She wanted to have some plan of action worked out before she reached home; if Pearl was in the kitchen, she would insist on talking about Jerome.

Midge was an unqualified bore, Amanda reminded herself. It was easy to sympathize with Lucie, who had to endure this dead weight as a neighbor. The mystery was how Daddy, admittedly a brain, could be attracted by a woman who was dull, and not even good-looking.

A phrase from a recent movie floated into Amanda's puzzled mind.

"The tug of the past," the hero had whispered sadly, and at first Amanda had thought he must be referring to a tugboat. Eventually he had cleared up her misconception by breaking his engagement to a wealthy fiancée and marrying the sweetheart of his school days.

Must Midge be labeled a tug from the past and could that be the reason why she appealed to a sensible man?

It would be easier for her mother to forgive Midge, Amanda thought with a flash of insight that would have astonished her elders, if she had happened to be young and beautiful. What any man, even her husband, could see in Midge Cutter, it was impossible to guess. Amanda stared at her empty glass and wondered if her mother could actually be jealous of Midge, or whether the talk of the Hallam divorce at school had put ideas into her head.

No, her mother was unhappy; Amanda knew that her imagination had not wholly tricked her. Something was worrying her mother, and although she might be pleased by her evident loss of weight, the dark circles under her eyes must present a make-up problem. She needed someone to take care of her, and if her husband was about to fail her, then her daughter's responsibility was clear.

"But what I want to know," Amanda said later to her grandmother, "was this Midge ever pretty? I mean when she was young?"

Pauline, who had not expected Amanda to stop in after school this afternoon, had only a box of chocolates and a bottle of root beer to offer as refreshments. She tried not to watch her guest enjoying the combination.

"Certainly Midge Sully was a pretty girl," she said. "Your father couldn't take his eyes off her when they were first engaged. At least so I've heard. Midge wasn't a beauty, but she had nice features and a lot of charm."

Amanda chewed on a caramel.

"How long was she engaged to my father?"

Vague disapproval colored Pauline's reply. It couldn't possibly matter, she said, but the engagement had lasted six months or so—certainly less than a year.

"They were totally unsuited to each other. Their horoscopes are incompatible at every point—not that either of them paid any attention to astrology. I didn't take it up myself until after your grandfather died."

Amanda poured herself a second glass of root beer.

"Why do you suppose she came back here—to this part of the country?"

Midge Sully couldn't very well remain in Japan when her husband was to be stationed in Washington, Pauline pointed out.

Amanda blew delicately on the root beer's beige collar of foam, and Pauline shuddered.

"It seems a little funny to me that she should come right *here*," Amanda said. "I mean she could have decided to live in Bethesda, or Georgetown, if she didn't like Washington."

Midge Sully probably had friends or relatives somewhere in the vicinity of Lyman; or she might have heard that the town schools had a high rating. There were dozens of reasons to explain her choice, but why should anyone care what they might be? Pauline eyed her granddaughter with sudden suspicion.

"Why are you so curious about Midge Sully? You're not likely to see much of her, especially since she's rented a house in Lyman. It must be all of a year since you've been out there, and Lucie's your own aunt."

Amanda had finished the root beer. She carried the empty bottle and her glass out to the kitchen with a rush of energy and loped back to pick up her books and help herself to two chocolate almonds.

"It's just possible that I may go out to Lyman and baby-sit

for Lucie this weekend," she said. "If I'm going to run into Midge, I ought to know something about her."

Pauline had just time enough to murmur, "You ought to call her Mrs. Cutter," before Amanda had kissed her and dashed into the hall. The door clicked behind her, and in the kitchen the glass she had hastily deposited on the drainboard crashed into the sink.

Dinner for Amanda that night was a waste of time, to be endured because one's parents were slaves to routine. It was psychologically wrong to force a person to eat three meals a day simply because it was the custom to serve food at set times. Babies were fed "on demand"—Amanda had heard Lucie expound that theory—and why shouldn't the rule be applied to all ages? It was only natural to suppose that a girl of fourteen was better able to judge when she was hungry than a baby two months old.

"Well, you don't have to eat, of course," Kelsey had responded to her argument. "No one should be compelled to swallow food. But you can surely sit at the table and let your mother and me enjoy your company. We don't see very much of you, except at mealtime."

Fortunately the question of having the living room redecorated was of absorbing interest to her mother this evening. Amanda could pretend to listen to the discussion of wallpapers, paint, and color schemes without being expected to have too definite opinions. She could, however, understand her father's evident bewilderment at being pressed to give immediate approval and consent.

"I don't think I can live another week with the room in its present condition," Elaine said with evident sincerity. "And there's so much to be done to it, I don't know where to begin."

Of course the living room looked all right to a man, she conceded, in answer to Kelsey's murmured protest. As long as there wasn't a hole in the middle of the rug and the chair he sat in didn't fall apart, he would see nothing that needed attention.

"You forget that we have a daughter who will be entertaining." Elaine glanced distractedly at Amanda, almost as if she didn't see her. "I think we should have a professional submit sketches and estimates."

"What do you mean, I'll be entertaining?" Amanda asked.

"You'll have dates," Elaine said. "Not right away, perhaps, but later. An attractive living room is important."

Amanda grumbled that she didn't have even a telephone, and Kelsey suggested that they were getting off the track.

"Two colors and a third for accent, I think." Elaine saw that Amanda was beginning to fold her napkin. "Chocolate cream pie for dessert, dear."

It would have been less trouble to have eaten the pie, Amanda thought, when she had finally escaped to her room. The trouble with parents was that they expected you to behave always exactly the same. Her mother had wanted to take her temperature simply because she wasn't interested in chocolate cream pie, but her father had managed to calm her. Amanda's indifference to her favorite dessert had surprised herself, but a moment's reflection had convinced her that it was probably a sign of maturity. She was probably outgrowing her taste for sweets.

The letter she had been planning to write to Mirabelle Marilyn Meeks was clearly outlined in her mind as she sat down at her desk. She had memorized the words of her sentences so that she could have recited them like a French translation.

". . . this time I am writing in behalf of my mother, who is unhappy. My father is seeing another woman and we do not know how far it has gone. My mother has said nothing to me as yet, but I am able to read between the lines—"

Amanda paused to wonder about that phrase, but she had no intention of changing a word of her composition.

"My mother is losing weight and she is crosser than usual, all due to her secret sorrow," Amanda had finished the first page. Her handwriting was too large, she decided.

"If there is any way I can help her, please tell me," she wrote in a weird scrawl, saving space by allowing no margins. "I feel a responsibility for keeping this marriage together."

144

She signed her name, added "Heartbroken," to be used for publication, and then thought of a postscript.

"My mother is anxious to change the decor of our living room because she feels that she has neglected to make an attractive home for my father. Do you think it is too late?"

She took the letter out to the elevator for Albert to mail and let herself into the kitchen through the back door. To Pearl, who was ready to leave, she said that she felt the need of something to eat.

"Chocolate cream pie—that's light. I'll take it in with me to keep me from getting a headache while I'm doing homework."

She could not, she had learned early in her correspondence with the columnist, expect to see a reply for at least a week. Mirabelle Marilyn Meeks disliked to be importuned to "answer in tomorrow's paper," and many of her readers suspected that any indication of impatience influenced her to prolong delay. Also, as Pearl had suggested, Mirabelle could be sure that no one waiting to hear from her would fail to buy the *Blaze* every night.

Amanda discovered the letter signed "Heartbroken" in the stock-market edition which reached the newsstands about four in the afternoon. She had bought a copy on her way home from school after a museum field trip and had taken a surreptitious peek while waiting for the traffic lights to change.

If she had to make small talk with any of the family before she could get to her room and lock the door, she would die, she assured herself as she dashed in front of a taxi whose driver had counted on beating the amber light.

Fortunately the apartment was empty when she opened the front door, left on the latch for her on school afternoons. Her mother was out, and Pearl was not in the kitchen; she could be making a swift trip to the supermarket, or she might be downstairs in Grandma's apartment, where she sometimes polished silver or made her a pie.

Amanda stopped in the kitchen long enough to gather up a box of cookies, two bananas, a bottle of olives, and two bottles of Coke. These edibles she arranged on her night table, and then, lying on her stomach on the bed, she gave herself up to the excitement of reading her letter in print.

She read it twice before she was ready to consider Mirabelle Marilyn Meeks's advice.

"Dear Heartbroken," Mirabelle wrote. "Your mother is indeed fortunate to have a loyal daughter like you. It would not be wise for you to discuss the subject of your father's unfaithfulness with your mother—that is her problem—but what you can do is to let her know, beyond any shadow of doubt, that you will not fail her. Divorce is so common in our society today that girls your age are fairly familiar with the subject. Try not to judge your parents; they are human beings as well as parents, you know."

# Chapter 10

"It's nothing—a touch of eye strain or something." Pauline shook two aspirins from the bottle into her hand. "I meant to ask Dr. Cannon for an appointment early this month, but I forgot."

Lucie suggested that "everyone" had migraine. She sat on the tiny love seat in Pauline's living room, her long legs drawn up so that her chin rested tidily on her knees. She looked a little like a castaway on a desert island, for the rug was strewn with cotton dresses, hatboxes, summer curtains, and bright-patterned slipcovers spilling out of packages delivered by the dry cleaner.

"I'm sorting things out for the summer," Pauline had explained to Lucie, whose habit of paying surprise calls seemed less endearing than ever.

Disorder of her own making never confused Pauline, and with her guest disposed of—above the water line, as it were—she felt free to continue with her work of examining, discarding, and putting aside. She couldn't ask the doctor for an appointment, she said in answer to Lucie's question, until the first of the month.

"There isn't a day favorable for medical consultation until July. I'm not willing to take a chance."

Lucie thought that by postponing a visit to the doctor one might be taking an even greater chance, but Pauline refused to agree.

"The stars are a reliable guide," she said. "And besides, I don't want any silly diet restrictions to interfere with the bus trip."

Pauline removed a small tower of three hatboxes from a chair and sat down. She was tired, but nothing would induce her to admit it. Her bridge club was to have its annual outing Saturday night, she said, and it would be just like Dr. Cannon to put her on a diet of cottage cheese or something equally drastic that would force her to stay at home.

"The girls count on me going, because I know the inn where we are to have dinner. Kelsey and Elaine took me there last year for my birthday. We've chartered a bus, each member can bring one guest, and it's something we look forward to for a year."

No, the affair couldn't be put off—Pauline was evidently prepared for the suggestion. In the first place, she had selected the date only after careful study and checking and rechecking of the stars. Saturday was perfect, in every way. Also, Saturday the buses were in great demand and the club couldn't be sure of getting transportation later in the season.

"And we probably couldn't fix on another Saturday that would be convenient for all the girls. I nearly went mad before we had everyone signed up. I certainly am not going to be the one to—what is it Amanda says?—to louse up the program."

Lucie hugged her knees and nodded in silent agreement. If Nana came down with appendicitis, she reflected, that would interfere with the plans of the bridge club, but short of an attack of intolerable pain, nothing would keep any of the old ladies from having their annual fling.

Pauline had lifted a black straw hat from one of the boxes and her fingers manipulated the white ribbon bows, but with an evident lack of interest; to sit idly in a room in which there was so much to be done would have hurt her conscience.

"It's nice you could have a morning in town," she said.

Immediately Lucie became apologetic—an attitude on which her psychiatrist had spent considerable expensive time. It hadn't been easy for her to get away, Lucie said. It was a struggle every time she had an appointment with the psychiatrist; he had no conception of what dozens of his women patients went through to enable them to shake off home duties long enough to fall into his office and out again.

"Some of us—friends and neighbors—have been trying to

form a group and have a psychiatrist handle us together, but the scheme doesn't seem to be working out. It would solve a lot of problems, but, as Royce says, getting a dozen women to stick to an agreement is going against nature."

Getting a baby sitter was her chronic problem, Lucie confided. She kicked off her pumps and they tumbled out of sight into a sea of tissue paper.

"Do you care if I smoke? You'll never guess who's baby-sitting for me today."

Although her tiny silver lighter had been a Christmas gift from Pauline, Lucie knew that she still thought that only men should smoke. Nana remained incurably old-fashioned in many of her ways.

"Midge Cutter and I have worked out a kind of system," Lucie said. "She really is a good soul, when you get to know her. Elaine can't stand her, but I don't believe in expecting too much of people. Then you're not so apt to be disappointed."

Midge was scrupulously fair about the exchange of time, Lucie went on, and that was the chief reason why they got on so well together. Some of the nicest girls among her friends cheated right and left when it came to keeping a record of baby-sitting hours.

"Don't you ever pay for a sitter?" Pauline remembered Amanda's criticism of relatives who refused to pay cash for services rendered.

She had no money to waste on sitters, Lucie answered, and neither had Midge. The saving was terrific—no boy friends to complicate situations, no raids on refrigerators, no teen-agers to be taken home. "Honestly, some of the parents are so demanding, you almost expect them to give you a signed receipt when you deliver Susie or Jane safely on the doorstep."

Midge gave all the children lunch—Lucie's two and two of her own (the oldest had lunch at school), and kept an eye on all of them, at least one day every week.

"She comes in to town one day a week and then I do the same for her. But now I'm worried about how I can manage; the psychiatrist thinks I'd be happier if I took a job."

Pauline said, "I thought he was a psychologist."

There wasn't much difference, Lucie assured her; she hadn't been able to afford the fees of a psychiatrist, but it sounded more convincing to say that she was "going to" a psychiatrist.

"Anyway, he thinks I ought to get a job. And of course we do need money. But Royce has it figured out that we'll have to have someone come in five days a week to look after the children. That's fifty dollars at least, plus her food. Then someone else would have to do laundry and cleaning, unless I did it Saturday and Sunday."

It was like Royce, Lucie said, to spoil her anticipation of escape from the drudgery of the house. You couldn't make a man understand that money wasn't everything.

"I suppose you'd have to pay commutation, too," Pauline said.

She didn't expect to make money the first year or two, Lucie admitted. She looked around for an ash tray, and Pauline hurriedly offered a china coaster. Eventually she expected to be earning a high salary, Lucie said, but it was important to start while she was still young.

"Well, your psychologist doesn't seem to be any more realistic than you are, if he thinks supplying you with a bushel-basket of new problems must have a soothing effect." Pauline reached down and dragged a flat box out from under a pile of folded slipcovers. "I thought the bedroom curtains were in it," she murmured when she found it empty.

Lucie said that psychology was not understood by the layman. She was progressing surely if slowly. The main value of her appointments lay in the knowledge that she had someone who would listen and advise. She had thought of working out a plan to have Midge and her children move in and share the house, but the psychologist had immediately pointed out the weakness in such a plan.

"We have only two bedrooms."

Pauline laughed. "I should have thought Royce could have pointed out that drawback."

But she secretly agreed that there could be no comparison between the impatient indifference of a tired, worried young husband and the sympathetic attention of a tactful, trained listener who apportioned his time in exchange for cash.

*150*

Pauline realized that she was making no headway in putting her living room in order and also that Lucie probably expected to be asked to stay for lunch.

"What kind of a job have you in mind?" She hoped that she sounded like a sympathetic listener.

The job didn't really matter, Lucie instructed her; it was a symbol. Presumably she would start with something in the clerical field, since the demand for office help appeared to be insatiable. She had thought of applying to Kelsey for a place in his office, but Kelsey had such odd ideas that she was reluctant to say anything to him until she had a definite plan worked out.

"Don't say a word to him, Nana. You never know how he'll take a new suggestion of mine. I don't suppose a man ever understands the inner life of a woman."

Pauline thought not. She had intended to accomplish a great deal this morning, for her daily horoscope had promised success in every undertaking. Now, surveying her unexpected guest and the unrelieved clutter in her living room, Pauline was assailed by doubts. She might easily have mixed her dates; all last week she had been reading her horoscope three days in advance, and a telephone call had interrupted her this morning before she had quite finished the day's forecast. It might be prudent to consult her calendar before she went any further.

"It's a good thing I looked," she told the bewildered Lucie. "We'll have to go up to Elaine's apartment for lunch. I'll telephone Pearl."

"Looked where?" stammered Lucie. "For what?"

She'd started the day with the wrong forecast, Pauline explained; the pages "had stuck together" and it was no wonder she couldn't find the bedroom curtains or that nothing was in the place where it was supposed to be.

"But Elaine doesn't believe in forecasts," Lucie protested. "What has she to do with it?"

Pauline, stepping over a hatbox on her way to the phone, said that Elaine had gone to the dentist's and wouldn't be home for lunch.

"Pearl always gets lunch for me on the days when I must avoid hazards in the home."

Pauline obligingly translated hazards in the home as accidents arising from handling household equipment or caused by general carelessness.

"The gas range might explode, or I might slip on a rug. Or I could burn or scald myself. You never know. Elaine isn't willing for me to take any chances and she's told Pearl to drop everything and help me on a dangerous day."

Pearl would come down in the afternoon and go through the various boxes, sort out the jumble of clothing, and send the heavy draperies to be stored.

"I'm glad I had sense enough to discover I had the date wrong," Pauline said innocently.

Apparently Pearl's adjustment to the stars included a cheerful willingness to cook a hot lunch on demand and the ability to rearrange her own schedule so that she could be free to "help out" in the afternoon. But she thought that Pauline had probably overexerted herself and that her slightly flushed face might be the forerunner of a "dizzy spell."

"Why don't you lie down for a few minutes, Miz Ives," Pearl suggested when Lucie, having finished lunch, announced that she must keep an appointment. "You take a little nap, while I do the dishes."

Pauline decided that it would be safe to nap in her own bed. She and Pearl both knew that she would wake to find chaos transformed into order. Lucie's understanding was more vague, but she had a shrewd idea that Pauline's domestic responsibilities seldom taxed her time or strength.

"It's always the people who don't need it who have help," she grumbled to herself as Albert in the creaking elevator took her down to the ground floor.

She made the same observation to Kelsey when, half an hour later, she discovered him eating a late lunch at his office desk. Lucie had intimated to his secretary that she was expected and had thought Miss Newman's distress rather amusing.

"Although I suppose I may be devoted to an employer myself one of these days," Lucie said with an indulgent smile for the secretary's little ways. "I'm going to take a job, Kelsey. That is, if I can get the help I need at home."

It was irritating, she continued in a deliberately controlled tone, to see how much easier some women had it than others. Not that she blamed Nana—or Elaine—and, to be quite fair, Pearl had a right to look after herself.

Kelsey took a final swallow of cold, weak coffee and said, "Are you sure you know what you're talking about?"

"If we lived in the city, I might be able to get a part-time maid, in spite of having two children." Lucie ignored the question. "You'll know how desperate I am when I tell you that I've been thinking of having Midge Cutter move in with us."

"Midge? Midge Sully—I never think of her as Midge Cutter." Kelsey was clearly bewildered. "Is there a housing shortage in Lyman?" he asked.

Lucie briefly outlined the plan, already rejected. She mentioned it, she said, merely to indicate the seriousness of her desperation.

"How can I take a job if I can't get anyone to look after the children? Nursery school is four hundred a year, and even then they wouldn't take Dilly—she isn't trained."

Royce, she added bitterly, forestalling Kelsey's next question, thought she should be willing to wait a few more years. She couldn't make him understand that it wasn't as much a matter of earning money—although heaven knew they owed positively staggering bills—as of enlarging her *space*.

"We all need an adequate amount of space in which to conduct our personal lives," she finished.

He preferred Royce's common-sense approach to the psychological, Kelsey said, whisking crumbs neatly into his wastebasket. "I assume you are quoting some authority?"

If she couldn't talk to someone with brains, she'd lose her mind, Lucie retorted. No one except a mother knew what it was to spend the entire day with two children under four years old.

"Anyone can give them physical care. They'll need an alert, informed mother later. I've got to get a job, as much for their ultimate good as for my mental balance."

She looked very pretty, very "alert," as she would have said, and she was beginning to lose her temper. Kelsey wondered how much of her patter had been picked up firsthand from some professor—he thought she had probably been taking extension courses in psychology—and how much she had memorized from her reading. It was all vaguely familiar, with an unconvincing quality that he seemed to have remembered, too. He let a threadbare phrase, which suggested itself as appropriate, drop off his tongue.

"We must face reality," he said. "If you can't get permanent help with the children, you can't take a job. Not yet. It may be hard, but there it is."

Lucie looked more alert than ever. She had no intention of giving up without further struggle, she informed him.

"I've already enrolled for an evening course in typing and shorthand—I thought you might be willing to lend me the money for that. Once I am prepared, have skills to offer, I'll be in a better position to plan for a full-time job."

"Stubborn as a mule," the principal of the boarding school from which she had eloped at eighteen had characterized her. But after all, she had been only eighteen, Kelsey thought; no wonder that at twenty-five she was restless and trying to discover what, if anything, she had missed.

"You ought to have had shorthand and typing in school," he said. "I'd make it required for all freshmen."

He'd pay for her business-school course, he promised, but Royce must not think that he was being undermined.

"As you say, it does no woman any harm to be prepared to be self-supporting and if he looks at it in that light, Royce can't be annoyed."

Lucie's blue eyes became pensive.

"Everyone says the big hurdle is lack of experience. You can't get a really good job without experience, and how can you get experience until you've been employed?"

Kelsey reminded her that she was putting the cart before the horse, a simile that, he told himself, dated him. Moreover, if Lucie was seriously contemplating an office career, she would have to learn the value of other people's time.

154

"I've a good many things to do." Kelsey took out his private checkbook. "How much do you need, dear?"

"Well, I ought to have some clothes, too," said Lucie. "I can't charge anything for the next two months, and Elaine isn't too cordial when I ask her to let me use her account."

Kelsey waited.

"I notice Miss Newman dresses very well. She must have paid at least sixty for that dress." Lucie fished up a compact from her bag. "I suppose in an office like this a secretary has to avoid anything cheap or flashy."

A faint alarm sounded in the far recesses of Kelsey's mind. "Lucie, I have work to do. How much money do you need?"

Unexpectedly she smiled.

"I needn't buy new clothes just yet, but of course I want to be a credit to you. Even if I just come for the experience." She began to powder her nose. "I ought to be ready in about six weeks—though of course I won't have much speed at first."

Kelsey shook his head. "No."

"No what?"

"No job for you here in the office. It's out of the question."

She didn't intend to *replace* anyone, Lucie insisted, so earnestly that he nearly laughed. All she asked was to be allowed to work a couple of months so that she could say she had had experience with a good firm. She might even be willing to forego a salary—nothing above her minimum expenses—and surely that was being reasonable.

"You've got everything wrong." Kelsey, pressed for time, braced himself to endure a flood of tears. "In the first place, I won't have any relative of mine applying for a place with my firm. In the second place, a legal stenographer or secretary must have thorough, long training. In the third place, you probably won't be able to manage a job and your home duties, too; your children are too young to be left. Here—"

He thrust a clean handkerchief at Lucie, who reached for it automatically and mopped her brimming eyes.

"I'm not going to be suf-suffocated," she sobbed. "I'm young; I have my life to live. If I don't get out of that house, I'll go crazy. You don't seem to realize that I have a mind!"

155

For one reckless moment Kelsey was tempted to argue. The obvious retort, that if she had a mind, why didn't she use it, was too childish to be considered and yet basically it was the simple truth. Had women, he wondered, always planned their lives on the pattern of a group, never as individuals? A few years ago the tide carried families from the city to the suburbs, where children had space to play and young mothers could practice the creed of neighborliness. A house in the suburbs became every woman's goal.

Now, if Lucie was a fair example, and, whatever her exaggerations, he had no doubt but that she represented hundreds of young, dissatisfied matrons of her own age and class, someone had altered the pattern again. Without individual thought, without individual study or analysis, the group conclusion was that women were being stifled by the suburban ménage. He didn't think Lucie was any more or less susceptible to mass suggestion than the average young woman who had never been trained to solve a single personal problem, but he did think that she and her friends were letting their brains go to seed.

And what was he going to do about it? He watched Lucie repairing the damage to her make-up and knew that he would give her a check. More money than he had at first intended, because he was sorry for her, but how could he set her life in order?

"You keep on with your evening course," he advised. "Do you more practical good than a psychologist. When you've finished will be time enough to find a job. Maybe you can get part-time work right in Lyman."

She didn't intend to work in that hateful place, Lucie said crossly, but her face brightened as she read the check pushed across the desk to her. The psychologist could wait, she told herself; she owed him for two appointments, but she would buy some new clothes and pay for the business-school course first.

"You're really sweet, Kelsey," she informed her brother. "But you're lucky, too—you don't know what it's like to be a woman."

# Chapter 11

The Saturday-night bus trip, in spite of the cheerful astrological predictions, was not an unqualified success. A series of minor mishaps plagued the bridge-club members, all of whom would have been classified by radio and television sponsors as "the young in heart." The motion of the bus made one woman slightly ill, another had forgotten her saccharin tablets, and a third accidentally dropped her soda mints out of the window.

Pauline Ives kept her secret miseries to herself. Her knee pained her, and she had brought her wrong glasses and couldn't see to read the menu. It began to rain while they were at dinner, and the trip home was subdued, even gloomy, for the bus driver had a raging toothache and was infuriated by the insistence of the committee chairman that he wait while she hunted for a lost glove.

Something, Pauline concluded as she wearily fell into bed, must be wrong with her charts. She hated to spend money on a visit to her astrologer—she ought to be able to work things out herself—but perhaps if Madame Titania put her once more on the right track, she could go on indefinitely needing no further help.

She would have liked to spend all day Sunday in bed, but as she frequently remarked to Pearl, no woman with children could ever call her life her own. Kelsey was worse than Elaine, and he wasn't even her child. The man was mad for medical check-ups, Pauline said, and if he had his way she would be a hypochondriac. Let her stay one day in bed, merely resting her bones and planning the next day, and Kelsey would have

Dr. Cannon dropping in, probably at the precise moment when she was having her third cup of coffee for lunch.

So Pauline rose and dressed, rubbed liniment into her knee, and swallowed a favorite remedy for the odd little pain in her stomach—at least she thought it must be her stomach—and ate dinner with the family. Amanda was spending the weekend in the country with a school friend, and Elaine and Kelsey had promised to drive up late in the afternoon to bring her home. Pauline, left free—she had no liking for motoring and her refusal to make the trip surprised no one—collapsed thankfully on her bed and roused only when fire apparatus thundering past the building awakened her.

She had had no supper and wanted none and she shared with Elaine a distaste for hot milk. The little clock on her dresser read nine o'clock, surely not too early to retire. If Elaine dropped in, she could say the bus trip had exhausted her. For a moment she waited expectantly, but the odd sensations, in reality twinges of acute pain, had apparently been cured by sleep. Rest was all she ever needed, she assured herself. Tomorrow she would visit Madame Titania—she might even invest in a five-year horoscope. She could call it a present from Kelsey, for she still had some of his birthday money left in her handkerchief box.

A familiar, pleasant excitement buoyed her up the next morning, enabling her to ignore the effort required to rise and dress. Ordinarily she enjoyed her breakfast, but when she had made coffee and toast she found that she had no appetite and ended by putting the toast in the garbage, pouring the coffee in the sink, and drinking only half a cup of weak tea.

Madame Titania, the astrologer, lived at the other end of the city. Pauline's original ideas of thrift would not allow her to take a taxi, although to reach the astrologer's apartment house she had to change buses twice. She usually had to wait from ten to twenty minutes for the third bus, a cross-town line.

"This a favorable day, Miz Ives?" Albert asked when she stepped into his elevator, forgetting her customary "Good morning."

"Oh—why yes, Albert. I didn't look at my guide today, but

I'm sure it's favorable." Pauline smiled at the good-natured anxious face turned toward her. "I think Jupiter's in my ninth house—that's favorable for travel."

Albert nodded assent. He had halted the car at the ground floor, but ignored the signals from the upper floors.

"I got Neptune adverse in my eighth house; someone's going to waste money, probably my wife," he said.

Pauline reminded him that he was using last year's "book."

"It's close enough for me." Albert reluctantly opened the gate. "The stars don't change much, if you ask me. You don't always hit it right, even with a new horoscope every year."

The admonition to "avoid arguments" which cropped up frequently in her readings was, according to Kelsey, astrology's pearl of wisdom. Pauline decided to abide by it.

"Have a favorable day anyway, Albert," she said far more cheerfully than she felt. "You're born lucky."

She had not phoned Madame Titania because of an uneasy recollection that somewhere, sometime, she had read that personal communication was more satisfactory for her sign than through any of the accepted mediums. It was annoying not to be able to catalogue fragmentary bits like this in her mind for useful reference. From time to time she had made vague attempts to start a file, or even a simple notebook, but without success. Her brain, like her bedroom, functioned in perpetual confusion, and although she could usually sort out what she needed in each, spasmodically she yearned to be more efficient.

Her disastrous experience with the purse-snatcher had forever discouraged her from entering into conversation with any talkative stranger. This morning she stared resolutely out of the window and ignored her seat mate on each successive bus, only murmuring an apology as she climbed over their knees.

She had a block to walk after leaving the last bus, and quite suddenly her feet began to ache. Doubts that this was really one of her favorable days stirred in her mind, but nothing would be accomplished by turning back. She continued to walk, slowly and doggedly, and not until she was turning in at the ornate entrance to the Quimby House did she remember the self-service elevators.

Pauline distrusted self-service elevators in principle. She usually began her explanations by saying that they put men (like Albert) out of work. They were also a hazard, a danger to unprotected women—she could recite newspaper stories to bolster that contention. Finally, she capitulated, she was afraid to operate them and suffered from claustrophobia when she found herself alone in one of them.

The lobby of Quimby House was elegantly imposing. Presumably the tenants were supposed to enjoy the pool, surrounded by tropical foliage, and the bright-colored murals that covered one wall and were reflected in the mirrors that covered the wall opposite, but only as they passed in and out. A single plastic chair shaped like a sugar scoop, at either end of the lobby, looked more decorative than practical.

Pauline had no desire to linger. She had never seen anyone moving about on the first floor, not even a porter with a bucket and mop. Immaculate and deserted, the place made her uneasy. Four empty elevators, gaping at her from the back of the hall, added to her anxiety.

She studied the directions, done in gold on a white panel in the handsome interior of the car, and breathed a sigh of relief as the door closed. If the elevator had gone down instead of up, it would not have surprised her, but it was reassuring to feel herself being carried smoothly upward. This pleasant emotion lasted until the car stopped, the door opened, and she saw the number twelve painted on the corridor wall. Madame Titania lived on the seventh floor.

For a moment she thought of walking down the stairs, if she could find the stairs. But she didn't trust her knees and her feet were already tired. Then, too, if she met the superintendent, or even a tenant, she might find it difficult to explain why she was limping down the stairways like a bandit. The fact that she had never seen a human being anywhere on the premises made it all the more likely—Fate being what it was—that she would run into people in *droves* once she placed herself in an embarrassing position.

Pauline stepped back into the elevator, read the white-and-gold panel over again, twice, pushed a button and closed her eyes. This time the car took her to the fifteenth floor, but the next attempt was successful and she hurriedly escaped at the seventh. The sight of Madame Titania's white-and-gold door had the soothing effect of a familiar landmark.

"Good morning," said the large, gray-haired woman who opened the door in response to the bell.

Pauline had expected Bessie, the neat, white-capped maid.

"Is Madame Titania reading this morning?" Pauline asked. "I haven't an appointment, but she takes me anyway."

"Oh, you're one of those; you'd better come in." The woman stepped back. "I've been doing nothing all week but explaining to people," she said.

She led the way into an overfurnished but comfortable reception room, and Pauline noticed that the door of the room across the hall was closed. Usually this door was open, because clients waited in the room which connected with the astrologer's office.

"I'm Madame Titania's niece," the gray-haired woman said. Having steered Pauline to a couch, she sat down beside her. "I suppose you came about your horoscope."

Pauline felt vaguely irritated. "Where is Madame Titania?" she demanded. "I've been coming to her for a number of years, Mrs. —" she floundered, glancing at the ringless hand.

She was "Miss Sadie," the niece said. (Evidently the family didn't care for last names.) For the last two weeks she had been taking care of Madame Titania's apartment, trying to keep track of her clients, a task complicated by Bessie's decision to take a month's vacation.

"Is Madame taking a vacation, too?" Pauline interrupted.

"A vacation? Mercy no," Miss Sadie said. "She had a nasty accident about three weeks ago and has been in the hospital ever since. The doctors say it'll be another two weeks before she can come home."

Pauline looked shocked.

"But—but she's always been so careful about accidents. I mean she has her horoscope and she follows the predictions. And she never makes mistakes the way I do. I don't see how it could possibly happen to her."

Miss Sadie said, "God give me strength!"

It was only that she had been listening to her aunt's "customers" for the last three weeks, until she was nearly out of her mind, she apologized.

"You'd think Aunt Tat was from outer space, to hear them talk. One woman told me that it was impossible for anyone in such close communion with the planets to have an accident. She as much as accused me of dreaming up the accident."

Pauline murmured, anxious to placate, yet unwilling to be intimidated. Madame Titania's clientele had great faith in her ability to read the stars. They came to her for advice, and she had saved many of them from disasters they would otherwise have been unable to avoid.

"So naturally we can't believe that a thing like this could happen to her—she would have had some warning." Pauline began to quail under Miss Sadie's fixed stare. "I'm sure you have benefited innumerable times by her predictions."

"Me? Ha!" Miss Sadie opened her mouth wide in derision, revealing very strong, white teeth. "Let me tell you, I have no truck with the stars. Aunt Tat's the only one in the family who goes in for this sort of thing. The stars don't do a thing for her when she's flat on her back; I have to leave my brother's butcher shop and come look after her."

Pauline said what she was obviously expected to say, that Madame was fortunate to have such a capable niece, but it was impossible not to help wondering if Miss Sadie could be trusted to keep her capable hands off the files and charts and rare books in the inner office. If in addition to her lack of sympathy, Miss Sadie proved to be a demon housekeeper, she might easily ruin the work of years by insisting on a thorough cleaning.

"What do you do about the people who have standing appointments?" Pauline asked. "I can't afford it, but lots of women—and men, I guess—come regularly once or twice a month."

There was nothing she could do, Miss Sadie said. Her aunt kept the rooms on the other side of the hall locked up and the keys were in her purse at the hospital.

162

"She won't give them to me—says she doesn't want me messing with her papers. And she's mad, anyway, because her horoscope didn't say a word about her being careful on the day she got caught between two cars on the Boulevard."

Madame Titania had been crossing a busy street against the signal lights, had panicked halfway from the opposite curb, and had apparently hoped to achieve almost invisible dimensions as the onrushing traffic hastily split to bypass her.

"Two cars kind of sandwiched her between them, but luckily they had slowed down," Miss Sadie reported. "She had three ribs broken and internal injuries. And not one word of it was in her stars."

Pauline said that she would send a get-well card, and when Madame Titania returned from the hospital—"the Down Town Hospital? Oh, thank you"—she would make an appointment. It was perfect nonsense, she told herself, to keep insisting that an astrologer of Madame's experience and standing had not been alerted to the need for caution on the date of such a serious accident.

"That woman," Pauline fumed inwardly when she had finally reached the street, "wouldn't call any prediction a warning unless it spelled out complete details in advance. Of course Madame Titania had warning; she forgot to be careful, that's all."

She had counted so heavily on advice from the astrologer that now her apprehension was intensified. It was certainly folly, she reasoned, to stay exposed to unnamed dangers: the day might be favorable, but it might as easily be difficult. It was the not knowing that gave her the horrors. The temptation to hurry home, get into bed, and pull the covers up over her head was stronger than she cared to admit. For her own self-respect she forced herself to stop for a cup of tea and a sweet roll. While she waited to be served, a sharp stab of pain directed her thoughts for a moment to the necessity of rationalizing these increasingly frequent twinges of anguish. She had read somewhere that "twinges" should be expected by the elderly, who were advised to think of others worse off than themselves.

She drank the lukewarm tea, reflecting that she could honestly say she had had her lunch, and then began the weary trip home, a journey haunted by the memory of Madame Titania's deplorable accident. Bus drivers, impatient, amazed, or frankly cynical, watched Pauline's excessively cautious progress without comment, but her fellow-passengers twice complained bitterly.

She was vaguely alarmed by the utter exhaustion that possessed her as she fitted the key into the lock of her quiet apartment. It was weariness with a new edge and she could be thankful that she lived alone in a privacy that allowed her to collapse in peace. There was nothing, she thought drowsily, stretching out on the bed and without energy enough even to kick off her shoes, as trying as to be under the constant surveillance of one's children.

She woke only when the phone rang. The invitation to have dinner with her neighbor across the hall, and to play a little bridge, pleased her. It had become important to avoid Elaine and Kelsey temporarily, although Pauline could not have told why. Her plan to spend the evening studying her forecast for the next day—her interpretation might be faulty, but it would be better than having no guidance at all—could wait. And certainly Grace Stewart's apartment would be as "safe" as her own.

A pleasant, informal dinner with the placid widow and her pretty spinster sister, followed by the card game in which a Stewart cousin made the fourth, in a measure helped Pauline to relax. Grace Stewart unconsciously created a tranquil atmosphere, perhaps because she habitually emphasized the present. In her company it was impossible to look beyond the next morning's breakfast, a limited horizon that Pauline sometimes found comforting.

The bridge game broke up fairly early because the Stewart cousin had to meet a seven o'clock plane at the airport, and Pauline permitted herself to drink a full cup of coffee, an indulgence that Grace optimistically predicted could keep no one awake.

"I ought to have known better!" Pauline scolded aloud when

164

she found herself wider awake at midnight than she had been at any time during the day. "The least I could have done was to have taken half a cup."

She had forgotten her intention to consult the horoscope predictions for the next day, and her books and charts were in the chest at the foot of her bed. The rollers on which she had wound her hair for the night interfered with the adjustment of her eyeglasses, but she put them on and began to search through the medley in the chest. Pearl's tidy habits compelled her to tuck all the astrology magazines out of sight and she paid no attention to the dates.

A half hour later Pauline, no nearer to sleep than before, pondered the hidden dangers inherent in the approaching day labeled succinctly "disturbing." She would be foolish to handle anything inflammable, she was warned. Liquids of all kinds should be avoided, impulses curbed.

"Start nothing new." The terse advice offered by three magazines impressed by the omission of detail.

Pauline lay down again. Usually she could take these predictions or leave them, but Madame Titania's accident had made her nervous. Miss Sadie had undoubtedly exaggerated the surprise element; the warning might have been veiled, but Madame was a trained interpreter and could not have missed it. It was as startling for an astrologer to have bad luck as for a doctor to be ill. Dr. Cannon, Pauline recollected, had been operated on for appendicitis. She didn't intend to let this forecast frighten her, but she did intend to exercise special care. In twenty-four hours the danger would be over, and the following day was simply filled with cheerful possibilities. She never could resist reading ahead and that was one reason why she confused her dates and tangled the predictions.

Tomorrow—tomorrow she must watch her step. Liquids, inflammables—have nothing to do with them. Curb impulses—that would be difficult. An impulse might last barely a second; to act without thinking, like moving a leg or an arm, could result in catastrophe, the forecast hinted. Could an impulse be controlled?

Pauline fell asleep.

Morning invariably surprised her. For a moment after waking she felt a sensation of having returned from a vague distance and usually had trouble recalling the calendar day. Her mind cleared quickly, however, and she chose to ignore the slight suggestion of panic. She liked to lie quietly, listening to the weather report and a summary of the news. To leap out of bed was to invite a heart attack, she firmly believed, and fortunately she had no reason to leap.

The recollection of her horoscope forecast of a "disturbing" day returned to her as she listened placidly to the hash of foreign and domestic news. Five minutes after the commentator had urged her to have a pleasant day and had subsided, she would not be able to remember a word he had spoken.

She forgot him completely now and did not even know when he read the weather report, to which she usually paid rapt attention.

"Handle nothing inflammable, avoid liquids of all kinds, curb impulses," she repeated aloud.

Interpreted, this presumably meant that the gas stove was a hazard. It would be inviting accident to take a shower—the newspapers had carried plenty of stories of people who were scalded in the shower. If she couldn't light the stove, she couldn't make coffee, which would be just as well since liquids were an issue.

It was, she decided, as difficult to analyze an impulse in the cold light of morning as it had been the night before. Her first impulse, if it was an impulse, was to stay in bed, where surely she could hope to keep the lurking dangers at bay. She even pictured them in her imagination as shadowy forms, dodging back and forth outside her bedroom door. If the temptation to remain in bed represented an impulse to be curbed, a bathless, breakfastless day must be spent elsewhere.

Another radio announcer's voice began its drone. Pauline closed her eyes, but not to sleep. If she concentrated, perhaps she could remember what Elaine's plans had outlined for the morning. Not that she wouldn't be delighted to have her mother come to breakfast, but she would naturally be curious, and Kelsey and Amanda would ask embarrassing questions.

Pearl—bless her heart—could always be counted upon for the practical sympathy that would include an extra breakfast as a matter of course.

"You can make this a bright day," the announcer insisted.

Pauline turned him off and sat up. At quarter of nine Kelsey and Amanda would already have gone. Elaine put in a full day at the Thrift Shop on Thursday—Pauline had finally straightened that out—and must leave early to open the shop at nine.

"I'll dress very slowly," Pauline said to the woman reflected in the dresser mirror. "I can use cold cream on my face, but I'll have to wash my hands."

She didn't feel hungry, but breakfast was a habit and she was devoted to routine. Apprehension caused her to move with exaggerated caution and it took her an hour to dress and to do her hair. A dull headache she ascribed to the need for a cup of coffee, but the general disinclination to move about she thought must be due to mental depression.

"You have to know the future, to be on guard," she explained to Albert, who asked as usual whether she could expect a favorable day. "But in some ways it's more cheerful not to see ahead."

"You can't live blindly," said Albert. "I got people right here in this house whose motto is 'Live a day at a time.' And what happens? Disaster comes up and hits 'em right in the face and maybe they jump out of the window. The stars could have warned 'em, but no, they think astronomy is superstitious."

"Astrology," Pauline corrected. "Who jumped out of a window?"

No one very recently, Albert admitted, but he had been thinking of stock-market crashes. He glanced impatiently at the signal board as the buzzer sounded.

"Now today for me is mixed," he confided. " 'Neutral,' the book calls it. I got Mars favorable in the ninth house, but I can be popular with the opposite sex."

Pauline looked significantly at the signal board, dotted with half a dozen floor numbers.

"You're using last year's magazines and you don't want to be popular with the opposite sex," she said.

Albert was devoted to his fat and cheery wife, whose one failing was her skeptical attitude toward the stars. An extraordinarily sustained pressure on the buzzer recalled him to his duties and he slammed back the heavy gates that released the door and let Pauline escape.

"That Mr. Hewitt on the twelfth, he's one of them," Albert mumbled as the car shot upward.

Pearl said that it would be no trouble at all to "fix up" a breakfast and that she would be glad to have someone to talk to while she finished the ironing and made the dinner dessert.

"You suppose it's all right for you to *drink* liquids?" she asked, when she had heard the outline of Pauline's disturbing day.

If Pearl had a fault, it was a too literal mind, Pauline thought, annoyed by her own irritation. She would feel in better humor after she had had a cup of coffee.

"How about bacon and eggs?" said Pearl. "Or ham?"

A sudden flare of nausea alarmed Pauline.

"For heaven's sake!" She swallowed convulsively and gripped the table edge, for the room had begun to swing in circles. "All I want is one cup of coffee and one slice of toast. And I think I won't have butter."

Pearl glanced at her sharply, but did not reply.

"My nerves are on edge," Pauline apologized. "I'll be glad when the day's over."

That was one impulse she hadn't curbed, she reminded herself, but Pearl was too good-natured to hold a grudge. Pauline opened her eyes to find the coffee and a slice of delicately browned toast before her. The room had stopped revolving, too.

"How is Jerome, Pearl?" She reflected that Pearl had not said much about her boy friend lately. "Remember he's Virgo —you have to lead him."

"Lead him!" Pearl, who had been setting up the ironing board, raised an indignant, flushed face. "He's got his mother leading him; isn't that enough?"

She plugged in her iron and opened a roll of table napkins. Her movements, jerky and emphatic, suggested repressed turmoil.

"Tell me," coaxed Pauline, safely fenced in by the breakfast nook and grateful for re-established normal routine. "What has Jerome's mother done now, Pearl?"

Pearl burst into a speech.

"Honest, Miz Ives, Jerome believes every word that woman tells him. A ninny would know she's having a fourth cousin of hers come to live with her for only one reason. But no, Jerome thinks she is doing it out of the goodness of her heart. What she has in mind, of course," Pearl went on, snapping open a napkin, "is to marry Jerome to this Ida Dern. I understand she has a little money of her own and of course she's a few years younger than me. I thought it looked funny to have a single woman come and stay in a house with a single man. I still think it looks funny. But Mrs. Van Antwerpt says the presence of the man's mother makes it all right."

Pauline suddenly moaned.

"It was the coffee—I should have avoided liquids!" she whispered. "Oh, Pearl, I feel awful."

Pearl managed to help her out of the breakfast nook and into the living room, where Pauline collapsed on the sofa, her face so white that Pearl's immediate thought was to telephone the Thrift Shop.

"I can get your daughter—she'll know what to do—" She broke off in alarm as Pauline struggled to sit up.

"Don't you dare telephone Mrs. Carpenter. There's nothing the matter with me." Pauline panted, and beads of moisture glistened on her forehead. "It's a bilious attack. I've had them before; you know I have. I'll be all right."

No, she didn't want Dr. Cannon either. She didn't need a doctor to tell her her liver was out of order. She should not have taken any liquids today—that was the whole trouble. And there were no favorable days for consulting medical men until next month.

"Let me get you a glass of water," Pearl said. "Or maybe a little baking soda—"

Pauline frowned. "No liquids."

She would lie quietly on the sofa until she felt better, she decided; then if she took a long nap in the afternoon, by dinnertime she would be all right. Pearl must go ahead with her work—finish the ironing, make the dessert—and not worry.

But Pearl had a shrewd idea that Miz Carpenter and Mr., too, would "take her head off" if the diagnosis of a bilious attack proved to be something more serious. Pearl knew that the family had several times been alarmed by Miz Ives's insistence on following the stars as a guide for making appointments with the doctor. Pearl didn't have that much faith in horoscopes herself. When you had a pain, the sensible thing was to let a doctor look at you, regardless of your chart.

She went back to the kitchen reluctantly, but half an hour later when she tiptoed into the living room she found the patient sleeping. Pearl adjusted the afghan with which she had covered her, and tiptoed back to start her upside-down cake.

She had it ready for the oven when a dull thud from the direction of the living room alarmed her.

"Pearl!" The trembling frightened call alarmed her, too.

"I thought you'd never come," said Pauline, rather unreasonably, but then she had been dreaming of looking everywhere in the apartment house for Pearl.

She lay on her side on the floor and made no attempt to move.

In her dream, she explained while Pearl knelt beside her, crooning sympathetically, she had even gone up on the roof and from there had heard Albert calling that he had found Pearl.

"I began to run—and the next thing I knew the rug slipped and I was here on the floor." Pauline sighed. "Do you know, I think something's broken," she said.

"Oh, no!" Poor Pearl was panic-stricken. "You mean you broke your leg, Miz Ives?"

Pauline thought it was her hip. "I guess you'll have to phone the Thrift Shop. But just say I have a bilious attack."

The Thrift Shop reported that Mrs. Carpenter had gone out "on a number of errands" and was not expected back until late that afternoon.

"How about the doctor?" Pearl made the suggestion timidly.

"He can't help me until next month," Pauline groaned. "I suppose you'll have to call Mr. Carpenter. But just say I don't feel very well."

Kelsey's speedy arrival almost coincided with that of Dr. Cannon, to whom he had phoned before leaving the office.

"I don't need a doctor," Pauline protested. "I planned to make an appointment early next month."

She heard that she had broken her hip, but angrily refused to be taken to the hospital.

"All the days are wrong," she told Kelsey. "The bones won't knit. Elaine wouldn't let me go; that's why you don't wait for her to come home."

"Elaine would never forgive me if I didn't take care of you." Kelsey saw the doctor approaching with a hypodermic. "You know you trust me, Pauline."

## Chapter 12

"He's very good-looking, much better-looking than Patty."
Amanda added a jar of mushroom paste to the catsup, butter,
and mayonnaise already on the table in the breakfast nook.

"You forgot the tartar sauce," Pearl said.

"I loathe people who are sarcastic. Why don't we ever have
enough cheese bread?" Amanda's retort was muffled because
she was speaking into the refrigerator.

Pearl watched her carry a bottle of Coke, a tomato, a jar of
guava jelly, and a tin of deviled ham to the table, leaving the
refrigerator open.

"I guess that's all." Amanda sighed. "Except the bread."

Silently Pearl fetched two large water rolls and closed the
refrigerator door.

"You must be in love," she suggested, offering the bottle
opener.

Amanda, going busily to work on the deviled-ham tin,
asked how a girl could be in love when her father refused to
let her date anyone old enough to be out of grammar school?

"Patty Wilson's brother is nineteen. I see him almost every
time I go to her house. Don't you think that looks as if he
was interested in me?"

Pearl had no finesse. "He ask you for a date?" she said.

Amanda admitted that Dave Wilson had not asked her for a
date. Not that it would have done any good, since her father
would have had a fit.

"But I think he's shy, too, and that's why he hangs around
when I go home with Patty. He doesn't have to stay around,
you know."

"Well, he lives there," Pearl said.

This was so unlike her—usually she was the most sympathetic of listeners—that Amanda was shocked and alarmed.

"You sick or something?"

She was worse than a doctor, Pearl grumbled. Just because Miz Ives had landed in the hospital was no sign that everyone else was falling apart.

"Then what makes you such a crab?" Amanda gulped a generous amount of Coke. "Mother thinks you're losing weight, Pearl."

"I got plenty of troubles to make me cranky. An angel couldn't bear what I have to bear and keep its wings," Pearl said.

"Oh, Pearl!" Amanda was instantly contrite, but she continued to fish for an elusive pickle in the almost empty jar. "Did Jerome's cousin come?"

The creature's name was Ida Dern and she wasn't one to stand out in a crowd, Pearl said. Jerome's mother had had the nerve to invite Pearl to supper, to meet her.

"If she thought I wouldn't come, I fooled her. I wore my best silk jersey and the pin Jerome gave me a year ago. I saw his mother looking at it."

"Well, you've known Jerome longer than she has," Amanda pointed out, eyeing her second roll happily. "You must have the inside track."

It wasn't Jerome, it was his mother, who worried her, Pearl said. She hadn't needed Mrs. Van Antwerpt to tell her that Jerome was a mama's boy.

"But she seems to think I can win out, if I don't stoop to his mother's low tactics. I was going to send his mother an anonymous letter, but Mrs. Van said you can't fight fire with fire."

Amanda chewed thoughtfully and allowed her thoughts to return to Dave Wilson. Jerome's mother was an old story, but Pearl probably missed Grandmother and Mother, too, who now spent so much time at the hospital.

"I got to start dinner. You through, or do you want to take it with you?" Pearl asked. "Don't leave me one pickle in the bottle."

Amanda obligingly ate the solitary pickle, helped herself to a fresh bottle of Coke, and wandered off in the direction of her room. She was composing a letter that required considerable thought, since Patty Wilson was also a devoted reader of the column edited by Mirabelle Marilyn Meeks.

It was to be hoped that Mirabelle appreciated how much a girl had on her mind. Amanda settled herself on the bed with the Coke bottle and a straw. She had been able to do very little about Midge Cutter, not only because she had no idea what to do, and Mirabelle's advice, comforting on the first reading, didn't "get anywhere" when carefully studied, but because her grandmother's accident had upset the household routine.

Amanda reflected that even if Midge should be taking advantage of Daddy while his wife visited her poor sick mother in the hospital, her mother was undoubtedly too busy to take any steps to right her wrongs. Originally Amanda had had some idea of following Midge, to establish whether she actually visited the law office, but the attendance rules at Miss Mary's were strict and Amanda could not be expected to spend her Saturdays as an amateur detective.

She swallowed Coke contentedly and let her thoughts dwell on the broken marriage of her father and mother. Her parents, she supposed, would stay together for her sake; Tully's father and mother had been willing to save Tully from the evil effects of a broken home. Parents owed that to their children—Mirabelle Marilyn Meeks had said so repeatedly—but Amanda, remembering the girls at school whose parents had been divorced, wondered exactly what the evil effects might be. That was the trouble with all the information she was able to collect—it stopped short just when it promised to be interesting.

If her parents refused to consider a divorce, what would happen to Midge? Presumably she would have to go on living with her husband, although she couldn't be very fond of him. But Midge and the major would also be saving their children from the evil effects of a broken home.

Tully's parents had parted after her death. Amanda hastily

deposited the empty bottle on the floor. The thought of dying, so as to set her unhappy parents free, did not appeal to her. But if she married, they need no longer pretend. How she was ever to get married with a father who represented a persistent stumbling block was a problem, and she had more problems now than she could handle.

Without getting off the bed she could fish a pad and pencil from one of the drawers in her desk. She settled back against the pillows and began the draft of an important letter.

"Dear Mirabelle," she began conventionally, "I am in urgent need of advice. Is a boy of nineteen too old for me? I am going to be fifteen on my next birthday and he may feel that I am childish, although he treats me as if I am mature."

Amanda reread the scrawl, trying to decide whether Patty would be able to recognize the writer. Dave would be nineteen in a week's time, and Amanda's birthday was months away, but the essentials were true enough for Mirabelle to make a decision.

"Is it ever all right for a girl to let a boy see that she is interested in him?" Amanda's dark eyes reflected her anxiety. "I cannot invite him to my home because my parents, my father especially, are terribly old-fashioned and out of touch with reality. They are on the verge of divorce—" The pencil halted, crossed out the sentence. "How can I get this boy to notice me?" Amanda finished.

A half hour later, at the dinner table, she thought of another question to be added to her letter when she made the final copy. Did eye shadow, she would ask Mirabelle, make a girl look older?

## II

"I'm sure I don't know what else you could expect," Pauline Ives said, speaking rather indistinctly because of the bobby pins in her mouth. "A doctor only examines you in the hope of finding something wrong."

"Don't hold them in your mouth, Gram," Amanda scolded.

"You'll have the whole staff here if you swallow—what do they call it?—a foreign body."

She had offered to set her grandmother's hair in pin curls, and Pauline, whose recovery from the hip fracture had been complicated by a series of operations, first for appendicitis and then for gallstones, had agreed that she might feel better if she looked better. She had fought stubbornly to live through the hot, weary summer, and now, late in November, was still unable to walk.

"Dr. Cannon has his heart set on putting my ankle in a new cast. Perhaps your mother told you?" Pauline put a thin hand up to her hair. "It pulls," she complained.

Amanda adjusted the offending pin, murmured that the doctor was willing to wait. She wasn't sure that her grandmother understood that the small bones broken in her ankle obstinately refused to mend.

"Good afternoon, Mrs. Ives. Would you like some nice fruit juice?"

A very pretty blonde girl in the "candy-stripers" uniform stood at the foot of the bed, holding a tray.

"I had orange juice for breakfast," said Pauline, whom the fruit juice routine frankly bored. "You're Judy, aren't you? Judy, this is my granddaughter, Amanda."

"You want some juice?" Judy thrust the tray forward in a hospitable gesture.

Amanda accepted a paper cup of grape juice, and Judy departed, the tray lurching alarmingly as she turned to catch a glimpse of herself in the dresser mirror.

"She's a junior aide," Pauline said. "They work afternoons and Saturdays. She must be about your age."

A good many of the girls at Miss Mary's were candy-stripers, Amanda said. She supposed she ought to do something to help other people, and the uniforms were cute.

"Miss Berry, the night nurse, says there's a new class forming. You ought to ask about it." Pauline yawned. "I never saw them do anything but carry fruit juice, but Miss Berry says they're quick learners."

Amanda finished her drink and carried the paper cup out

176

to the waste container in the corridor, because her grandmother was vehement on the subject of "garbage" left in the room.

"You want more?" Judy came out of the room opposite as Amanda returned.

Amanda specified Coke or root beer, declined grape juice. She learned that Judy's ambition was to be a nurse and that she had a sister who had been a nurse's aide for two years.

"She met her boy friend that way," Judy said.

"You mean he was sick and she took him grape juice?" the literal-minded Amanda asked.

Judy giggled. There were other liquids served the patients; in fact, orange juice was more popular than grape.

"My sister was helping take care of a patient in for observation; Gin can give back rubs and everything," Judy said. "Her brother came to see her the night before the operation and he was real cute. He and Gin hit it off and now they're going steady."

Amanda remembered that she had not finished making pin curls, and the sight of an approaching nurse reminded Judy that she had not completed her rounds. They smiled uncertainly at each other, murmured "So long," and abruptly retreated.

"I didn't mean to be so long—I was talking to Judy," Amanda apologized. "I should think it would be more exciting to work in a hospital at night."

But asked why, she could say only that more "things" happened at night than during the day.

"Besides, there are more visitors at night. You don't see any men in the daytime. I mean patients have their brothers and things come to see them in the evening visiting hours."

### III

Pauline said that no woman could ever have too many earrings and that if she couldn't wear pretty shoes, it was more important than ever to accent "above the table interest."

"You're sweet to bring me such pretty ones, Lucie," she

added gratefully. "I'll put them on now, so you can get the effect."

Lucie made a nice effect herself in a black knit that set off her shining hair. She said that she had been trying to get into town for two weeks, but that she had been frustrated at every turn.

"You mean the children?" Pauline admired her silver earrings in a hand glass.

"No, I mean the shop." Lucie looked as pleased as a child who had set off a firecracker. "I haven't told even Kelsey yet —he's so seldom sympathetic."

Pauline's patter of questions gratified her. Yes, she was now a businesswoman and found the job thrilling. For the present it was part-time and that was just as well, since the eternal question of who would look after the children continued to haunt her.

"Midge Cutter takes care of them for me three mornings a week. Of course I have to look after her youngsters whenever she wants to come to town. It's the best I can do, until I get hold of some money."

For the present she was being paid nothing, Lucie said, but the benefits of the training couldn't be calculated in dollars and cents. She worked in a decorating shop, newly established in Lyman, and the woman interior decorator was an artist and a superb teacher.

"I've discovered what has been making me restless ever since we moved into the house," Lucie said. "The colors are all wrong, but then, neither Royce nor I knew anything about the principles of decoration. Mrs. Beach has taught me more in a week than I could have learned in a year at one of the art schools."

Pauline thought of suggesting that she had learned a great deal about interior decoration, too, but decided that the joke was too feeble.

"You think the wrong colors make you restless?" she inquired politely.

She knew it, Lucie said, the light of a crusader in her aqua eyes. Her bedroom had been done in yellow, and blonds

178

had to be careful about yellow. The living room was uninspired, the halls drab, and the children's room actually invited quarrels.

"I'm going to do the entire house over. Mrs. Beach is letting me select wallpapers, draperies, and upholstery material at half price, which is a terrific saving. You won't know the place."

Pauline wondered about the labor costs.

"Kelsey always says the painters and paper hangers charge so much. And Elaine had a chair reupholstered; I forget what the bill was, but it made a deep impression."

She hoped to be able to do some of the work herself, Lucie said rather hurriedly. Of course it would be fine if Royce could be one of those husbands who had a well-equipped workshop in the cellar and could do carpentering and paint and repair.

"He couldn't even put on a washer until the man next door showed him how. And I can't get him to go to the extension classes—I've enrolled for one in upholstering this fall. It's an evening class and he'll have to look after the children."

"Well, I suppose you can do a room at a time, the way we used to do our spring and fall house cleaning—" Pauline broke off to smile at someone who had come up behind Lucie. "Elaine, darling, I was afraid you weren't coming today," she said.

"I'm to ask you if the pin curls lasted. They look fine to me." Elaine kissed her mother, gave Lucie's shoulder an affectionate pat. "What pretty earrings, sweetie—are they new?"

"Lucie brought them." Pauline felt of the little silver acorn dangling from her ear. "My chart said this would be a favorable day," she added.

"Pearl sent you a lemon pudding—the nurse put it in the icebox for your supper—and Kelsey is coming over tonight." Elaine had moved around to the other side of the bed.

There was no use in telling Elaine that she was losing weight, Pauline reflected. She probably would be delighted to lose a few pounds—any woman would—and it was unfortunate that loss in weight registered in one's face and throat,

**179**

never in the thighs and hips. Pauline had even discussed this annoying trick of nature's with Dr. Cannon, who had stubbornly maintained that loss of weight was loss of weight and that only the total registered on the scales concerned him.

Lucie murmured that she must be on her way, but made no movement to go. She planned to drop in to see Kelsey, if she had time, she said.

"You know, it's the funniest thing, but the last two or three times I stopped in at his office, I ran into Midge Cutter. Once in the elevator in his building and another time she was coming out of the lobby as I went in. And, oh yes, I thought I saw her another time, but I wasn't too sure. The starter closed the elevator gates just as I got there and a woman who looked like Midge was standing in back of a man with a green bow tie."

Elaine, avoiding her mother's eyes, turned to the dresser and began to rearrange the white and purple asters in a pottery vase.

"Didn't she speak to you, Lucie?" she asked in a deliberately casual voice.

"Well, do you know, she acted so queer, I couldn't be sure she saw me," Lucie said. "I got the impression she was trying to duck me. But when you think that over, it doesn't make sense, because we see each other practically every day now."

Midge had been—well, furtive, Lucie continued. She might not have given the incidents a second thought, but each time had coincided with the previous refusal of Midge to baby-sit, on the plea that she had to keep a dentist's appointment.

"We have dentists in Lyman; in fact, I gave Midge Dr. Erdman's phone number weeks ago. I meant to look at the directory in Kelsey's building. Do you know whether there are any dentists there, Elaine?"

Elaine didn't know. She gave a white aster a final twitch and stood back to judge the result.

"Of course you may be mistaken, especially if the woman you saw wears dark glasses—they are a wonderful disguise," she said.

Lucie stood up and stretched delicately to adjust the knit

to the best advantage. She intended to ask Kelsey about the dentists, for the simple reason that she hated to be made a fool of, she said.

"Midge is tricky. I've learned that much about her. She likes to hear all about my business, but she's terribly close-mouthed when it comes to discussing her own."

Lucie leaned over the bed and dropped a light kiss on Pauline's cheek.

"I'll let you know if I find out anything," she promised. "Nana, I could almost envy you, knowing that your supper will be brought you on a tray. I'd have to have a baby to get a meal served me in bed."

Pauline said nothing until the clatter of high heels on the corridor tiles could no longer be heard.

"Kind of takes my interest for granted, doesn't she? I don't believe she saw Midge at all, do you, Elaine?"

Elaine said, "Lucie has twenty-twenty vision. I think I'll have Midge in for dinner some night soon, Mama. I feel that I owe it to Kelsey. I wouldn't want her to think that I neglect his friends."

Luckily Kelsey hadn't that much imagination, Pauline retorted; one imagination working overtime was enough in any family, and Lucie had enough imagination for three women.

"I never knew a Libra person who could stick to a plan. Lucie doesn't know her own mind and can be persuaded to switch over at the drop of a hat. The one description of herself she believes is always the last."

Elaine, confused, glanced at her mother in some alarm.

"You're not feverish, are you, Mama?"

"The reason I'm talking so much is because I had a tranquilizer," Pauline explained. "It's wearing off."

She insisted on repeating Lucie's account of her part-time work, unconsciously revealing a motive for Lucie's planned visit to Kelsey's office. Elaine knew that Kelsey loaned his sister money fairly frequently, loans that were in effect gifts, for Lucie was seldom able to repay. It was his own money, Elaine reasoned, and he was as generous to her mother as to his own. Only occasionally did she wonder whether Royce might not resent Lucie's reliance on Kelsey's help, but then she doubted that Lucie would consider Royce's protests seriously.

"Do you want me to bring you anything, Mama?" she asked when Pauline finally leaned back against her pillows, if not exhausted, at least willing to rest.

She needed more "materials," Pauline said, materials being the term that covered her astrological dabbling. Already she had promised to work out horoscopes for a dozen nurses, and her daily forecasts interested the skeptical and the believers alike, since even what Kelsey called "a cockeyed view of the future" was a challenge to monotony.

Elaine wrote out the list, and reminded her mother again of the lemon pudding and of Kelsey's impending visit. Pauline murmured drowsily when she kissed her good-by; the nurse, who noticed Elaine leaving the room, said that Mrs. Ives was usually asleep when the supper trays came up.

After a long, chilly walk home, taken on the vague assumption that exercise must calm her nerves, Elaine was displeased to find the apartment dark.

"I dreamt I dwelt in marble halls" came Pearl's uncertain soprano from the kitchen. "With vassals and serfs at my side—"

"Isn't Amanda home yet? Why didn't you turn on the lights?" Elaine demanded of the singer, isolated in a brilliantly illuminated kitchen.

Pearl said that she had forgotten the lights and that Amanda had not come in.

"How is your mother, Miz Carpenter?"

Elaine, her irritability rebuked, said that her mother was very comfortable.

"I don't think she'll care too much if she isn't home for Christmas."

Pearl smoothed her apron and asked if anything had been said about her horoscope.

"I'd like to know a little more, but I don't suppose your mother thought to tell you."

A familiar apprehension nudged Elaine, who was hungry and tired.

"Pearl, don't pin your hopes to any predictions. Mama's calculations aren't too good when she's well, and now she must be more mixed up than ever. There's no sense in expecting her forecasts to come true."

She had a hunch that this time Miz Ives was right, Pearl said. According to her chart something was going to happen in December that she had been expecting for a long time.

"Either before Christmas, or after," Pearl said, her round face bright with anticipation. "I think Jerome is going to give me my ring. Miz Ives has a feeling it's going to be that, too."

"I can't stand it if she doesn't get the ring," Elaine told her husband and daughter at the dinner table that night. "I wish Mama wouldn't make these positive predictions."

Kelsey argued that Pearl was jumping to conclusions.

"Your mother says 'something' is going to happen—that leaves wide possibilities."

"Pearl ought to go see Madame Titania," Amanda said. "Gram gets her readings all mixed up."

She wished "someone with influence" would talk to her mother about astrology, Elaine sighed. Dr. Cannon was losing all patience; you couldn't expect a doctor to arrange his operations to fit a personal horoscope. By the time Mama had the day and the hour worked out to her satisfaction, she might be stricken by a fatal attack.

Amanda did not listen to her parents' discussion of the stubbornness of old ladies, a familiar theme. She hoped that Pearl would get her ring, which according to Pearl was a symbol that would put Jerome's mother in her proper place. Pearl had confided that unless Jerome could "make a home for her" apart from his mother, she intended to work after marriage.

"Your grandmother says his mother's birth sign and mine will never get along together," Pearl had said. "So in a way we're neither of us to blame. It's Fate."

Amanda had shrewdly attributed that charitable conclusion

to Pearl's renewed hopes. Pearl already visualized herself as wearing Jerome's ring, and her improved status, though imaginary, made forgiveness easy.

"She hasn't filled the salt shakers," Kelsey said. "I suppose she'll be living in marble halls from now till Christmas."

Jerome wasn't likely to give Pearl a very large diamond, Amanda thought. But she was determined to have some kind of a diamond; her first two engagement rings had been pearls.

"My first two husbands thought it was cute," she told Amanda. "I'd like a diamond for a change."

"Cute" was the word all the girls used to describe Dave Wilson. Amanda's thoughts moved on to her favorite daydream, a dramatic interlude in which Dave asked her for a date. She knew that he had asked Patty who her friend "with the big eyes" was, and Mirabelle Marilyn Meeks had considered that a sign, a definite sign, of interest on his part. She had advised Amanda to be "friendly, natural and not self-conscious," and had not thought the difference in ages much of an obstacle.

"Your father will always be critical of your boy friends and a natural jealousy is likely to impair his judgments," Mirabelle Marilyn had written. "As you break away gradually from the restrictions of home, he will learn to accept your independence."

"I don't suppose you saw Midge Sully today, Kelsey," Elaine said.

Kelsey looked bewildered, and Amanda promptly forgot Dave Wilson.

"Where would I see Midge Sully?" Kelsey asked.

Elaine said, "Well, I didn't think she would be in town today, but I wasn't sure. Lucie didn't exactly say she was baby-sitting for her."

"Lucie dropped in at the office." Kelsey spoke carefully in an evident attempt to find a clue. "Midge wasn't with her."

"She's having a lot of dental work done with a dentist in your building," Elaine told him. "I thought she'd probably mentioned it to you."

184

He had not known of a dentist with offices in his building, Kelsey said.

"And I understood Lucie thinks the world of what's-his-name—Erdman, out in Lyman. She's never said anything to me about changing dentists."

"Not Lucie, Midge," said Elaine.

Kelsey braced himself with a swallow of coffee.

"Look, we ought to have an interpreter," he suggested. "Are we talking about Lucie, or Midge? And whose dentist?"

He hadn't seen Midge since the time she had been at the apartment for dinner, he said, when finally set straight. Elaine and Lucie both seemed to think that she wandered in and out of his office daily, simply because the poor woman had been seen in the lobby of his firm's office building.

"If she doesn't go to see a dentist there, she must go to see someone else," Amanda said, her face expressionless to indicate neutrality.

Unexpectedly her father laughed.

"We could have her to dinner and ask her," he said.

Elaine resolved to consult Naida Steckner before she committed herself, but secretly she was dismayed. She had thought that the opportunity to study Midge and Kelsey together might easily provide her with what Naida called a blueprint for action, and that once she knew how to handle the situation, anxiety would vanish. Now she discovered that she felt inadequate basically and that the prospect of trying to analyze Midge frightened her.

She wondered if she could invite Naida Steckner to dinner without arousing Kelsey's curiosity, or resentment, and whether Naida would come. The blissful dream of having Naida present to make an expert analysis of the predatory Midge and to decide how deeply Kelsey might be involved was shattered by Pearl's dejected announcement that she had forgotten a dessert, and would canned peaches do?

## Chapter 13

Fortunately the approach of the holidays served to absorb Elaine's time and attention to such an extent that Midge retreated as a central figure. Elaine loved to shop, and constructed elaborate lists which she checked off with painstaking care. This year she had her mother's shopping to do, and gradually, in some manner not quite clear to her, she found herself handling shopping requests for many of the nurses and patients. They had, her mother explained, so little opportunity and time. The hospital gift shop was wonderful, Pauline added, as far as it went, but was hampered by restrictions of space and price.

Amanda, having had a part in the school's Christmas play thrust upon her, was an hour later than usual every other afternoon in reaching home. She grumbled that she couldn't afford to spend money at the snack bar in November, but that if she let Pearl ply her with food she had to listen to the endless story of Jerome, his mother, and the hoped-for ring.

It was therefore a pleasant surprise to be greeted by Pearl one afternoon with the information that she had had a phone call. Getting messages straight was not one of Pearl's gifts and she preferred to carry numbers and names in her mind, a system that naturally often resulted in confusion.

"It was a boy," she told Amanda this afternoon. "He's going to call you again, after dinner tonight."

"A boy!" Amanda's radiant face would have caused any woman a stab of pity. "Oh, Pearl, can't you remember his name?"

186

Pearl, only vaguely aware of emotion, insisted that it didn't matter.

"He's just a boy—the world's full of them. And he's going to call you back; he said so. No, he didn't leave a number. What difference does it make?"

It made a lot of difference, Amanda said, jerking open the refrigerator door. Talking on the phone was more fun if she knew the family were out of earshot.

"I wish I had a phone of my own."

Santa Claus might oblige, Pearl said, but it could do no harm to ask her grandmother if the stars promised any sort of co-operation.

"You're not going to eat cranberry sauce with root beer, are you?"

Amanda considered this a rhetorical question needing no reply.

"I should think you could remember a boy's name," she said. "Did it sound like Chick? Chick Little goes to our church. Mother likes him, but I don't."

Since she was roasting chicken for dinner, the name of Chick Little would have "stuck," Pearl said.

"I hope Jerome has sense enough not to mention my ring to that Ida Dern. In some ways Jerome is too trusting for his own good. If he thought Ida was sympathetic, he'd tell her all about my ring and of course she'd go right to his mother. I'll be glad when the holidays are over."

"You say that every year," Amanda reminded her. "I think I'll have some peanut butter and toast."

It was annoying to have her parents credit her loss of appetite at dinner that night to the small snack she had eaten in the kitchen, but she was too excited to enter into argument. It would be terrible if the phone should ring during the meal. As Tully had once said, some fathers had a fixation about their steak and potatoes.

Mercifully, when the phone did ring, Amanda was crossing the hall. Her heart leaped, but she managed to steady her voice.

"Tried to get you this afternoon," said Dave Wilson's voice.

Amanda listened in a mesmerized silence. The airy bantering she had practiced in imaginary conversations with Dave floated away like tufts of cotton, leaving her mind the consistency of melted jelly. She understood that Dave was asking to take her to a New Year's Eve party, she even realized that he must have been turned down by two or three older girls before he had thought of her, but the one solid, indisputable fact to which she clung was that she had a date for New Year's Eve.

"You'll go?" Dave concluded, a shade too briskly.

Amanda said, "Yes, of course," which was not at all what she meant to say.

It was too late to temporize, or to pretend that she had refused earlier bids, but apparently Dave had no desire to prolong the discussion. He said that he would pick her up at nine o'clock—she was to be waiting for him in the lobby—and then hung up.

Amanda gazed at the silent phone for a moment in rapture. She had never expected to have a date for New Year's Eve, and her feeling for Dave Wilson was uncomplicated, unabashed gratitude. Moving like a sleepwalker, she reached the living room and made her announcement from the doorway.

"I've got a date for New Year's Eve!"

Elaine sat at her desk, working on her Christmas-card list. The sight of Amanda's glowing face stirred up buried apprehensions in her mind.

"But, dear, your father thinks you're too young. New Year's Eve is so—so hectic. You can have a party here—" she broke off before the storm signals flashing in Amanda's eyes.

"I'm not going to have my whole life ruined!" Amanda's tone was fierce, but she kept her voice down, knowing that the study door was not soundproof. "I won't have a stupid party here with you and Daddy hovering. I'm going out with a boy and have some real fun."

Elaine said, "Who is the boy? You didn't seem very enthusiastic on the phone."

She hoped she didn't have to act like a kid, simply because

Patty Wilson's brother asked her for a date, Amanda said with great dignity. Daddy couldn't possibly object to Dave; he knew Mr. Wilson. And, anyway, it was to be a double date, because Dave had the car.

"You mean he's old enough to drive and the other couple isn't." Elaine frowned. "I remember him now—he's nineteen or twenty and too old for you. Your father won't like it."

She wasn't going to have her life ruined, Amanda repeated, her angry, tragic eyes too old in her young face. Christmas would mean nothing to her unless she could look forward to New Year's Eve. Her prestige at school would be assured for the spring term; she would be envied by her whole class.

"Mother, you've got to talk Daddy into letting me go. The more boys I know, the better chance I have of making a successful marriage. Perhaps you didn't know enough boys when you were young."

Elaine said automatically, "What are you talking about?" but to Amanda's relief she did not make an issue of the remark. She did promise to plead for Amanda and, if successful, to see to it that she had a new dress.

"Not too babyish," Amanda specified. "And you can call it my Christmas present. I'm way over my budget now—I couldn't buy a handkerchief out of my allowance. Maybe you'll lend me your pearl necklace, Mother?"

The New Year's party took precedence in Amanda's mind over all the usual holiday preparations. After she had obtained her father's reluctant consent—an older boy, Elaine had pointed out, might be more reliable than one too young— it became imperative to make Dave understand that he would have to call for her. The difficulties of finding parking space would have no effect on her father's rule that an escort must present himself at the apartment. Amanda searched her scrapbook for a bit of advice remembered from Mirabelle Marilyn Meeks's column.

"If your date balks at having to make conversation with your parents, be ready, down to the last bobby pin, when he rings the bell," Mirabelle advised. "He need only say a pleasant 'Good evening' and you can be off."

Amanda resolved to be ready. She sent word through Patty that Dave must come up to the apartment, but that the parked car would furnish an excuse for leaving at once.

Christmas became something to be lived through, but every night she lay awake for hours, too excited to sleep, planning her dress, her slippers, devising new styles of wearing her hair, and wondering how much make-up she dared use. She visited her grandmother, now in the convalescent wing, where she must learn to walk again before the doctors would approve her release. New Year's Eve, Pauline assured Amanda, was an exceptionally favorable period in her birth chart, but if she had predicted a holocaust, it would have made no difference.

Because she had what she wanted most in the world—or so she told herself happily—she found it little trouble to accede to her parents' wishes; indeed, she decided they were almost absurdly easy to please. She accompanied them to the midnight mass at All Souls, went with them to carry gifts to the hospital, and during holiday week gave an afternoon to the Thrift Shop's party for its faithful customers, although she was frankly critical of "middle-aged women who had parties on the brain."

It was a mercy, Elaine observed on Christmas Day, that they had planned to have their dinner at one of the good restaurants, to leave Pearl free. As it happened, Pearl would have been in no condition to cook a holiday dinner, and her sister telephoned during the morning to say that Pearl had needed the services of a doctor.

"It's that wretched Jerome!" Elaine, who had taken the phone call, reported. "He didn't give her a ring—he gave her an umbrella!"

Kelsey laughed, and Elaine turned on him furiously.

"How can you be so heartless! On Christmas Day, too! Meta says Pearl had hysterics and the doctor had to give her a sedative. Pearl had her heart set on a ring."

He hadn't meant to be heartless, Kelsey apologized. It was probably a nervous reaction.

"I was keyed up about the ring," he explained, when his wife still looked suspicious. "Pearl talked so much about it, it's been on my mind. An umbrella seems deliberately insulting, doesn't it? If I was Pearl, I'd cross Jerome off my list."

Amanda found Pearl vaguely irritating in the slow march of days that led from Christmas to the new year. A figure of gloom in the background was the way she thought of her, for unconsciously she had counted on Pearl to be a sympathetic listener. After one attempt to interest her in the glories of the delectable white chiffon with a silver belt and the silver pumps with high heels that represented a battle fought and won, Amanda gave up.

"We have to have dinner at five thirty tonight," Elaine warned her husband on New Year's Eve. "No, not because Pearl is going out. It's Amanda."

Kelsey remonstrated that Amanda wouldn't be leaving before nine or half past. "She's been washing her hair all day to have it dry by nine."

"Well, she wants plenty of time, so she won't feel rushed. Don't upset her at the table, or she won't eat a thing. And be sure to tell her she looks lovely when she's dressed."

Amanda said that she didn't see why people had to eat dinner "regardless."

"I'll bet if the world was falling apart, we'd sit down to dinner and Daddy would say the salt shakers weren't filled just before the roof was blown off," she grumbled, taking her place at the table that night.

Elaine said, "Don't say a word about the salt. Pearl has enough to bear." She glanced apprehensively toward the swinging door. "I'd like to take that umbrella and beat Jerome over the head with it."

"You couldn't," Amanda said.

She wore a blue robe and kept pushing the sleeves up. Her hair was set on rollers, and Kelsey, whose list of instructions had included an admonition not to mention *hair*, averted his eyes after one look.

"Why can't your mother beat Jerome with the umbrella?" Kelsey asked, with a substitute flourish of the carving knife.

Pearl had burned the umbrella, Amanda said. She had paid the building superintendent to break it up in small pieces and then had dropped them, one by one, into the incinerator.

"Like a kind of funeral service," Amanda said. "The super

wanted the umbrella to give his wife, but Pearl wouldn't let him have it."

Elaine protested that it was wicked to destroy something useful, but Kelsey insisted that the news of the umbrella's funeral was a relief.

"Pearl's a wise woman. That umbrella was unlucky—probably had a curse put on it at the factory," he said. "Amanda, you're not eating your dinner."

"I can't eat any more—I have too much to do." Amanda sounded alarmed. "Besides, I'm not hungry."

They let her go, and Pearl, bringing in the dessert and coffee a quarter of an hour later, asked if it would be safe to take down the ironing board.

"Amanda set it up before dinner, in case she needed to use it in a hurry," Pearl explained. "And I had to move everything off the second shelf in my refrigerator—she had to have space for the box with her corsage in it. If the pudding isn't set, it's because she's opened the refrigerator door twenty times to look at her orchid."

"Hideous flower," said Kelsey absently. "I hope this Dave Wilson isn't a show-off."

Two couples made everything much safer, Elaine assured him. In a group of four young people, each pair influenced the other. Double dating encouraged steadiness, she urged, beginning to flounder under her husband's skeptical gaze.

"Well, I want a word with Amanda before this young man gets here," Kelsey said. "You know the people who are giving the party, Pussy?"

"The Gilvey Hunters. They have a son and daughter, and the girl goes to Miss Mary's." Elaine broke off as Amanda, still in the blue robe, appeared in the doorway.

"Is that your best perfume in the atomizer, Mother?" Amanda's eyes were enormous, dark and sad.

"Come here a minute—you have plenty of time," said Kelsey. "I want to impress something on your mind. Sit down and listen to me."

She seated herself obediently in a chair near him and folded her hands in her lap. He was going to be tiresome, but she had no intention of opposing anything he said. One of Mirabelle Marilyn Meeks's most repeated warnings was not to quarrel with parents just before going out on a date.

"Your mother and I," Kelsey said, "are not going out this evening. We plan to stay at home. We'll be right here, all the time. If anything happens, if you need help of any kind, phone home—we'll be here and awake. Will you remember?"

Amanda blinked. "Nothing is going to happen."

"The car might break down," Elaine said.

"Yes, the car might break down," Kelsey repeated. "Or you might not want Dave Wilson to bring you home—I don't think you know him very well. You can always phone home. That's what we want you to remember."

"I hope I'm fat enough next year to wear an off-shoulder dress," Amanda said.

By nine o'clock, she could admit that she was ready. From her thick, dark hair, brushed high without a parting and rolled into a page-boy bob, to her silver-slippered feet, she looked unbearably vulnerable and shining with the glimmer of expectant dreams.

"High heels come natural to me; I could wear them every day," she said hopefully.

She had brought her gloves, the white silk evening bag that had been her grandmother's Christmas gift, and the black velvet coat, borrowed from her mother, into the living room, so that she would be ready for instant flight.

"Why not be a little more subtle?" suggested Elaine, eyeing these preparations with obvious surprise. "Or isn't it the thing to keep him waiting a few moments?"

Amanda, intensely nervous, flushed. She was still not sure that Dave would come up to the apartment, or, not finding her in the lobby, would not go to the party without her—or with another girl. Patty had reported that he had been "furious" to hear that he was expected to meet Amanda's parents, and in her momentary irritation Patty had revealed that Amanda, as she had suspected, had not been Dave's first choice.

"He's been going with Helena Carr; she's eighteen and in the first year of college," Patty had said. "They had a fight—

and well, you know he must like you, or you wouldn't have come into his mind."

The familiar creaking sound made by the elevator set Amanda's heart to beating rapidly. The palms of her hands felt damp. Her eyes turned frantically to her mother, and Elaine smiled.

"You look absolutely lovely, darling. Have a grand time." Heroically Elaine kept still about the mascara, which she loathed.

Dave Wilson, tall and handsome, was wearing a tuxedo, Elaine thought. She couldn't be certain. The speed with which he bowed to her, shook hands with Kelsey, whisked Amanda into her coat and out of the door left both parents slightly dazed. He must have tipped Albert to hold the elevator, because it was waiting when the young people dashed into the hall.

"He did call for her, didn't he?" asked Kelsey, closing the door.

Elaine murmured that Dave Wilson might have been trying to catch a plane.

"He muttered something about his car—I think. I wanted to ask him if the other couple were downstairs, or if he is going to pick them up."

It was one way to avoid the boring conversation of the aged, Kelsey admitted, but he didn't like it.

"I'd give something to know whether he put Amanda up to that trick of being ready to take off like a bat out of hell. Well, Pussy, at least we must face it—we are now on the sunset path."

It would be nice, Elaine thought, if Midge Sully could hear him. Not that the nonsense about the sunset path meant anything, but such remarks tended to rule out romance. Middle age had its compensations, she supposed, and one would be the knowledge that she no longer had to worry about her husband's attraction for an old sweetheart.

Unfortunately, the dangerous age for Kelsey might be expected to last for several more years, according to Naida Steckner and to the various magazine writers who upheld her analysis. The fact that he spoke of growing old showed his psychological need for reassurance, Naida said.

"As a rule, another woman's flattery will carry more weight than yours, but you have twice the opportunity to inflate his ego," Naida had elaborated. "A man your husband's age may not look old or feel old, but he's getting the early shocks, mostly from young people to whom he *is* old."

Kelsey, reading under the light of the living-room lamp, didn't look old. He was forty-five, and Amanda might think him ancient. Elaine, who would be forty on her next birthday, reflected that Amanda probably expected her to crumble soon. Had Mama seemed elderly to her teen-aged daughter? Elaine had a guilty feeling that one's mother never had been young.

The evening passed quickly. Neither she nor Kelsey had ever entertained much or gone to gay parties on New Year's Eve. Elaine put Amanda's tangled room in order and turned down the bed for her—the child would be dead for sleep. An hour's work on the needlepoint for the dining-room chairs— she might be nearly forty, but she didn't need glasses—and then she and Kelsey toasted each other in sherry because for years her mother had made it a part of the ceremony she cherished. They called her at the hospital—the indulgent convalescent wing had given consent—and after that they had only to wait for Amanda.

"I should have told that kid to bring her home at a definite time," Kelsey growled when the mantel clock chimed half past one.

Elaine was reminded of Amanda's complaint that a striking clock called too much attention to the time.

"Why didn't you want him to have a deadline?" Kelsey asked, having compared his watch with the clock.

Elaine murmured uneasily that New Year's Eve was a special occasion.

"Mirabelle Marilyn Meeks says you have to make exceptions. I don't suppose the party really began until midnight."

"Damn Mirabelle Marilyn!" Kelsey glared. "It's bad enough to have Amanda quote her at every turn, without you repeating her nauseating drivel. The woman's a fool."

"I'll make some coffee," Elaine said.

She was in the kitchen when the phone rang. Her heart lurched in sudden, sickening fear and she ran through the dining room, back into the living room, pursued by a definite terror.

"Right! We'll be there in twenty minutes," Kelsey said and replaced the handset.

"Amanda?" Elaine gulped for air.

"She's all right. That is, there's been no accident." Kelsey pushed her gently into a chair. "I'll get the car out—no use trying to ring up a cab tonight."

Elaine shivered.

"Where is she? What happened? Where are you going?"

"We have to go to Homewood," Kelsey said, mentioning one of the nearer suburbs. "Put on your fur coat and drink a cup of coffee if it's ready. You'll feel better if you walk to the garage with me than if you waited for me to bring the car around."

The absence of excitement in his face and voice steadied her. Something had happened, but Amanda was safe, or he would not be so quiet. At the same time the grim set of his jaw discouraged further questions. She hurriedly made two cups of instant coffee and left Kelsey to drink his scalding and black while she shrugged on her beaver coat and tied a scarf over her hair.

They walked the two blocks to the brilliantly lighted garage, and Elaine noticed how quickly the surprised attendant switched from jocular comment to subdued efficient service. Evidently he was practiced in reading Kelsey's moods, too.

Snow had been predicted, but fortunately the weather remained dry and clear. It was bitterly cold, and Kelsey switched on the heater. He seemed not to hear the blaring horns, or to notice the heavy traffic and the crowds still milling noisily through the downtown streets.

Elaine kept silent until they were on the throughway leading to the string of suburban towns.

"Who telephoned?" she ventured.

Kelsey, his eyes fixed on a sports car full of shouting, singing youngsters that had just passed him, said, "The police."

Amanda was all right, he repeated; there had been no accident. Trouble, of course, or they wouldn't have been sent for, but he didn't know what they would find. It had seemed more important to get to the police station than to ask questions.

"But, the police!" Elaine floundered helplessly. "It sounds horrible. Amanda must be scared to death."

According to the police lieutenant, she had been very much alive, Kelsey said. He made a right turn, and an instant later two green lights glowed steadily among the flickering neon signs of Homewood's main street.

The interior of the police station was neat and orderly; just what Elaine had expected she could not have told, but presumably she had connected law offenders with dust and dirt. She and Kelsey walked directly into a room where a young man in uniform was seated at a long table, with two other policemen watching him as he talked into a phone.

At the other end of the table Amanda sat with Dave Wilson and another girl and a young man. Elaine realized that she had never before seen this couple, the other half of the double date.

The man at the phone held up his hand to signal Kelsey to wait. Amanda stared woodenly at her parents, her face so white that the lipstick made a grotesque smear, like blood. Dave Wilson seemed to have trouble in focusing his eyes and he blinked stupidly. The other girl was crying in deep, gasping gulps, painful to hear. Amanda kept patting her on the shoulder, an automatic gesture that might have been going on a long time. On the other side of the girl, her escort huddled in a chair, one arm on the table, his head on his arm.

"Mr. Carpenter?" The handset dropped into place, and the police officer stood up. "Will you and your wife come in here for a moment? I'd like to talk to you."

He crossed the room, opened a door, and stood aside for them to enter a small, well-lighted room, evidently his office. The door closed with a decisive click.

197

"I'm Lieutenant Vail," the young man said, indicating two chairs near the flat-topped desk. "So far you're the only parents I've been able to reach."

He waited for a moment after they were seated, his gray eyes appraising them.

"You know where I can get hold of Mr. and Mrs. Wilson, or Mr. and Mrs. Dykes?" he asked. "No, if their phones don't answer, I suppose it's anyone's guess."

Kelsey said very quietly, "Was it the car?"

"Your daughter was driving," the lieutenant said.

Elaine cried out in protest. "She doesn't know how to drive."

"There must be a mistake. Amanda is not quite fifteen," Kelsey said.

The lieutenant had heard the complete story from Amanda herself. He had gathered from her account that the party had been more sophisticated than she had expected. Some of the guests had brought extra liquor, and the parents of the young host had stayed only long enough to welcome the guests before going on to some entertainment of their own.

"Well, this Dave Wilson is a decent young fellow, I think, but he's the type who gets sick after one drink. He was your girl's date?" The lieutenant nodded. "I thought so. The other lad—Hal Conway—doesn't know when to stop. He passed out and never did hear the New Year's bells."

Dave Wilson had known at the end of the celebration that he was in no condition to drive. He could get no help from his buddy. Neither of the girls knew how to drive; both were under age, anyway.

"But Amanda has never handled a car," Kelsey broke in. "It would be bad enough in the daytime, but at night—I just can't believe it. She'd be terrified."

"She was," the lieutenant said. "The kid has guts."

Dave Wilson had had a brain storm, the matter-of-fact policeman-voice continued. He told Amanda that she would have to drive and that he would tell her what to do. They bundled Hal Conway and his girl into the back seat and Amanda took the wheel.

"One of my men spotted this car zigzagging down the highway and he says it was God's mercy that it didn't hit something—a tree, a light pole, or another car full of other crazy kids. When he signaled them to pull over, he thought it was going in the ditch."

The lieutenant cleared his throat and looked away from the tense, absorbed faces confronting him.

"Your daughter's hands gripped the steering wheel so hard, we had to pry them loose. The other girl was having hysterics and screaming at the top of her lungs. But all of them except Hal Conway, who still doesn't know what happened, were indignant to think that the police would stoop so low as to try to get into communication with their parents."

The office was still for a moment then. Elaine, her throat dry, felt as if she had been sitting there so long that her body might have turned to stone.

"We were at home. We stayed at home so that if Amanda needed help, we would be there."

Kelsey broke the silence. "She knew it. Can you tell me, Lieutenant, why children will risk their lives rather than turn to a parent for help? Can you tell me why?"

# Chapter 14

"She was glad to see us, I think." Elaine looked about her mother's room for a place to put a Japanese garden—the sixth, planted in a pottery bowl, that Pauline had received —but saw no vacant spot. "You'd think they might have window sills in a hospital," Elaine grumbled.

Pauline said that the children's ward doted on Japanese gardens. The others had gone down there, and a nurse would be glad to take this one.

"Are you worrying about Amanda, Elaine? You're losing weight."

"Well, I haven't lost twenty pounds and you have." Elaine took the chair beside the bed. "Dr. Cannon doesn't want you to lose any more, does he?"

There was no pleasing a doctor, Pauline said. Dr. Cannon had been after her for years to lose pounds, and now that she had obliged, he was even more insistent that she build herself up.

"For minor surgery. One more little item and then I can go home, he says. My chart indicates that this trying interval is about over." Pauline ruffled the magazines strewn on the bed. "Amanda phoned me during her lunch period today, when I was in the sun parlor. She has a cold, hasn't she?"

Amanda had caught cold New Year's Eve, but she had been more fortunate than Mary Dykes, who had just missed having pneumonia.

"She was the other girl in the car, Mama. The Wilsons have done everything they could. They have a daughter, you know, and they realize how we feel. Dave Wilson apologized to Kelsey—I'm sure his father sent him. And Amanda has been so quiet. The police lieutenant's talk made a deep impression on her. I guess on all of them except that boy who was too drunk to hear a word."

Lucie had been shocked when she heard that the police had lectured the culprits severely, Elaine continued; Kelsey and his sister had had a violent argument. It was, Lucie had said, all wrong to frighten a child, no matter what the circumstances. If the police had had the faintest smattering of child psychology, they would have known that blaming a child taught him nothing.

"Of course Lucie really knows a lot about psychology," Elaine admitted. "And the lieutenant did frighten them. I never saw Amanda so frightened before."

Pauline said that Lucie was a fool and that to be afraid of the law might be considered proof of Amanda's common sense.

"Kelsey says it's a relief to know that someone besides Mirabelle Marilyn Meeks can influence Amanda," Elaine said. "But the truth is, Mama, that he was more frightened that night than Amanda was—we both were. I had Tully Hallam on my mind every minute after that phone call."

She had more on her mind than Tully Hallam now, but it was nothing that she could talk over with her mother. Mama, Elaine reflected when she had left the hospital, was devoted to Kelsey; it would be cruel to shake her faith in him. Mama was probably incapable of imagining Kelsey vulnerable to the—the wiles of Midge, and the fact that Kelsey stubbornly refused to confer with a marriage counselor would not change Mama's opinion of him.

Although a light snow was falling, Elaine decided to walk home. She needed time to put her thoughts in order. All that Naida Steckner ever suggested was that Kelsey agree "to look at the situation objectively." Certainly that was not much to ask of a husband. But after breakfast that morning, when she had as tactfully as possible asked him if he wouldn't consent to at least one interview with a marriage counselor—any counselor—he had heatedly refused.

"Why should I?" He had been standing by his desk, checking his briefcase, when she followed him into his study.

"It never hurts to talk over a situation objectively." Elaine had practiced that sentence.

Kelsey, without glancing up from his papers, had said, "What situation?"

"Oh, if you're going to be like that!" Elaine forgot to be objective. "How can you be so stubborn!"

He had closed the briefcase then and looked at her, his blue eyes concerned.

"I don't think this Steckner woman is good for you, Pussy," he had said. "I've never thought so, but you seemed to like to talk to her. Now you're a bundle of nerves; you haven't recovered from the shock Amanda gave us. How would you like to take your mother south for a couple of months? Or, if the responsibility is too much, go down for a rest alone."

Elaine stepped off a curb with a jolt, recovered her balance, and stepped back as the light changed. She had not expected Kelsey to be so crude; in her mind she had thought of all his moves as being adroit. He must think that he had married a fool if he believed that he could dispose of her so easily, leaving him free to play around with Midge.

Unfortunately Naida Steckner had gone to Florida for a short stay—widowed, she had no marital problems—and was not available for consultation. Elaine wondered for a moment whether she could accomplish anything by asking someone else for advice, perhaps Lucie's psychologist. But it would be something like changing doctors, and repeating the history of her marriage to a stranger might be tedious and difficult. And apparently the magazines, too, would be satisfied with nothing less than her life story, so it was useless to think of obtaining a prompt response from the marriage "directors" on their staffs.

II

"Where do you get your perfectly awful ideas?" Pauline asked, trying to speak sternly and at the same time keep her voice low.

She sat in a wheel chair in the convalescents' sun parlor and Amanda perched on a hassock beside her. The room was comfortably filled with patients and their visiting friends.

Amanda bit carefully into a chocolate cookie. Grandmother's friends seemed to think that the hospital starved her and that it was up to them to help her gain weight.

"You don't realize that I'm interested in human relationships," Amanda said. "Anyone can tell that Mother hates the sight of Midge Cutter. And why?"

"Your mother wants you to call her Mrs. Cutter," mumbled Pauline in a frantic attempt to assume her grandmotherly role.

Amanda smiled tolerantly. Her mother, she said, was jealous of Midge and the reason she was jealous was because Midge had once been engaged to Daddy.

"It's the tug of the past that calls to them both. I mean Daddy and Midge. Mostly Midge, I think. But I'm loyal to Mother, and if they're divorced, I shall ask the judge to let me live with her."

"Your father and mother are a devoted couple." Pauline's quiet authority was impressive. "You must be out of your mind."

Amanda sampled a cream-filled cookie, but said nothing.

"Do you know Mrs. Cutter's birth date?" Pauline sat up straighter. "Or even which month she was born in?"

She thought it was November, Amanda said. But it could be May. Something Lucie had once said made her connect May with Midge.

"You could look up both signs, Gram. I don't suppose there's any use in me trying to talk to Daddy. Do you think I ought to say anything to him?"

Pauline surveyed her granddaughter for a moment in speechless astonishment. Amanda, in a bright-red jersey dress, a box of cookies on her lap, looked nearer twelve than fifteen. In spite of her serious expression, Pauline was irresistibly reminded of a little girl pretending to be grown up. She thought of a great many things that might be said, but settled for the simplest negative.

"No!"

Amanda nodded, and helped herself to another cookie.

"That's what Mirabelle Marilyn Meeks told me," she said.

For a moment she seemed depressed, but then remembered that she had been charged with a message from Pearl.

"She's through with Jerome, she says, and she wants to know if there's anything new in sight for her. She's coming to see you tomorrow."

But Pearl, who arrived the next afternoon, bringing a chocolate cake—Jerome's favorite, she remarked gloomily—revealed that she had not been so definite. She was not one to burn her bridges, she said, until she could see a little ahead.

"You're coming into better vibrations next month," Pauline comforted her. "A good time to start new ventures. Romance is favored."

Pearl, perhaps recalling the umbrella episode, was cautious.

"You're not making it up?" she said.

"Amanda told me you were coming today—I've been working on your horoscope for an hour. I must say you're not very grateful—"

Pearl's quick apology appeased Pauline, who began to wonder if she herself had expressed convincing gratitude for the mammoth cake.

"It's a beautiful cake, but you know I can't begin to finish it before it gets dry," she said. "Pearl, don't you think it would be nice to give some of it to those four ladies in the room at the end of the hall? You know them—I was in talking with them the last time you came to see me."

She added that the daily forecast for Pearl's sign indicated that new friends might be helpful.

Pearl, sociable by nature, approved the suggestion. Under Pauline's direction she cut four generous wedges of the three-layer cake, arranged them on a plate, and covered it with a paper napkin. All the patients, Pauline said, had plastic forks handy; they were prepared to welcome snacks in the convalescent wing.

Pauline had expected Pearl to return within a few minutes after delivering the cake, but it was nearly an hour before she came back. Her eyes were bright, her face flushed, and she moved with a kind of buoyancy that Amanda had once described as her "hop-skip step." It had been weeks since Pearl had shown any inclination to hop-skip.

"Guess you thought I was lost, Miz Ives." The rejuvenated Pearl seated herself in a chair close to the bed. "We got to talking, and you know how time flies."

Most visitors loved to talk, Pauline thought, moving one leg tentatively to see if her hip still ached. It did. She had walked too much that morning, in an effort to prove that the wheel chair could be discarded, and in consequence must lie on the bed for the rest of the day.

"Did they like your cake?" she asked.

The ladies had been crazy about the cake, Pearl said modestly. But she had been a little embarrassed, because one of them had had a visitor.

"I wanted to come back and cut him a piece—I knew you wouldn't mind and, anyway, I can always make you another cake," Pearl said. "But he wouldn't hear of it. Happened that his aunt can't eat much sweet stuff, so she gave him her piece. He said he never ate better cake in his life."

Pauline blinked. "He? Was there a man there?"

A very nice fellow, Pearl assured her. Not too young, middle-aged, in fact, easygoing, and a great kidder.

"He drives a light truck and he's in the neighborhood almost every day. He drops in to see his aunt—Miz Hermer, the little blonde woman who had a hysterectomy and then broke her arm."

Pearl had learned that one of the other patients in the four-bed room—a Mrs. Frazer, whose husband had "walked out on her"—would be forty-six years old the next day.

"The ladies want to give her a party—they know her husband won't show up—and I promised I'd make a cake and bring it tomorrow afternoon. A little later than this. Luckily it's my day off. You sure were right about my horoscope, Miz Ives. The nephew's name is Nelse Turner. He's coming to the party."

"I'm not surprised," Elaine said that night when at dinner Kelsey discovered that the salt shakers had been filled with pepper. "Pearl has a new beau."

*205*

Kelsey said, "Good for her!" and Amanda asked if she had "ditched" Jerome.

It was still in the tentative stage, Elaine admitted, but her mother had telephoned her the details and they added up to one of Pearl's romances.

"I don't think I can stand it, Kelsey. I simply haven't the strength to go through with another of Pearl's affairs. The man's middle-aged, she told Mama, and that means he's married or divorced or something. It takes so little to start Pearl off."

Every cloud had a silver lining, Kelsey reminded his wife. True, Pearl in love was apt to be annoyingly absent-minded, and when the course of romance met rough going, she was less than a ray of sunshine around the house.

"But, in the beginning at least, when the clouds are pink and she's sure *this* is the right man, she can't do enough for us. Her energy is boundless, her cooking improves. And that's more than can be said for most of those who dream they dwelt in marble halls and wake to reality."

Elaine said, "You don't have to listen to her. I got so sick of hearing Jerome's name, I was ready to scream. Now it will be Nelse Turner, and I'm shuddering in advance."

Amanda asked if anyone had ever heard Jerome's last name and, answered in the negative, said that Pearl had psychological reasons for concealing it. Psychological reasons were always extremely interesting, Amanda informed her parents, and explained "everything."

Kelsey, who had sprinkled his salad heavily with pepper, looked irritated.

"What do you mean by 'everything'?" he demanded.

"I mean what a person does," Amanda said. "It may look wrong, but it isn't, not if you understand his psychological reasons for doing it."

Pearl came in with a fresh plate of hot biscuits—she made hot breads three times a day when in love—and Amanda returned to the contemplation of her hopelessly confused thoughts. According to Mirabelle Marilyn Meeks's latest advice, it would be wrong to blame Midge for her mother's distress. No one was to blame, no one was ever to blame for anything that happened, and that was a little difficult to think out. Amanda would have liked to talk it over with her father, but Mirabelle had pointed out that adults, especially parents, were conservatives who shrank from examining new ideas. It was the young, with flexible minds, who must refuse to conform. "Accept nothing, examine everything" had been Mirabelle's conclusion to a long column that had been inspired, she said, by a letter from a teen-ager and signed "Bewildered."

Amanda had been more bewildered than ever after reading this response, because it made no attempt to answer her question: Should she have a talk with Midge? Mirabelle evidently did not have much faith in the value of the spoken word. Amanda resolved to write to her again and ask her opinion of anonymous letters. Or, if she disliked anonymous letters, she might approve a letter with the address given and name signed.

## III

Naida Steckner, lightly tanned from the Florida sun, said that yes, she had had a complete rest, and yes, she was glad to get back to her office.

"There's something about helping people that can't be disregarded," she confided. "I can stay away just so long, and then the knowledge that I am needed draws me and leisure becomes almost intolerable."

She smiled at Elaine, visibly relaxing in the high-backed consultant's chair.

"And now, my dear, what can I do for you?"

She listened without interruption. Probably none of her clients realized it, but they talked to no one else who listened to them in complete silence. Doctors and lawyers asked a hundred questions, bosom friends made hysterical comments, husbands, of course, plunged into argument. Naida Steckner simply listened.

She said, when Elaine had finished, "This sister-in-law of yours—how reliable is she?"

"Lucie? She knows Midge Sully—she can't be mistaken."

"But is she the hysterical type? Given to dramatization? I think you told me she lives in the suburbs, and young matrons in the suburbs are frequently victims of monotonous routine. Your sister-in-law, perhaps unconsciously, may be trying to inject a little drama into her daily program."

Elaine recollected that Lucie complained of being stifled by her deadly round of duties as a suburban housewife. Still . . .

"I just don't think she's the type to dream things up. She has to *see* a thing before she believes it."

"Lacks imagination." Naida's long forefinger pigeonholed Lucie with a gesture. "Well, if this Midge is seeing your husband, I don't feel it's advisable for you to do anything about it. Not yet."

Elaine shook her head. "I can't wait forever. Kelsey wants me to go south and stay a couple of months. I'm sure Midge put that idea in his mind."

She didn't have to go, Naida pointed out. And nothing would be lost by postponing all action for another week or so.

"Say nothing to your husband. Make no contacts with Midge. And do come in, say a week or ten days from today, and we'll talk it over and devise a plan." Naida made a note on her calendar. "Don't worry," she said.

Her secretary at the desk in the outer office was a young woman with cocoa-brown hair and eyes to match. She had made the appointment on the phone for Elaine, explaining that Miss Bittel, who had been with Naida for years, had taken a six months' leave.

"The fee is now twenty dollars, Mrs. Carpenter," the young secretary said with a carefully arranged smile.

She was silly to let the extra five dollars be so irritating, Elaine scolded herself, but if Naida Steckner thought that she intended to keep that second appointment when nothing, absolutely nothing, had been accomplished in this morning's interview, she wasn't much of a psychologist. Elaine, halfway home on the bus, remembered one of her mother's old-fashioned axioms: "If you want something done, do it yourself." She had wasted all the time she intended to; from now on she would be committed to a course of action. The realization that there was no one to whom she could tell what she intended to do—and what she intended to do she didn't know—gave her a feeling of momentary panic. No matter how desperately she needed advice, there was no one to whom she could turn. She considered briefly the wisdom of seeking another marriage counselor, a stranger, but again a reluctance to spend time filling in the marital background deterred her. Besides, they probably all charged twenty dollars for a half hour now.

Over her solitary lunch—waffles with cherry sauce, because Pearl and the truck driver had had their first movie date— Elaine tried to reach a decision. She had Lucie's assurance that Midge Sully came into town three mornings a week— Monday, Wednesday, Friday—and Lucie was sure that each time she went to Kelsey's building. Very odd, Lucie thought, but if she connected the routine with Kelsey or his office, she had never said so.

"All I want to know," Elaine had told Naida Steckner, "is whether she goes to Kelsey's office and why. She rushes right home; at least Lucie says she's always back by two thirty."

The Thrift Shop would have to manage without her for three mornings—she would give them the afternoons. Tomorrow was Wednesday and she intended to be in the lobby of Kelsey's office building by half past nine. Lucie had recollected vaguely that she had seen Midge usually "around ten o'clock." Lucie herself liked to reach Kelsey in his office before he would be tied up with tiresome appointments.

It was essential, of course, that Midge should not recognize her. Elaine, planning a disguise, found it annoying to remember that both Pearl and Albert were likely to notice any drastic changes in her appearance. She solved that problem by taking her dark glasses and a shabby coat—saved for the Thrift Shop collection of carpet rags—and a pair of scuffed shoes down to her mother's apartment. After breakfast the next morning, she dressed there; then, to escape Albert's sharp eyes, she walked down the service stairs and through the tradesmen's entrance to the street.

She had put on more lipstick than usual and had used rouge and felt confident that the make-up, together with the flowered scarf she had tied over her hair, would successfully disguise her. But she had not been prepared for the possibility of attracting unwelcome interest, and when, at the bus stop, a bearded old man with watery eyes mumbled, "Hi, Toots, going my way?" she yanked open the door of an empty cab that was waiting for the traffic light to change, and stepped in blindly.

The driver shot forward into traffic as Elaine slammed the door shut. "That'll learn him," he said, without turning his head.

She gave Kelsey's office address. When she studied her face in the mirror of her compact, the rouge had deepened to a violent purplish-red that shocked her. She scrubbed at it surreptitiously with a tissue, but decided to leave the lipstick alone. Mama would have said that she had enough on to paint a barn, but plenty of women had heavily lipsticked mouths.

The cab stopped before she realized they had reached the Talbot Building. Remembering that Kelsey had told her a cabby disliked "short hauls," she increased her customary tip, and to her fury the man winked at her as she handed him the change. Her hands were shaking as she felt in her bag for her dark glasses, and she dashed into the entrance of the building so fast that she found herself jammed into a compartment of the revolving door with a man obviously not expecting to share the space.

Elaine's murmured apology scarcely dented his annoyed astonishment, but she extricated herself thankfully and strolled with forced composure to the directory framed on one of the long walls. She studied this, with her back to the elevators, until her flushed face cooled and she could be sure that she was no longer nervous.

The lobby cut through the building to an entrance on another street, and a constant stream of pedestrians flowed both ways. Elaine stood quietly beside a drinking fountain recessed in the wall opposite the bank of elevators. It had not occurred to her that Kelsey might have business outside his office, and when he stepped from an elevator, passing so close to her that she could have put her hand on his sleeve, she almost betrayed herself. He did glance over his shoulder at the odd, half-strangled noise that rose in her throat, but continued to walk briskly on.

Irritation and gloom descended upon Elaine. Had she wasted her time? Presumably Kelsey did not expect Midge this morning, or he would have remained at his desk where he belonged. On the other hand, he might be keeping an appointment that would allow him to return for a rendezvous only slightly delayed. He and Midge undoubtedly knew what they were doing, but she, Elaine, was left in maddening uncertainty.

Fifteen minutes later her feet had begun to hurt. She imagined that the elevator starter was eying her with suspicion. Midge was late, or perhaps Lucie had been mistaken about her routine. Elaine decided that at the end of another five minutes she would give up, at least for that day.

She looked toward the revolving doors and saw a compact contingent of women spilling out; the three doors turned in unison, and at each revolution a woman popped into view, until the lobby seemed to be filled with them. In spite of the dark glasses, Elaine recognized Midge at once—"I'd know her feet anywhere," she later told Lucie. Nearly all the women wore dark glasses; they were almost a year-round fad, and Amanda had asked for a pair and been refused. Elaine suspected that she wore them on her way to and from school.

The chattering crowd surged forward to the elevators, and Elaine deftly inserted herself between two short, stout figures and was carried along directly behind Midge, who talked in a low voice to another woman wearing a towering fur hat. Elaine relaxed, confident that she would know when Midge left the elevator at Kelsey's floor—the sixteenth. But the elevator had passed the sixteenth floor before she realized that it had made no stops. When, an instant later, the door slid back, she trooped into the twentieth-floor corridor with the others, simply because she could think of nothing else to do.

"Lovely day, isn't it?" said a woman beside her, peering

at her through dark glasses, mouth shaped into a friendly smile.

Where was Midge going? Where were they all going? Elaine had once been caught in an undertow at the beach, and she had the same sensation now of having lost her footing and of being sucked down into water that whirled.

"Did I talk to you last week?" A smartly dressed young woman, beautifully made up, her dark glasses framed in wide gold bands, spoke to Elaine as the crowd struggled through an office doorway. "No? Well I shouldn't ask of course—we're not supposed to know."

The office was large, carpeted in gray broadloom, and furnished simply with a small table desk and rows of chairs of the type used in lecture classrooms. A woman whose resemblance to Naida Steckner was so marked that Elaine was startled sat at the desk. She said nothing until everyone was seated and then touched a bell on the desk which rang a single, soft note. Immediately the room was stilled.

"We have a number of new members added to our circle today," she said in the voice of a trained speaker. "For that reason, before roll call, I will outline, very briefly, our methods and aims."

Elaine looked away—the woman couldn't be a sister of Naida's, could she?—and saw that Midge Sully was staring at her with disconcerting intentness.

". . . organized as a circle for self-help," the woman at the desk was saying. "These sessions afford each member an opportunity to seek advice and to give it. Each of you is expected alternately to talk freely of your problems and to listen sympathetically to another's troubles. When you bring your secret fears out into the open, you will find that they dissolve."

According to routine, she said, she would first read the names of those who were to discuss their problems, then the names of those who were to serve as listeners. The reading was also to serve as a roll call, since it was necessary to make sure that the group would be evenly paired off.

Elaine listened as if mesmerized. She realized vaguely that she must be witnessing a class in what Lucie had called group psychiatry, or psychology; the terms remained hopelessly mixed in Elaine's mind. Not until four or five of the women had answered to their names did she begin to wonder how she was to account for her attendance in a class in which her registration was apparently taken for granted.

"Mrs. Stanley—" The speaker paused. "Mrs. Stanley?"

A small, blonde woman leaned forward and touched Elaine lightly on the knee.

"Oh!" Elaine gulped. "Here!" she said and was vexed because all the others had said "Present!"

As the last name was called, the women began to bustle about, rearranging the chairs. The little blonde who had saved Elaine awkward explanations evidently liked to talk.

"I knew you must be Mrs. Stanley when no one else answered. I remember you signing up last week. It's so much less expensive than individual treatments, don't you think? Isn't it funny, we're both assigned to be listeners today—your first and my fifth time. But if you're in a bad way, you can get a transfer. Mrs. Wade will assign someone to listen to you."

She was very young, Elaine decided, probably about Lucie's age.

"What do you mean, if I'm in a bad way?"

"Desperate," said the girl with relish. "I've been that way myself. In my case it comes from living shut up with the children. Middle-aged women are mostly worried about their husbands—I think I've got one heading my way now."

A stout, gray-haired woman, dragging a chair behind her, halted, her eyes behind the dark glasses turning from Elaine to the blond.

"Mrs. Parker?" she ventured.

The blond identified herself and they retreated to a cleared space along the window wall. Elaine turned and found Midge at her elbow.

"You're alloted to me, Mrs. Stanley," Midge said.

"I'm allotted to you?" Elaine repeated.

"You're my listener," Midge said. "I've got two chairs lined up in a corner, if someone hasn't grabbed them."

She started off across the room, and Elaine followed her,

brushing past women already seated and talking to each other in low tones. A confused feeling that it was all some kind of a masquerade and that presently the woman who looked so much like Naida Steckner would have them all dancing to music made Elaine glance nervously at the blank faces around her. A room filled with women dancing somberly in dark glasses would have a ghostly effect.

"We mustn't waste time, Mrs. Stanley." Midge indicated two empty chairs backed into a corner. "I have to catch an early train today. I have made up my mind to hold nothing back—Mrs. Wade urges a complete catharsis."

Panic assailed Elaine. She wanted to turn and run, but instead she sat down, then jumped convulsively as Midge pulled her chair so close that they were knee to knee.

*If she tells me about Kelsey, I shall scream!* Elaine thought, and the idea was intolerable.

"Look, you ought to know something before you begin." She took a deep breath, put up a hand to her glasses, but left them in place—she would feel naked under the gaze of all those strangers. "I'm not Mrs. Stanley," she whispered.

Midge said, "Don't be an utter fool. Of course you're not Mrs. Stanley; you're Elaine Carpenter. We all use fictitious names. Mrs. Wade thinks anonymity releases inhibitions. I knew you right away."

"But you don't want to talk to me," Elaine protested.

"Why not?"

"Well, I should think—that is—it seems to me it might be embarrassing to—to both of us."

She couldn't afford to waste time arguing, Midge said, and her brisk tone suggested a woman rolling up her mental sleeves, preparatory to tackling a job that demanded effort.

"If you'd ever taken any of Mrs. Wade's lectures, you'd know that it doesn't matter a damn who I talk to. Or should that be whom?"

"I think it's 'whom,'" Elaine said.

"Whom, then." Midge stared intently through her dark glasses. "I have an hour to talk, then the bell rings and you have half an hour for comment, and after that Mrs. Wade

214

gives group counsel for half an hour. You understand the setup now?"

Elaine nodded and instinctively closed her eyes.

"It's Lige, my husband. I'm almost certain he's growing tired of me," said Midge in a sudden rush of words. "He's a wonderful man in many ways, and I've never felt that I deserved him. But I don't feel that the woman who's trying to get him—Washington is full of prowling cats—is any better than I am, or that she can make him happy."

Midge paused long enough to take a silver pillbox from her bag and help herself to a cough drop.

"This woman who's making a play for Lige in Washington," she resumed, "is good-looking, in a brassy kind of way. But she has such homely feet, she toes out to the extent you might call her deformed. . . ."

## IV

Elaine, floating homeward in a kind of delicious daze, stopped in several little shops along the way. In one she bought a sheaf of pussy willows, a nuisance to carry, but Kelsey was fond of them. In a second store she picked up his favorite imported cheese, and in a third she selected half a dozen colored blotters for his desk pad and then, impulsively, a new wastebasket for his study. This was even more awkward than the willows to carry, but it suddenly seemed essential to replace his shabby old basket, and she could not wait for the next day's delivery.

She had forgotten her key and had to ask Albert to let her into the apartment. It was too early for Amanda to be home from school, and Pearl had planned to take lunch and clean laundry to the hospital. Pearl had become expert in devising hospital errands, and Kelsey said that the truck driver's aunt probably didn't have the heart to get well and leave.

But Pearl was not at the hospital. She sat at the table in the kitchen, crying into a cup of coffee. Poor Pearl—the kitchen was more her home than the room she had in her sister's house.

Elaine, still a little groggy from Midge's recital, braced herself for the report of a familiar disaster.

"He's gone, Miz Carpenter—out to Oregon to work for his wife's father."

Pearl's hands groped pathetically, and Elaine saw that she had a pad of ruled paper and a pencil on the table.

Elaine could only say, "His wife's father? Oh, Pearl, I'm so sorry."

She wasn't one to cry over spilt milk, Pearl said, ignoring tears already shed.

"I'm writing to Mrs. Torrington Van Antwerpt to ask her how a lady can make the first move to renew an old friendship. Without being criticized by the mother of the man."